10 August 2011

Mr. JUSTICE

SCOTT DOUGLAS GERBER

Mr. JUSTICE

NOTE: This is a work of fiction. Names, characters, places and incidents are the product of the author's imagination or are used fictitiously, and any resemblance to actual persons, living or dead, business establishments, events or locales is entirely coincidental.

For information about special discounts for bulk purchases, please contact Sunbury Press, Inc. Wholesale Dept. at (717) 254-7274 or orders@sunburypress.com.

To request one of our authors for speaking engagements or book signings, please contact Sunbury Press, Inc. Publicity Dept. at publicity@sunburypress.com.

FIRST SUNBURY PRESS EDITION
Printed in the United States of America
May 2011

ISBN 978-1-934597-35-4

Published by:
Sunbury Press
Camp Hill, PA
www.sunburypress.com

Camp Hill, Pennsylvania USA

Also By Scott Douglas Gerber

Fiction

The Law Clerk: A Novel

The Ivory Tower: A Novel

Nonfiction

A Distinct Judicial Power: The Origins of an Independent Judiciary, 1606-1787

The Declaration of Independence: Origins and Impact (editor)

First Principles: The Jurisprudence of Clarence Thomas

Seriatim: The Supreme Court Before John Marshall (editor)

To Secure These Rights: The Declaration of Independence and Constitutional Interpretation

For my brothers and sisters

(Better late than never)

"We are very quiet there, but it is the quiet of a storm center."

—U.S. Supreme Court Justice Oliver Wendell Holmes Jr.

PART I

Advice and Consent

CHAPTER 1

Lights from TV cameras blazed like the summer sun. Still cameras popped and hissed like firecrackers on the Fourth of July. Reporters packed together as tightly as teenagers in a speed-metal mosh pit flooded the hearing room.

Professor Peter McDonald nevertheless felt alone in the world. It didn't matter that *he* was the focus of all the attention. It didn't matter that *he* was only moments away from the start of his confirmation hearing to become an associate justice of the Supreme Court of the United States.

It was every law professor's dream to serve on the Supreme Court—every law professor but Peter McDonald, that is. It might have mattered to him once, but nothing had mattered since Valentine's Day—the day on which his beloved wife Jenny and his precious daughter Megan had been ripped from his life by an assassin's bullets ... bullets that had been meant for *him.*

Peter McDonald—Phi Beta Kappa graduate from Harvard College, Order of the Coif recipient at Yale Law School, former law clerk to the chief justice of the United States, youngest professor awarded tenure in the history of the University of Virginia School of Law, most frequently cited constitutional law scholar in the nation—had met the former Jenny O'Keefe on the first day of their first year of college. Peter was a "legacy" at Harvard: his father, grandfather, and great-grandfather all had attended the famed Ivy League institution. Jenny, in contrast, was a scholarship student from South Boston—a "Southie," as locals were called. She was the first member of her family to attend college, let alone graduate from the most prestigious college of them all.

Peter and Jenny came from different worlds, but Peter knew he was a goner the instant Jenny walked into Introduction to American History on that crisp day in September and sat in the seat directly across the classroom from him. *She* didn't seem to notice *him*, but *he* noticed *her*. And *she* certainly noticed that. How could she not? He spent most of the semester stealing awkward glances at her from behind his textbook.

Eventually, after more than a few false starts—"Uh, Jenny, what did the professor say about the Articles of Confederation?"; "Er, Jenny, did the professor say whether the midterm is open book?"; "Excuse me, Jenny, can I xerox your notes?"—Peter McDonald somehow managed to convince Jenny O'Keefe to have a cup of coffee with him. And, eventually, coffee somehow turned into lunch, lunch somehow turned into dinner, dinner somehow turned into a weekend on Cape Cod, a weekend on the Cape somehow turned into summer jobs in the same city, and summer jobs in the same city somehow turned into a marriage proposal—a proposal that turned into the happiest twenty years of Peter McDonald's life.

The last five years had been the best. After fifteen long years of trying—fifteen years of near-bankruptcy inducing visits to fertility clinic after fertility clinic and down-to-the-minute time management of their procreative activities—Peter and Jenny McDonald became the proud parents of Megan Mallory McDonald.

Megan looked almost exactly like her mother. She had a wall of chestnut hair, sparkling green eyes, a face full of freckles, and a smile that could make an angel sing. She also had her father wrapped around her little finger. All she had to do was ask, "Daddy, can I ... ?" and McDonald would answer, "Yes, sweetheart." He didn't need to hear the end of her question. The answer was always, "Yes, sweetheart." In fact, McDonald spent as much time as he could with Megan. Perhaps more time than he should, those who had long been championing his rise to the top kept telling him. But he wouldn't listen to them. He cared more, *far* more, about Megan and Jenny than he did about securing a high-level government post—including one on the Supreme Court of the United States.

CHAPTER 2

"All rise!" the clerk called out.

The nineteen members of the Senate Judiciary Committee were led into the hearing room by Alexandra Rutledge Burton, the senior U.S. senator from, in her favorite phrase, "the great state of South Carolina." Burton was a legend on Capitol Hill. With a thick mane of silver hair, a Grecian profile, and shoulders as broad as those of the All-American basketball player she once was, the senator looked every bit the force of nature she was reputed to be. But those who knew her best—the handful of managing partners in D.C.'s most influential law firms, the CEOs of Wall Street's most highly capitalized corporations, the editors in chief of the nation's most widely circulated newspapers—understood that the senator hadn't recovered from the trauma of witnessing her grandson commit suicide after being rejected for admission to her home state's flagship institution of higher education.

My grandson had dreamed of attending the University of South Carolina since he was nine years old, Senator Burton had written in an op-ed piece for the *Charleston Post and Courier* six months after her grandson's death. *He wasn't interested in applying to Harvard, or Yale, or some other fancy New England college. He was a South Carolina boy through and through. He never missed a Gamecocks' football game. His bedroom was chock-full of SC memorabilia. He bled garnet and black. He wanted to follow in his parents' footsteps. They had met at SC. He wanted to follow in* my *footsteps.*

A flattering photograph of the senator's grandson separated the paragraphs of her article. The text continued: *My grandson's tragic death has revealed more powerfully than anything could that affirmative action—what is best described as "reverse discrimination"—has profound human costs. Academic administrators continually trumpet the importance of "diversity" in our nation's colleges and universities, but what about the more qualified applicants who are denied admission to those same institutions solely because of the color of their skin? Make no mistake about it,* Senator Burton continued, *my grandson was more qualified than many of the minority students who were granted admission to the university ahead of him. My grandson graduated with a 3.6 grade point average from Charleston High School and scored in the top 15% on the Law School Admissions Test. Three-quarters of the minority students in this fall's entering class—the entering class my grandson should have been a part of—have GPAs* of *less than 3.0 and LSAT scores in the fortieth percentile or below. Where's the justice in that? Where's the justice for my daughter and son-in-law, who have lost their only child to his own hand? Where's the justice for my grandson?*

Burton assured her readers that she wasn't writing the op-ed to exact some sort of revenge on the university. *After all,* she reminded them, *I am a proud alumna of SC. Rather, I am writing to announce to the nation that I am behind my daughter and son-in-law one hundred percent in their appeal of the U.S. District Court's recent decision dismissing their lawsuit against the university on the grounds that, one, the U.S. Supreme Court held in 2003, in* Grutter v. Bollinger, *that "diversity" in the student body is a "compelling" interest and, two, colleges and universities may consider race as a factor when deciding which applicants to accept.*

The senator then addressed the elephant in the room—namely, why she hadn't used her considerable influence to guarantee her grandson's admission to SC. *To be honest,* she wrote, *I didn't think he needed my help. That goes to show how naive I was about how aggressively reverse discrimination is being practiced by college admissions officers today. Moreover, I felt it would be inappropriate for me to pressure the university. My grandson, God rest his soul, agreed. In fact, he begged me not to intervene. He was a young man of uncommon integrity—he omitted any reference to me whatsoever on his application—and we will miss him dearly.* The senator closed her opinion piece by writing: *As the saying goes, we will take my grandson's case "all the way to the Supreme Court" if we must.*

Senator Burton's op-ed had drawn more letters to the editor than any other article in the long history of the *Charleston Post and Courier.* All of the letters expressed sympathy for the family's loss, and the vast majority—nearly eighty percent—supported the family's decision to appeal the trial court's ruling. *Give 'em hell, Senator,* a particularly ebullient letter writer said. *Show those pinkos at the university that you mean business.*

And the senator did mean business. She had a plan. Two plans, actually.

The first plan was to request an expedited appeal to the U.S. Supreme Court, a maneuver that would bypass the hopelessly Left-leaning U.S. Court of Appeals for the Fourth Circuit. Although the Supreme Court tended to frown upon such requests, the close vote in *Grutter v. Bollinger* (five to four) coupled with the high profile nature of the dispute (*the* hot button issue of American civil rights law), gave Burton hope—especially when one of the justices who had voted in favor of affirmative action had recently retired from the bench.

Burton's second plan required the assistance of a particular constituency who was considerably more reliable than the prima donnas with whom she worked in Washington. That constituency wasn't comprised of high-priced lawyers, corporate honchos, or opinion makers. No, it was made up of a group of men who were far more powerful.

CHAPTER 3

His name was Lincoln Jefferson. He was seventeen, and he was black. His parents had named him after the two U.S. presidents who had done the most for African Americans: Abraham Lincoln, who had helped to free the slaves by winning the Civil War; and Thomas Jefferson, who had written in the Declaration of Independence that "all men are created equal."

Lincoln Jefferson's "crime"? Sleeping with a high school classmate who happened to be white.

He had been pulled from his bed in the middle of the night, stripped naked, and dragged kicking and screaming deep into the woods on the outskirts of Charleston. The large bonfire was already ablaze underneath a tall oak tree when he arrived. He was immersed in coal oil, hoisted up onto the tree, and slowly lowered into the fire. Some of the spectators cut off fingers and toes from his corpse as souvenirs. Others punched and spat at his disfigured body. His remains were dumped into a burlap bag and hung from the tree while many in the crowd cheered.

Earl Smith drained a bottle of Budweiser in one long gulp. He shattered the empty bottle against the tree. Shards of glass scattered into the fire. "'King of beers,'" he said to his brother. He belched. "Ain't nuthin' like it."

"Amen to that," Billy Joe Collier said. He threw a log onto the fire. He tossed his brother another beer and grabbed one for himself.

Earl Smith and Billy Joe Collier weren't blood brothers. They were, however, brothers in the Knights of the Ku Klux Klan, a self-proclaimed "fraternal organization" that grew out of the Civil War to protect and preserve the white race and ensure voluntary separation of the races and even extinction of blacks, Catholics, and Jews. Smith, the grand dragon of the Klan's South Carolina chapter, liked to joke, "We don't burn crosses; we light 'em. It's just a religious ceremony."

Of course no one believed him. The Justice Department certainly didn't. The FBI had tried to keep Smith and company under close surveillance ever since Charles Jackson had become the first African American president of the United States. Prior to that watershed event the Klan had essentially disappeared from view, and the Feds' attention had been dominated by Al-Qaeda, the Taliban, and other foreign terrorist groups. But it was amazing how quickly the Klan had sprung back to life after President Jackson's victory. Indeed, the Feds had named their reconstituted Klan watch unit *Phoenix*, after the mythical bird that rose from the ashes.

Chief among Earl Smith's cohorts was Billy Joe Collier. Collier was the second highest ranking official—the klaliff—in the South Carolina Realm. Smith had asked him to call a konklave—a meeting—of the Charleston den.

The konklave was being held in a location nearly impossible to access. The Klan was like the Mafia: everyone knew it was there, but no one knew how to find it. Secrecy was the Klan's cardinal rule—secrecy and the destruction of anyone who threatened the supremacy of the white race. The rationale for the Klan's most visible characteristic—the uniform of long white robes and tall white pasteboard hats —was secrecy.

"Akia. Kigy," Smith said. That was Klan nomenclature for "A klansman I am" and "Klansmen, I greet you."

"Akia. Kigy," the konklave replied.

Smith said, "Kludd Bates will now read from the Kloran."

Johnny Bates, the den chaplain, opened the ritual book and said, "Your Excellency, the sacred altar of the Klan is prepared; the fiery cross illumines the konklave."

Smith said, "Faithful kludd, why the fiery cross?"

Bates said, "Sir, it is the emblem of that sincere, unselfish devotedness of all klansmen to the sacred purpose and principles we have espoused."

Smith said, "My terrors and klansmen, what means the fiery cross?"

The konklave said, "We serve and sacrifice for the right."

Smith said, "Klansmen all: You will gather for our opening devotions."

The konklave sang the Klan's sacred song. The chorus rang out:

Home, home, country and home,
Klansmen we'll live and die
For our country and home.

Kludd Bates read more from the Kloran.

When Bates had finished, Smith said, "Amen." Then Smith said, "I've called this konklave because our good friend Senator Burton needs our help."

"Name it, and we'll do it," one of the hydras said. "Anything for Senator Burton."

A hydra was an assistant to the grand dragon. This particular hydra worked at Wal-Mart during the day.

"Akia! Akia!" the konklave cried out.

Alexandra Burton had been a good friend to South Carolina klansmen over the years. She always made sure they had enough money to keep their organization afloat, and she always did her best to keep federal authorities from investigating them when black men were found hanging from ropes on trees. Black men such as Lincoln Jefferson ...

"That's what I told the senator," Smith said.

"What does she need for us to do?" the same hydra asked. He threw a rock at the burlap bag that contained Lincoln Jefferson's disfigured body.

"She needs us to scare off some nigger lovin' law professor," Smith answered.

"Why would Senator Burton give a shit about some goddamn egghead?" the hydra asked next. He picked up another rock.

Smith answered, "Because he might become a judge on the Supreme Court. If he does, the senator said he can make more nigger-friendly laws."

"Death to the nigger lover!" the konklave shouted.

CHAPTER 4

Jeffrey Oates handed Senator Burton the folder that contained the list of questions the senator planned to ask Peter McDonald during the confirmation hearing. Oates, Burton's top legislative assistant, was hoping for an acknowledgment—a "Thank you" ideally, although an audible grunt would have sufficed—but he didn't receive one. He never did anymore. The pleasantries had stopped when Oates had failed to kill McDonald six months earlier, shortly after the professor's nomination to the Supreme Court had been announced by the president. Frankly, Oates was surprised that Burton hadn't fired him. The only reason that Oates could think of for why he still had a job was that the senator knew Oates could tie her to the plot. Consequently, Burton could only go *so* far in expressing her displeasure with her chief aide because he had gone *too* far when his careless mistakes left their target unscathed, killing his wife and child instead.

Oates would never forget that day. He had driven from Washington to Charlottesville in order to get a feel for McDonald's movements ... for a typical day in the life of one of America's most celebrated law professors. Oates actually enjoyed some of his trip. Most of the one-hundred-mile drive between the nation's capital and the University of Virginia wended through rolling hills and pastoral farmlands at the foot of the Blue Ridge Mountains and the headwaters of the Rivanna River. Monticello, Thomas Jefferson's magnificent home, was visible on the horizon about ten miles outside of town. Charlottesville, a city of approximately forty thousand people, looked like a postcard of a college town. The university itself—locals, in fact, referred to UVA as "*the* university"—was one of the most scenic campuses in the nation. The Lawn, a/k/a "Mr. Jefferson's Academical Village," was the heart of the university. The Rotunda, a scale replica of the Roman Pantheon, sat at the top of the Lawn, and rows of student rooms and professors' residences proceeded down it. The Lawn was a beautiful sight on a good day. During a 1993 visit to the university, Mikhail Gorbachev, the former president of the Soviet Union, had said, "You people live in paradise."

The law school was located about a mile from the Lawn, in a part of the campus known as the North Grounds. And it was on the North Grounds where Jeffrey Oates found Jenny and Megan McDonald waiting for the man that Oates had been told to kill.

Peter McDonald's wife and daughter looked like they had just finished posing for a Hallmark card. Jenny, McDonald's wife, was wearing an emerald green Laura Ashley dress spotted with yellow daises. It was a striking choice for a woman of her porcelain complexion and chestnut hair color. Megan, the little girl, had on an identical outfit. She was carrying a heart-shaped box of chocolates in her tiny hand.

Valentine's Day! Oates said to himself after taking in the scene. He had forgotten all about it. Why wouldn't he? He had no one to share it with. He had spent his entire adult life serving Senator Alexandra Burton, one of the most powerful women in the country and, someday, perhaps the first female president of the United States. Oates didn't know why the senator wanted him to kill Professor McDonald, but it wasn't his job to ask why. It was his job to do it.

CHAPTER 5

Peter McDonald exited the law school's back entrance and spotted his wife and daughter standing in the faculty parking lot next to the family's new Volvo station wagon. A huge smile spread across his handsome face. He waved hello to his wife and then called out to his daughter. "Hiya, June Bug," he said. Megan had been a June baby. "Are you ready for lunch?"

"Yeth!" Megan bubbled. The recent loss of her two front teeth had turned her s's into th's. It had made her even more adorable than she already was. "Pitha!"

Jenny McDonald said, "I thought we decided to take Daddy someplace special for Valentine's Day, sweetheart." She stroked her daughter's chestnut hair.

"Pitha ith thpethal, Mommy." Megan decided that now would be a good time to start spinning like a top. "Pitha! Pitha! Pitha!"

Peter McDonald said, still smiling, "Pizza it is, June Bug."

Jenny said, "But I've got reservations at the C&O, Peter. I wanted today to be special. You've been so busy since the nomination was announced."

The C&O was the most expensive restaurant in Charlottesville. It specialized in French cuisine. Julia Child had called it the finest French restaurant south of the Mason-Dixon line in her classic book, *Mastering the Art of French Cooking.*

McDonald took his wife by the hand. He looked directly into her sparkling green eyes. "Any day with you and Megan is special, hon. It doesn't matter where we eat."

Jenny's eyes misted. "'Pitha,' here we come." She kissed her husband on the cheek and hugged him like there was no tomorrow.

"Pitha! Pitha! Pitha!" Megan sang as the happy family headed for the car.

The McDonalds meandered down Route 250 on their way to Crozet Pizza, one of the hidden gems of the area. UVA students in the know understood that a trip to Crozet for a hand-tossed pie was as sacred as a naked sprint across the Lawn.

Fortunately for Jeffrey Oates, Route 250 was a back road and wasn't heavily trafficked. He followed closely behind the McDonalds' Volvo, but not so close as to be conspicuous. He had borrowed a colleague's car with Virginia license plates for the same reason. It was a late-model Mustang, and unlike his ten-year-old Taurus, it had speed to burn. That was crucial because Oates would need to make a quick getaway.

Oates followed the McDonalds for the better part of ten miles. Where the heck were they going? he said to himself more than once. He wasn't from Charlottesville, but he knew that a college town of its size and significance must have a number of quality restaurants.

Finally, the Volvo turned into a gravel parking lot about a quarter of a mile west of a small wooden sign that read CROZET at the top and INCORPORATED 1791 at the bottom. In a way, Oates thought, it was good that the McDonalds had decided to celebrate Valentine's Day outside of town. There would be fewer witnesses this way. He knew it took only *one* witness, though. One person who could identify him. He needed to be careful.

Jenny McDonald was the first to exit the car. She placed her purse on the roof, tucked her hair behind her ears, and opened the back door. She leaned over and unbuckled the child safety seat that held her slumbering daughter. Megan never stayed awake for more than five minutes in the car. Jenny and Peter had discovered that when Megan was a baby and wouldn't sleep through the night. One evening, at about half past eleven, Peter decided to drive his crying daughter around the block. Five minutes later, she was sleeping as soundly as a senior citizen after a Wheel of Fortune marathon on the Game Show Network.

"Come on, Professor," Oates muttered. He bit his lip. He had picked the wrong time to try to quit smoking. "Get out of the car. Get out of the goddamn car."

Oates felt more than a little guilty about the prospect of shooting McDonald in front of his wife and daughter, but he had no choice. Senator Burton had insisted that the deed be done ASAP. And what the senator wanted, the senator got. Everyone on the senator's staff knew that. Jeffrey Oates certainly did.

McDonald finally exited the car. He locked the doors with the press of a button on his key chain and then did a quick sprint to where his wife and sleeping daughter were waiting. He eased his daughter from his wife's tired arms, positioned her comfortably on his shoulder, and took his wife by the hand. He still got tingles when Jenny caressed his hand with the back of her thumb, and he still felt all warm inside when Megan wrapped her tiny arms around his neck.

No, Peter McDonald said to himself, life doesn't get any better than this. Then ...

A shot! McDonald heard a *shot*!

He felt his wife's grip loosen from his own. He watched her knees buckle as she crumbled to the sidewalk like one of Megan's rag dolls.

"Jenny!" he cried out. "Jenny!"

Then ...

A second shot!

He heard a sharp squeal.

Megan! The second shot had hit *Megan*!

"No!" he cried out. "Please God, *no*!" McDonald dropped to the sidewalk. Megan lay limply across her mother's chest. Jenny had a hole in the side of her head the size of a quarter. Both McDonald's wife and daughter were soaked in blood, and both had their eyes open. "No!" he said again.

It didn't take long for people to start pouring out of the pizzeria to find out what the commotion was about.

"Oh my God!" a middle-aged woman said. She had a slice of pepperoni in her pudgy hand.

"Call an ambulance!" McDonald said. "*Please*! Someone call an ambulance!"

A young man in a starched polo shirt and jeans—a UVA student, most likely—reached into his pocket and pulled out a cell phone. He dialed 911 and said, "A lady and her daughter have been shot! They need an ambulance!" He paused briefly, and then in obvious response to an obvious question, said, "Crozet Pizza on Route 250."

Another young man—he, too, wearing a starched polo shirt and jeans, and he, too, most likely a UVA student—pointed across the road and said, "Look! I bet the shots came from that car!"

But before anyone could do anything about it, Jeffrey Oates hammered down on the Mustang's accelerator and disappeared into the horizon. More importantly, there was no need for an ambulance. Jenny and Megan McDonald were dead.

CHAPTER 6

"This hearing will please come to order," Senator Alexandra Burton said with a loud rap of her gavel.

All nineteen members of the Judiciary Committee were in their seats. Usually, only two or three members were present at the same time. But, usually, the committee was being asked to assess the qualifications of a nominee for a federal district court judgeship or for a seat on the U.S. court of appeals. Under the doctrine of senatorial courtesy, the senator from the state in which the judicial vacancy existed made the appointment. The Constitution specified otherwise—the president was to "nominate" and the Senate was to provide "advice and consent"—but the Senate rarely confirmed a presidential appointment if the nominee's own senators disapproved. As a result, the practice had developed in such a way that now the home state senator told the president who should fill the seat. There was one notable exception to this longstanding custom: when the vacancy was on the Supreme Court of the United States, the nation's highest court.

"Good morning, Professor," Burton said.

"Good morning, Senator," McDonald said.

"Let me assure you, Professor, that I intend to bend over backwards to make sure you get a fair hearing before this committee." Burton glanced toward the press gallery. "I know that our colleagues in the Fourth Estate probably don't believe me, but it's true."

The members of the press didn't "probably" not believe Burton—they *definitely* didn't. A slew of stories in the morning's newspapers had reminded readers that the senator's daughter and son-in-law had filed a request for an expedited appeal to the Supreme Court asking that the Court reverse its 2003 decision permitting colleges and universities to consider the race of an applicant when deciding whom to admit and that, if confirmed, Peter McDonald would be the swing vote in the case. The talking heads who had been hired by the television networks to provide play-by-play for the confirmation hearing—apparently, there wasn't much difference anymore between TV coverage of a confirmation hearing for a high-level government post and a football game between division rivals—had opened their morning broadcasts by expressing the same sentiment.

"Thank you, Senator," McDonald said, struggling to keep his eyes from rolling. He didn't believe that Burton would be impartial, either.

"Would you like to make an opening statement before we begin the morning's questioning?"

"Yes, Senator. Thank you." McDonald swiveled in his seat and retrieved a thin manila folder from Kelsi Shelton's quivering hand.

Kelsi Shelton was a third-year law student at the University of Virginia. She was Peter McDonald's research assistant. Working for McDonald was a coveted assignment for any UVA law student: he was brilliant, productive, and less pretentious than any other member of the faculty. Kelsi had applied to work for him because the principal focus of his scholarship over the past several years had been capital punishment, and she hoped to become a public defender when she graduated in May. Those plans might need to be placed on hold for a year. McDonald had told Kelsi that if he was confirmed by the Senate for a seat on the Supreme Court, he wanted her to clerk for him.

Some of Kelsi's classmates—the jealous ones, mostly—were saying that McDonald wanted Kelsi to continue to work for him because she was beautiful and he was now single. Everyone knew how devoted McDonald had been to his wife, but his wife was dead. McDonald was human, the argument went, and even *he* couldn't avoid noticing how attractive Kelsi was. She was tall with blonde hair that shined like sunflowers on a summer day, and she possessed a smile that put everyone around her at ease. She tended to favor sweatshirts and jeans around the corridors of the law school, but even a loose fitting sweatshirt couldn't conceal the eye-popping figure that lay beneath.

McDonald, plainly aware that Kelsi was more than mildly overwhelmed by the spectacle being played out before her, flashed his research assistant a reassuring smile.

Kelsi returned his smile, swept her hair from her face, and settled back into the seat behind the large walnut table at which McDonald sat. Kelsi, in short, was sitting where Jenny McDonald was supposed to be.

"Professor?" Burton said. It was remarkable how patient the senator was being.

"Sorry, Senator. My assistant had my notes."

The myriad of TV cameras crammed into the hearing room all panned to Kelsi. Her face turned the color of the most prominent third of the American flag towering over the dais occupied by the members of the Judiciary Committee: *r-e-d*.

"Professor McDonald's assistant certainly is beautiful," a blithering head of hair spray could be heard reporting live for FOX News. Like it mattered to Article II, Section 2, Clause 2 of the Constitution of the United States—the provision that spoke to the Senate's "advice and consent" power over presidential nominees to the federal bench—what Peter McDonald's assistant looked like.

It did matter, though. In politics, as in life, it always mattered whether someone was attractive.

Kelsi Shelton would soon be learning that lesson for herself.

CHAPTER 7

Billy Joe Collier had arrived at The Rebel Bar and Grill an hour earlier than Earl Smith had told him to. But Collier was stoked for a fight, and he always liked to have a nice buzz going before he got down and dirty. He had already drunk three beers. The number would have been greater—Collier was known to inhale a six-pack an hour on a good night—but he was distracted by the couple at the bar.

Collier didn't know the couple. That didn't matter. He knew he didn't like them. He hated them, in fact. Why? Because the woman was white and the man was black.

Earl Smith entered the bar. He removed his baseball cap and raked his hands through his hair. He plopped his cap back on his head. He scanned the room. He spotted Billy Joe Collier sitting in a booth near the back of the bar with a table full of empty beer bottles to keep him company.

"Sorry I'm late," Smith said to his top lieutenant. "How long have you been here?"

Collier checked his watch, a dollar store special. "About two hours." He chugged another beer. "Where the fuck have you been?"

The Ku Klux Klan wasn't the military or the Mafia—although it patterned itself a bit after both—so Collier could get away with being disrespectful to his higher-up.

Smith fidgeted again with his baseball cap. He said, "Lost track of time is all." That wasn't true. But he couldn't afford to tell Collier the real reason he was late: he had been with Cat Wilson.

"Have a seat, boss."

Smith sat. He removed his cap and placed it on the table. The cap had Taylor Tires embossed across the front. He worked at the tire plant as a line foreman. Collier was part of his crew there, too.

Collier's attention was again drawn to the couple at the bar. The man had placed his hand on the woman's thigh. "Stick to your own kind, nigger!" Collier shouted.

Both the couple and Smith were startled by Collier's outburst. The remainder of the bar's patrons seemed used to it.

The couple paid their tab and quickly left the bar.

Smith thanked his lucky stars that he hadn't told Collier about Cat. Frankly, he knew he shouldn't have been surprised by Collier's outburst about the couple at the bar. Nothing made a klansman angrier than an interracial romance.

"Fuckin' cunt," Collier spat. He drained another beer. "A piece of pussy that fine shouldn't be wasting herself on no nigger." He smiled. "She should give me a taste of that sweet thang. God knows I could use me a taste."

Smith played along. "You and me both, Billy Joe. You and me both." He signaled for the waitress. "Now let's talk about McDonald."

CHAPTER 8

Peter McDonald said, "I realize that custom dictates that I begin by introducing my family. But, as the committee knows, my wife and daughter were murdered six months ago."

Whispers of sadness and sympathy filled the committee room. Everyone already knew about the tragic deaths of McDonald's wife and daughter, but hearing him mention it for the first time publicly was one of the most gut-wrenching moments in the history of the Supreme Court appointment process.

McDonald added, "I would like to take this opportunity to thank the chair for the kindness she showed when she was first apprised of that awful news. I especially appreciate her generous offer to postpone this hearing until I felt ready to proceed."

Senator Burton said, "You're welcome."

Actually, the senator had initially inquired about whether the professor might wish to reconsider his acceptance of the president's nomination to the Court. "Everyone would understand if you changed your mind," Burton had said at the time, her voice dripping with southern charm. "Losing your wife and daughter is a lot to bear. I know. I still haven't recovered from losing my grandson two years ago."

Unfortunately for Burton, McDonald had said that he owed it to the president—and to the country—to honor his commitment and press forward with the confirmation process.

McDonald took a sip of water. "I'd also like to thank the committee for the serious attention it has afforded to my nomination. I'm a law professor, and we law professors tend to put pen to paper quite a lot. I thank each and every member for the time you've invested in reading my books and articles."

Members of the committee nodded, and a few smiled. The members weren't used to reading so much scholarship from a nominee. Most modern presidents tended to appoint stealth candidates to the bench—men and women with no paper trail to criticize.

McDonald continued, "I'm especially grateful to President Jackson for nominating me to a position that I find humbling to even think about. If I'm confirmed, I'll try to become a justice whose work will justify the confidence that he and you have placed in me."

The committee nodded again. The fourteen men and five women who composed it looked like a collection of antique bobble-head dolls.

"As my writings make clear, I believe that a judge's authority derives entirely from the fact that he or she is applying the law and not his or her personal values. No one, including a judge, is above the law. Only in that way will justice be done and the freedom of the American people secured."

McDonald took another sip of water. "How should a judge go about finding the law? By attempting to discern what those who made the law intended. I realize that many of my colleagues in academia, and more than a few members of the judiciary, believe that the law means what judges 'need it to mean' in order to do justice, but I believe, and I have stated so in print, that if a judge abandons intention as his guide there is no law available to him, and he begins to legislate a social agenda for the American people. That goes well beyond his legitimate power. He diminishes liberty instead of enhancing it."

The FOX News reporter could be heard saying, "He sounds like a conservative."

Of course any journalist worth his salt would have read at least *some* of McDonald's writings and known that wasn't true. But this particular reporter was too busy getting his hair styled to read anything more detailed than a Clairol box.

McDonald said next, "The past, however, includes not only the intentions of those who wrote the law; it also includes the opinions of previous judges who interpreted it and applied it to prior cases. That is why a judge must have great respect for precedent. It is one thing as a legal theorist to criticize the reasoning of a prior decision—even to criticize it severely, as I have done. It is another and more serious thing altogether for a judge to ignore or overturn a prior decision. That requires much more careful thought. That doesn't mean that constitutional law is static. It will evolve as judges modify doctrine to meet new circumstances and technologies. Thus, today we apply the First Amendment's guarantee of freedom of the press to radio and television—and even to the Internet—and we apply to electronic surveillance the Fourth Amendment's guarantee of privacy for the individual against unreasonable searches of his or her home."

The FOX News reporter told the television audience, "This guy really knows his stuff. I should know. I went to law school myself."

A new personal record: the reporter had waited a full ten minutes before mentioning that he, too, was a lawyer.

"But there are limits on how the law should evolve, at least judicially," McDonald said. "When a judge reads entirely new values into the Constitution, values the framers and ratifiers did not put there, he deprives the people of their liberty. That liberty, which the Constitution clearly envisions, is the liberty of the people to set their own social agenda through the processes of democracy. In short, my philosophy of judging is neither liberal nor conservative. It's simply a philosophy that gives the Constitution a full and fair interpretation but, where the Constitution is silent, leaves policy struggles to the Congress, the president, the legislatures and executives of the fifty states ... and to the American people writ large."

McDonald reached again for the glass of water that stood alone on the elegant table at which he was sitting. "I welcome this opportunity to come before the committee and answer whatever questions the members may have. I am more than willing to discuss with you my judicial philosophy and the approach I would take to deciding cases. I cannot, of course, commit myself as to how I might vote on any particular case, and I know you wouldn't wish me to do that."

The FOX News reporter said, "Senator Burton 'wishes' the nominee would discuss at least one 'particular case': *Tucker v. University of South Carolina*. That's the case her daughter and son-in-law are appealing to the Supreme Court."

It was the first insightful comment the TV pretty boy had made all morning.

CHAPTER 9

Billy Joe Collier left The Rebel Bar and Grill feeling two things: (1) drunk as a skunk and (2) disappointed about his meeting with Earl Smith. The first was no big deal. Collier spent most of his evenings on the south side of sobriety. Why shouldn't he? His life was on the fast track to nowhere. Booze helped him to forget that fact. However, when Smith had suggested that they meet about the matter Senator Burton wanted them to address, Collier had assumed that meant he would get to take part in the killing. But Smith had said that he would handle the matter alone. "I think it's best if the Realm keeps a low profile on this one," Smith had said. "The heat hasn't died down yet from the Harvey Gates thing."

Harvey Gates had been the wildly popular black mayor of Charleston. Three years earlier he had provided Alexandra Burton with a stiff challenge for reelection to the U.S. Senate. Gates had called Burton's dedication to civil rights enforcement into question and accused the five-term incumbent of being out of touch with the "new South Carolina." Gates had been right, of course. Conveniently for Burton, though, the mayor had turned up dead in a fleabag motel in a seedy part of the city. The Klan had shot him at the senator's request, and Billy Joe Collier had been the trigger man. Consequently, Earl Smith had suggested that Collier sit this one out.

Collier understood his place in the chain of command and was willing to do what his grand dragon had asked him to do; namely, nothing. But he wasn't happy about it. The Gates murder had been almost three years ago, and the lynchings that had taken place since then—that of Lincoln Jefferson, for example—had been a group effort.

Billy Joe Collier liked to kill alone.

CHAPTER 10

The morning session had gone as expected: the senators who supported the president had asked nothing but softball questions, while those who opposed the president had come about as close to accusing Peter McDonald of wanting to rewrite the Constitution as good taste would permit. "Is it true, Professor McDonald, that you graduated at the top of your law school class?" Hamilton Holt, a pro-Jackson senator from New Hampshire, had asked. McDonald had answered, "Yes, Senator." Meanwhile, Susan Armstrong, an anti-Jackson senator from Georgia, had wanted to know why the professor had written an article "calling for the end of the death penalty."

McDonald had written nothing of the kind. He had simply concluded in an essay for the *Harvard Law Review* that the death penalty was sometimes misapplied by jurors who didn't understand the law and that, as a consequence, judges needed to do a better job of explaining the law to them. But subtleties such as that were often lost in the hardball politics of the Supreme Court confirmation process. Just ask Robert Bork, the brilliant conservative jurist whose nomination went down in flames after liberal interest groups spent millions of dollars on television ads distorting his record.

Then came the confrontation for which everyone had been waiting: that between the nominee and Senator Gregory Carpenter.

"This should be good," the FOX News reporter said to his TV audience.

Gregory Carpenter was the junior senator from South Carolina. He previously had served as Alexandra Burton's top legislative aid, the post currently occupied by Jeffrey Oates. It was no secret in Washington power circles that Oates was jealous of Carpenter because Burton had recommended Carpenter rather than Oates when the South Carolina Republican Party had been looking for a candidate to challenge the state's then-incumbent Democratic senator in the most recent election. Thanks both to Burton's tireless efforts on Carpenter's behalf and the increasingly conservative makeup of the South Carolina electorate, Carpenter had won by a landslide. As a result, he was now a member of the nation's most exclusive club—the United States Senate—while Oates was forced to continue serving a woman he no longer respected.

Given the fact that Carpenter owed his Senate seat to Burton, he was more than willing to ask the question that Burton herself couldn't ask—the question about affirmative action. "Good afternoon, Professor McDonald," Carpenter said.

"Good afternoon, Senator." McDonald squeezed his water glass.

"I very much benefited from listening to your answers to my colleagues' questions about the death penalty, privacy, abortion, and so forth, but I'd like to take up another issue for a few moments if it's all right with you." Senator Carpenter flashed a tobacco-stained smile. Big Tobacco paid the bills in South Carolina politics. "It is, of course, the issue that almost everyone in this room has been waiting with bated breath to hear about: your views on affirmative action."

McDonald said in a voice that for the first time sounded rehearsed, "As I mentioned in my opening statement, it would be inappropriate for me to comment on litigation that is currently pending before the Court."

It was a predictable response from the nominee—no nominee in recent history had failed to respond in a similar fashion to thinly-veiled questions about how he or she might vote in a potentially landmark case wending its way to the high Court—and Carpenter replied in an equally predictable manner. He asked for McDonald's "theory" for deciding such cases. "You are, of course, an academic, Professor. As your responses to my colleagues' questions made plain, you have theories about most issues of constitutional law. I assume affirmative action is no different."

McDonald said, "You are correct, Senator. I've got a theory on the subject." The nominee fidgeted in his seat. "My theory is this: a tension underlies all facets of equal protection jurisprudence involving race. That tension is between government neutrality and anti-subordination. Is it better to have a flat per se rule of invalidity of all racial classifications? If you believe in the primacy of government neutrality on matters of race, this might be appealing. It's what the first Justice John Marshall Harlan referred to as 'color-blindness' in his legendary dissent in the Court's infamous 1896 segregation decision, *Plessy v. Ferguson.* But if you believe that anti-subordination is at the heart of the equal protection clause, you may be skeptical. Anti-subordination is a theme that Justice Harlan also embraced in his *Plessy* dissent when he insisted that the Constitution does not tolerate a 'caste system.' In short, Senator, whether a judge accepts or rejects affirmative action turns on which principle—color-blindness or anti-subordination—the judge emphasizes." McDonald cleared a tickle from his throat and then said, "If the judge emphasizes color-blindness, then affirmative action would violate the equal protection clause. But if he emphasizes anti-subordination, affirmative action would likely pass constitutional muster."

Senator Carpenter leaned forward in his chair and frowned. "*That's* my question, though. Which do you emphasize?"

McDonald leaned back in his chair and smiled. It was the first time he had smiled—*truly* smiled—since Jenny and Megan had been killed. "And *that* I'm afraid I can't answer, no matter how much Senator Burton might wish I could."

CHAPTER 11

Billy Joe Collier pulled into the Exxon station down the street from The Rebel Bar and Grill. He needed to refill the tank on his aging Ford Monte Carlo. The car was a gas guzzler, but he liked how much power it had. He also liked how large the trunk was; there was room enough to fit two bodies inside. Usually, he killed only one person at a time. Tonight, he felt the urge to kill two.

Collier swiped his Visa card through the designated slot on the gas pump, removed the nozzle, punched the regular unleaded button with his index finger, and began to fill his tank. A Toyota Pathfinder pulled up to the pump at the far end of the service island. Out jumped the black man who had been in The Rebel with the white woman—the guy Collier had called a nigger and chased from the bar.

The black man's eyes met Collier's. Talk about shitty luck, he seemed to be saying to himself. He said to Collier, "We don't want any trouble."

The white woman turned to see what the commotion was about.

Collier said, "Me neither." Of course he was lying. He lived for trouble.

The white woman said, "Let's get out of here, hon. There's a Chevron near my apartment."

The black man said, "It'll be OK."

He couldn't have been more wrong.

Collier allowed the couple to pay for their gas and exit the station. He followed them to the woman's apartment. It was in a nice part of town. That made him wonder why the two had shown up at The Rebel in the first place. He was glad they had, though.

He killed the black man first. He smashed the man's head with a seven iron he had removed from the white woman's golf bag. "Is your nigger's dick as long as this golf club?" he asked the woman while he drove the club into her boyfriend's skull. "Fore!"

The white woman simply sat and cried. She was too frightened to move or scream.

Collier stuffed the black man's body into a laundry bag he found under the sink. He turned and faced the white woman. "It's your turn, bitch. But first I'll show you what a real man is like. Niggers ain't nuthin' but animals with big dicks."

Collier ripped open the woman's blouse. He removed her skirt. She was still too frightened to scream. "Don't you know it's against God's will to fuck a nigger?"

Collier proceeded to rape the woman for forty-five minutes. When he was done, he smashed her skull with the same golf club he had used on the black man. "I see why golf is such a popular sport," he said to the now empty room.

He felt good. He always felt good after a kill. He couldn't wait to tell Earl Smith all about it.

CHAPTER 12

Earl Smith watched out of the corner of his eye while the young woman dressed. He was lying on the bed of a twenty-dollar-a-night motel room on the south side of Charleston draining a bottle of warm beer.

The young woman was in the bathroom struggling to pull on a pair of nylons in a space only a bit larger than a broom closet. Her raven hair and chocolate skin reflected off the mirror like freshly polished coins tossed into a fountain.

"Hurry up," Smith said to her. "I've gotta get going." There was a surprising amount of tenderness in his voice.

The young woman picked up on Smith's welcoming tone. This wasn't the first time they had slept together—not by a long shot. She said, "You gonna come by and see me later?" She smiled and reached for her bra. "I'll treat you to a piece of strawberry pie."

"You know I can't do that." Smith flipped on the Weather Channel to see what the temperature was in D.C. He would be heading there soon.

The young woman knew why they couldn't be seen in public together: she was black. She liked to tease Smith about it, though. It was a running joke between them. "Don't your Cat do it like you like? Don't I always?"

Smith lifted the beer bottle in the young woman's direction and smiled.

Cat Wilson waited tables at the Waffle House off of exit 39. She had worked there for about two years. It wasn't a good job, but she needed something to support herself and her infant daughter. High school dropouts weren't in much demand in the information age. Hard luck stories weren't, either. She was lucky she was pretty. At least she got good tips.

Smith had met Cat—short for Catherine—late one night after the graveyard shift at the tire plant had gotten out. He had stopped in for a plate of eggs but ended up leaving with a lot more than that.

At first, Smith had approached his relationship with the young waitress as a rite of passage. Every klansman believed that blacks were animals, and every klansman was permitted one opportunity to experience for himself what sex with an animal was like. But for Smith, one opportunity had turned into two, and two had quickly become a weekly rendezvous at the Interstate 26 Motor Inn.

Smith had tried to rationalize his relationship with Cat as nothing more than a red-blooded male's weakness for good sex—and Cat certainly was good in the sack—but he knew it was more than that. He actually cared about her. He actually loved her.

Of course, he knew he was a dead man if Billy Joe Collier and the rest of his brothers in the South Carolina Realm found out. The image of Lincoln Jefferson's lifeless body dangling from a tree flashed through Earl Smith's mind as he kissed Cat Wilson good-bye.

CHAPTER 13

Kelsi Shelton tucked her hair behind her ears so that she could see what she was doing. She owned only two business suits, and she couldn't afford to spill coffee on either of them. The dry cleaning bill alone would put a serious dent in her already paltry bank account. Law school research assistants might be future lawyers, but they were paid like grocery store clerks.

Kelsi removed the carafe from the four-cup coffeemaker that came with the room and filled two plastic cups with steaming joe. She added a packet of Carnation Non-Dairy Creamer to one of them and then carried both cups to the small wooden table near the window at which Peter McDonald was working.

"Sorry they only had the chalky stuff," she said as she placed the cup with the artificial creamer in front of her favorite professor. "I guess the budget cuts are affecting everything."

McDonald chuckled at Kelsi's remark. "I don't think it's that," he said. "I think the Republicans are trying to send me a message: stay in academia, Professor; the coffee's better there."

Kelsi chuckled this time.

McDonald motioned for her to take the seat across from him. "How do you think it went today?" He stirred his coffee with the top half of a plastic hotel pen.

Kelsi sat. "I think it went really well." She took a sip of her coffee. She liked hers black. "You certainly showed that you know a lot about the law and that you're not an ideologue."

McDonald said, "Thanks."

Kelsi said, "That wasn't the best part, though. You know what was?"

"What?"

"What you said at the end about Senator Burton. Her face got so red that I thought she was having a heart attack."

McDonald smiled. "I know. I probably shouldn't have said it, but I couldn't help myself. Shoot, I'd bet the farm that Burton's staff wrote the questions that Senator Carpenter was asking."

"That would be a good bet." Kelsi glanced at the notepad in front of her professor. "Do you need any help with that?"

McDonald was working on his closing statement. Given how tight the vote on his confirmation was likely going to be, he had been spending even more time on it than he otherwise might have spent.

Peter McDonald had always been one of those last-minute wonders—someone who could wait until the deadline to get started and then manage to produce a work product that was better than that of anyone else. His law school classmates used to tease him about it. His law faculty colleagues resented him for it.

He said to Kelsi, "Aren't you missing too many classes as it is? I feel guilty about that, you know."

"Don't. I've learned more about the law in the two and a half days we've been here than I've learned in two and a half years of law school." Kelsi blushed and then said, "Except in your class, of course."

"Good save, kiddo." McDonald smiled. He seemed to be smiling a lot lately, and it always seemed to be when Kelsi Shelton was around. "Then maybe I could read my closing statement to you when I've finished with it, and you can tell me what you think."

"I'd love that," Kelsi said. She glanced out the window and wondered what it meant.

CHAPTER 14

Jeffrey Oates decided to walk to the Hilton Hotel. Traffic in the nation's capital was almost always a nightmare, and he didn't want to get caught up in a high-speed chase with the D.C. metro police in the middle of DuPont Circle. Evading local cops through the back roads of rural Virginia had been difficult enough. He wasn't a cat. He didn't have nine lives. After failing to take out Peter McDonald in Charlottesville, Oates was thankful that he still had one. He knew how vindictive Senator Burton could be. He also knew the rumors about the senator's alleged KKK connections. He didn't believe them, but he couldn't take the chance that they might be true. If they were, he might be dead soon. Unless he took out McDonald ...

Oates could have taken a taxi from his Georgetown apartment to the Adams-Morgan neighborhood, where the Hilton was located, but he didn't want to risk being identified by the cab driver after the fact. It didn't take a rocket scientist to figure out that the D.C. police wouldn't be the only ones turning over every stone to try to discover who had just assassinated a Supreme Court nominee. The FBI, the Secret Service, and perhaps even the CIA itself almost certainly would devote their vast resources to the investigation.

The weather had turned for the season. The wind blew hard from the east, and snowflakes frosted the cityscape. Oates picked up the pace as he drew closer to his destination. The cold air—not to mention the adrenaline rushing through his body—propelled him forward like a power walker during a morning workout. He zigzagged through the sea of cars that converged around the many traffic circles that made D.C. such a hazardous city to navigate. More than a few horns blared as he dashed in front of more than a few irate drivers.

"Ouch!" a pedestrian said.

Oates had knocked a young man to the pavement in his haste to avoid being mowed down by oncoming traffic.

Lucky for both of them, the young man was a Georgetown University undergraduate student who was used to getting knocked to the ground at weekend fraternity parties. Consequently, he knew how to take a fall.

It wasn't all good news for Oates, though. The collision had caused his pistol to fly out of his pocket.

"Is this your *gun*, man?" the Georgetown student said as he rose to his feet. He was dangling the gun between his forefinger and thumb like it was a dirty rag.

"Uh ... yeah," Oates said.

"What the fuck are you doing with a *gun*?"

Oates's eyes danced through the throng of passersby. The college kid had quickly returned the gun to Oates, and Oates had quickly returned it to his coat pocket. No one else seemed to have noticed the gun. One good thing about big cities, Oates knew, was that nobody seemed to notice anything.

Oates said, "D.C.'s a dangerous place. 'Murder capital of the world.' Or so the *Washington Post* always says. I got it for protection."

"I guess," the Georgetown student said. "Be careful with it, though. The fuckin' thing could've gone off when it hit the sidewalk."

"Don't worry. I'll be careful. But I've got to get going. I'm supposed to meet someone in a couple of minutes." Oates re-buttoned his coat and left in a rush.

CHAPTER 15

Peter McDonald held the door.

Kelsi Shelton ducked under his arm. "Thank you," she said.

"I could've done that, sir," said the Secret Service agent assigned to protect McDonald. The agent pulled up the collar on his trench coat to shield himself from the freezing rain that had begun to fall.

McDonald said, "I know. But in case you haven't figured it out yet, I'm not too comfortable with this whole bodyguard thing. I'm not Kevin Costner."

The Secret Service agent smiled. "Whitney Houston, sir. You're not Whitney Houston. Kevin Costner played the bodyguard in that movie. Whitney Houston played the celebrity. But with all due respect, you had better get used to it. Once you're confirmed, there'll be two of us assigned to you."

"*If* I'm confirmed," McDonald said. "*If* ..."

Kelsi Shelton spun on her heel and flashed a thousand-watt smile. It was the sort of smile that made her male classmates weak in the knees. "There's no 'if' about it, Professor McDonald. You're a shoo-in."

"I thought I told you to call me Peter? ... And how do you know I'm a 'shoo-in'?" McDonald returned Kelsi's smile.

She said, still smiling, "I've got my sources, too, you know." She giggled.

The Secret Service agent didn't seem to know what to make of the playful banter between his assigned "body" and the law student with the fantastic *body*. He just watched and listened. That's what he was paid to do. But, boy, did he have stories he wished he could tell. He used to work for Bill Clinton.

Jeffrey Oates bumped into several more pedestrians in his haste to arrive at the Hilton in time to catch Peter McDonald. Fortunately for everyone involved, the scene with the Georgetown student didn't repeat itself; no one else was knocked to the pavement, and Oates's pistol remained securely in his pocket.

Oates turned the corner onto California Street. He hustled to the end of the block. The Hilton was in plain view across the street on Connecticut Avenue. He surveyed the area. He suddenly realized that he had forgotten the most important part of his plan: *how* he was going to get a shot off without someone seeing him do it. As anyone who had been to the nation's capital could attest, there weren't many moments during the day when no one else was on the sidewalk. That was especially the case around the capital's luxury hotels.

Oates knew he had to take a chance, though. He had overheard Senator Burton say on the phone recently that she had lost faith in her top aide's ability to finish sensitive assignments. And that meant that Oates's opportunity to one day become White House chief of staff in a Burton administration was out the window, too—unless, of course, he could show the senator that the Charlottesville screw-up had been an isolated incident.

Oates spotted a mailbox directly in front of the hotel's taxi stand. Cabs were lined up like yellow chicks behind their mother, but the drivers themselves were standing underneath the hotel's canopy smoking cigarettes and trying to keep out of the rain.

Oates reached into his pocket to make sure the gun was still there. It was. A young mother pushing a jogging stroller dashed before his eyes. Thank God he hadn't pulled out the gun, he said to himself. Thank God he hadn't *fired* the gun.

The young mother smiled as she went jogging on her way.

Oates returned her smile. He double- and triple-checked Connecticut Avenue to make sure that no one else was about to flash before him. The coast was clear. Finally, the coast was clear.

Peter McDonald stepped onto the sidewalk. An attractive young woman who Oates recognized as McDonald's research assistant was at the professor's side. The Secret Service agent assigned to McDonald was two paces behind them.

Oates pulled the pistol from his pocket. He cupped it between his palm and forearm. He checked again to make sure that no one was about to jump into his line of fire. He took a deep breath, wiped the raindrops from his brow with the back of his hand, and raised the pistol to eye level. He pulled the trigger. The recoil caused him to stumble back a step. He regained his balance in time to see that this time he hadn't missed: Professor Peter McDonald, the president's nominee to the Supreme Court of the United States, collapsed to the pavement like a pile of bricks at a city-run construction site.

CHAPTER 16

John Gilstrap penned a best-selling novel a decade or so ago called *Nathan's Run* that was essentially nothing but one long chase scene. The novel wasn't literature, and the author wasn't a new Charles Dickens, but the book had an engaging, plucky hero and a breakneck pace.

Jeffrey Oates felt like a much older version of twelve-year-old Nathan Bailey as he coughed and wheezed his way through the tangled streets of the nation's capital. The cold rain had begun to fall harder, which was actually a good thing for Oates because it meant that fewer people were in his way than there ordinarily would have been.

Several people seemed curious about why Oates was in such a hurry—one soaking wet FedEx driver asked if Oates was afraid he would melt—but most Washingtonians were used to stepping aside while someone sprinted past them like George Foreman at the sound of the dinner bell. After all, D.C. was dominated by people—lawyers, lobbyists, politicians—who spent most of their lives rushing from one meeting to the next.

Oates hadn't traveled more than three blocks before police sirens began to blare. It was far from uncommon to hear sirens on the crime-infested streets of Washington, D.C. However, these particular sirens were more numerous and louder than usual. In fact, Oates couldn't recall hearing so much cacophony since the day President Reagan had been shot. Oates had just arrived in the nation's capital to join Senator Burton's legislative staff, but he remembered that day like it was yesterday.

Ironically, President Reagan had been shot in front of the very same hotel at which Professor McDonald had been shot. The only difference was that Oates had pulled the trigger that felled McDonald.

Oates slowed his pace while police cruiser after police cruiser whirred past. He slowed down both because he didn't want to appear suspicious and because he, like everyone else on the street at that moment, was transfixed by the chaos unfolding before him. He no longer felt like a character in a suspense novel; he felt like a villain in a horror movie.

What have I done? he said to himself. More importantly, where could he hide?

His eyes danced through the crowd that had formed on the sidewalk. Men in business suits caucused with shop clerks and women on their way to work. Then it hit him: the best place to hide was in plain view. He hailed a cab and told the driver to head for the Capitol.

Senator Burton would be waiting.

CHAPTER 17

Kelsi Shelton paced the crowded corridor like she was waiting for final grades to be posted. She had been keeping vigil at Bethesda Naval Hospital for more than five hours. She had changed from the blood-spattered blouse she had been wearing at the hotel into hospital scrubs that one of the nurses had kindly provided for her. The scrapes and bruises on her arms and cheek had been cleaned and bandaged, and now all she had to do was wait. But for someone whose plate was always full—the running joke at school was that Kelsi must have a secret twin because she took on so many projects—waiting was unfamiliar territory. And *what* she was waiting for made the situation unbearable: news about whether Professor McDonald had survived the shooting.

The Secret Service agent who had been assigned to protect the professor from precisely the sort of catastrophe that had transpired outside the Hilton was guzzling coffee as if it were water. He said, "Why don't you go back to the hotel, Kelsi? There's nothing you can do here."

Kelsi froze in her tracks. Her face was flush and tense. "But there was something that *you* could've done *there!* Wh ... what are my tax dollars paying for? He ... he might *die*, you know!"

Traffic in the corridor screeched to a halt. Nurses, orderlies, and families waiting for news about loved ones all directed their attention to the beautiful young woman having a meltdown in the middle of the room.

The Secret Service agent rose from his seat in the waiting area. He walked toward Kelsi. "I did the best I could," he said. "I screwed up. I'm sorry."

"Sorry! Sorry!! *Sorry* doesn't save Peter!" Kelsi collapsed into the Secret Service agent's arms and began to sob like a little girl.

Kelsi Shelton had never called Professor McDonald "Peter" before. She knew what that meant: she loved him. She knew she shouldn't, but she did.

Bethesda Naval Hospital was where many high-ranking government officials received medical care. The president's widely publicized annual physical examination was always administered at Bethesda, and numerous emergency procedures had been performed on various members of Congress and a myriad of federal judges over the years. Peter McDonald was still a private citizen, but no one questioned the decision by Secret Service Agent Brian Neal to have the professor transported to the nation's most sophisticated and secure government hospital.

Agent Neal had returned to his seat in the waiting area. He was inhaling yet another cup of stale vending machine coffee. Kelsi Shelton was asleep in the chair next to him. Her head had somehow managed to end up resting on his powerful shoulder.

An orderly dropped a tray of surgical instruments. They clattered to the floor like milk bottles during a carnival game. The noise startled Kelsi back to consciousness. She blushed when she realized where her head had been resting during her nap.

"Sorry," she said.

Agent Neal smiled. "Don't worry about it." He took a sip of coffee. "You don't know my name, do you?"

"Yes, I do." Kelsi tucked a loose strand of hair behind her ear. She flinched when her fingers brushed against the cut on her cheek. She had hit the sidewalk face first when the gun had fired.

"What is it?"

"B ... Bill N ... Nelson."

Agent Neal smiled again. "*Wrong*, Ms. Shelton. But thanks for playing. Hey, at least you got the initials right."

"Brian Neal!" Kelsi said. "Your name is Brian Neal!"

"Right. I didn't think you knew."

"I'm not a complete bitch, you know. It's just that I've been really busy working on Professor McDonald's confirmation. I'm a nice person. Really, I am. Just ask my mother... . "

They shared a nervous laugh.

Agent Neal said, "I know you are. Besides, it's a testament to my skills as an agent if I blended into the background. It's *good* that you had a hard time remembering my name. It's *good* that most women do. That's what I keep telling myself, anyway."

They laughed again. Then the surgeon who had operated on Peter McDonald marched in their direction.

CHAPTER 18

Four television sets were adding to the taxpayers' electric bill in Senator Alexandra Burton's elegant suite in the southwest corner of the Dirksen Congressional Center. U.S. senators, being political animals, felt compelled to stay in constant touch with the nation's leading media outlets. If a senator was allocated only one television, the argument went, he or she might miss a breaking news story being uncovered by one of the networks his or her TV wasn't tuned in to. On this particular afternoon, however, all the networks were covering the same event: the president's news conference on the status of Professor Peter McDonald.

Charles Jackson, the first African American president of the United States, was born for the television age. His eyes were the color of Swiss chocolate, his cheekbones looked as if they had been sculpted from Italian marble, and his smile glistened like that of a model from a Crest Whitestrips commercial. He bore a striking resemblance to a young Sidney Poitier, which helped explain why he had captured an unprecedented seventy-five percent of the female vote in the most recent presidential election. President Jackson wasn't trading on his looks this time, though. He was trying to reassure a nation in shock.

"This morning brought tragic news to the people of the United States," the president began. "An assassination attempt on the life of Professor Peter McDonald occurred outside the Hilton Hotel here in Washington at approximately 8:45 A.M. As the American people are well aware, I've nominated Professor McDonald for a seat on the U.S. Supreme Court. I'm proud to have done so, for Professor McDonald is without question one of the nation's most brilliant legal minds. And as the American people also know, Professor McDonald suffered the devastating loss of his beloved wife and daughter nine months ago. He was strong enough to recover from that terrible tragedy, and with God's help and the prayers of the American people, he'll be strong enough to recover from this one too. I'll have more to say when I hear more from the fine doctors and nurses at Bethesda Naval Hospital. But until I do, please pray for Professor McDonald, and please pray for our great country. May God bless Peter McDonald, and may God bless America."

Alexandra Rutledge Burton—direct descendent of John Rutledge, the first governor of South Carolina and a signatory of the U.S. Constitution—sat back in her chair. That'll be *me* giving that speech one day, she said to herself. That'll be *me* speaking from the Oval Office. She rocked forward and punched her intercom button. "Tell Jeff Oates I need to see him right away," she told her secretary.

Jeffrey Oates stepped into the senator's office.

Burton said, "Why are you wet?"

After a brief silence, Oates said, "I ... I walked to work this morning." He patted his head dry with a clump of paper towels that he had retrieved from the break room.

"From Georgetown? That's four or five miles from the Capitol."

Oates stayed silent.

Burton said, "Close the door."

Oates did. He returned to the spot in front of the senator's desk where he so often stood waiting for the day's instructions.

"It was you, wasn't it?"

"Yeah." Oates pitched the paper towels into the wastebasket next to the senator's desk.

Burton smiled and shook her head. "You've got a lotta guts. No one can deny that." She sat back in her chair.

"I wanted to show you that what happened in Charlottesville was just bad luck." Oates brushed his hands through his hair. It was still wet, albeit not as wet as when he had first entered the senator's office. "I wanted to show you that I could do the job ... that I can do *any* job."

Both Oates and Burton knew that Oates was talking about *the* job—White House chief of staff. Oates always talked about that job. He was obsessed with it. Almost as obsessed as Burton was about becoming president... .

"Do you think you killed him this time?" the senator asked next.

"Yeah."

CHAPTER 19

The parking lot of the Waffle House at exit 39 off of Interstate 26 in Charleston, South Carolina, was jammed with aging sedans and rusty pickups. All were American made. It was tantamount to treason in the blue-collar haunts of the old Confederacy to drive a foreign car.

Earl Smith spun his Ford flatbed onto the concrete island next to the restaurant's fifty-foot-tall highway sign. He switched off the ignition, dropped his keys into his pocket, and snapped the door shut with a firm elbow.

He would need to be careful, he said to himself as he headed toward the entrance. It looked as if a lot of the guys from the tire plant were inside. He recognized their vehicles.

He and Cat were always careful. They were never seen in public together, and he had certainly never visited her at work after they had started sleeping together. The startled look on her face when he pushed open the door testified to that fact. Apparently, there really was a first time for everything.

But Cat Wilson was a pro. She regained her composure before anyone knew she had lost it.

"Hey, if it ain't old Earl," a middle-aged man called out from the booth closest to the door. The man was wearing a Taylor Tires cap, a grease-stained sweatshirt, and a pair of Wrangler jeans. He made Brett Favre seem well groomed by comparison. "I didn't think you worked the graveyard no more." He stubbed out his cigarette on the soiled plate in front of him.

"Hey, Dex," Smith said to the man. "How ya doin'?"

"Aces, Earl. Frickin' aces."

Smith grabbed a stool at the far end of the counter.

Another coworker who was seated on the stool next to the one that Smith had selected leaned in and said, "Back on the graveyard, huh?" He soaked up the egg yolk on his plate with a piece of whole wheat toast.

Smith said, "Nah. Just hungry's all."

"But don't you live clear across town?" The man had moved on to his grits. He shoveled a spoonful into his mouth. "There's dozens of places to eat closer than this dive."

Smith smiled. "I know. But I like the hash browns here. Speaking of which," he said, shifting his attention from his seatmate to his soul mate, "could I get a number five, girlie?"

Cat glanced up from the cash register. "Sure." There wasn't a hint in her voice that she knew Smith, let alone that she was sleeping with him.

The guy seated next to Smith elbowed Smith in the ribs. "Make sure you get some brown sugar with that." He cackled and then inhaled another spoonful of grits.

Cat Wilson placed Earl Smith's order on the counter in front of him. The number five was Smith's favorite: two eggs over easy, two link sausages, a double side of hash browns, and two of the Waffle House's eponymic waffles.

Again, not a hint of recognition came from the waitress. "Enjoy" was all she said. She returned to the cash register.

The guy seated next to Smith nudged him again and said, "I know I would." He was leering at Cat's fabulous ass. It put Beyonce's to shame.

Smith didn't say a word. He couldn't take his eyes off Cat, though. He never could.

The guy seated next to him picked up on it. "I didn't think the Klan got hot for nigger women." Food crumbs dotted the guy's whiskered face.

"Shut the fuck up."

"Hey. Mellow out, Earl. I'm just messin' with ya." The guy spun on his stool and announced to his coworkers scattered around the diner, "Earl here don't like it when you say he's got the hots for the nigger waitress."

"I said shut the fuck up!" Smith sprang from his stool. He grabbed the guy by the collar and shook him like a bottle of ketchup.

The guy broke free from Smith's grip and lurched to his feet. He was a full six inches taller than Smith, which suggested that Smith was thinking with his heart rather than his head at the moment. "You stickin' up for niggers now, Earl?" The guy shoved Smith hard into the counter.

Smith stumbled back a bit but quickly regained his balance. His eyes danced around the room. He counted four klansmen in attendance. He reminded himself that he needed to be careful. Even grand dragons had been killed for less than what he was being accused of. He said, "Of course I ain't stickin' up for no nigger. Niggers ain't nuthin' but trash."

The klansmen who were present said, "Akia. Kigy."

Smith nodded to each of them. His eyes met Cat's.

Her eyes weren't locked on his for long, but it was long enough to let Smith know how hurt she was.

CHAPTER 20

Billy Joe Collier tossed his lunch pail and thermos onto the table in the break room. He was halfway through his shift at the Taylor Tires plant on the west side of Charleston. He snatched the copy of the *Charleston Post and Courier* that one of his coworkers had left behind. He couldn't read well, but the pictures told the story: gruesome front-page photographs of the black man and white woman he had murdered for simply being in love. Most of the black man's face was gone, smashed with a golf club like a discarded jack-o'-lantern. The white woman hadn't fared much better.

Collier smiled. He always got a kick out of seeing the results of his handiwork. He snapped open his lunch pail and pulled out a bologna and cheese sandwich. He unscrewed the lid on his thermos and poured a cup of Dr. Pepper. He settled in to read the story. He was careful not to spill food or soda on it. He planned on adding it to his scrapbook.

The racism of men like Billy Joe Collier was crude. Its most overpowering element was the conviction that blacks and whites were utterly distinct. A person *was* a black or a white, just as a truck was a truck and a pencil was a pencil. Race was an absolute category and the presumed characteristics of a member of the racial group were taken as God-given and unalterable. Blacks, diehard klansmen such as Collier believed, were people who did not want to work, who gained money through bullying or cheating, who robbed, and who were violent. Blacks wanted to hurt whites ... to steal jobs from white males, to rape white females.

It was this latter issue of race mixing that upset Collier the most. He had recently been told by one of his brothers in the Charleston den about a new scientific discovery. A scientist had found out that certain substances in semen could be transmitted into the blood supply of a man's sexual partner and create long-lasting effects. The scientist reported that a white woman who had sex even one time with a black man might well find herself permanently altered as a result: she herself might change in her features and she might well find herself *three years later* giving birth to a black child.

So, Collier said to himself as he took another look at the newspaper photographs, he had done the white woman a favor by killing her. The rape was for him.

CHAPTER 21

President Charles Jackson's eyes were locked on a squirrel trying to pry an acorn loose from underneath one of the White House's famous rosebushes. The squirrel was scratching the dirt around the bush like a bulldozer reconfiguring the foundation of a dilapidated house. The president admired the squirrel's persistence; the acorn was as large as the squirrel's head and yet the squirrel "refused to give up on the dream," as the president's teenage son liked to say.

Charles Jackson had never given up on *his* dream. He was currently living it. Ever since the day his high school history teacher had played a videotape of one of John F. Kennedy's legendary press conferences, Jackson had wanted to be president. Now he was ... the first African American elected to the most powerful office in the world.

Jackson shifted his attention from the squirrel in the rose garden to the guard dog in the Oval Office. "What's the news from the hospital, Jim?"

Jim Westfall was the president's chief of staff. He had served Jackson in the same capacity when Jackson was governor of Connecticut. He had quickly acquired the reputation around Washington for being a highly skilled spokesman for the president and highly protective of him. Hence, he was often described as Jackson's "guard dog."

Westfall said, "Professor McDonald made it through surgery, so that's good news. Unfortunately, the bullet ruptured his spleen, and he's lost a tremendous amount of blood. Bottom line: we still don't know whether he's going to make it."

"Shit," the president said. "Hasn't this poor man been through enough? He lost his wife and daughter because of me." Jackson again stared out the window at the squirrel.

Westfall rose from his seat and walked over to the president. "You need to stop blaming yourself for that, Mr. President. Professor McDonald doesn't hold you responsible for what happened in Charlottesville."

The president continued to watch the squirrel try to pry the acorn loose. "But if I hadn't asked him to serve, his family wouldn't have been put at risk. Everybody knew that anyone nominated for Crandall's seat might be in jeopardy. I certainly did. I saw the Secret Service report. People feel very strongly about affirmative action, especially during tough economic times. Folks who can't find work often try to go back to school. If they're white, especially if they're white and male, it's tough to get into the best institutions."

Edwin Crandall was the Supreme Court justice whose seat Peter McDonald had been nominated to fill. Crandall was eighty-nine years old, and he had retired from the bench because he could no longer keep pace with the Court's workload. When asked by a reporter at the news conference announcing his retirement about why he was leaving the Court, Crandall had quipped, "Because I'm old and falling apart." It was a classic line from the sharp-tongued jurist. But the real interest around the nation was in how Crandall's replacement would vote in *Tucker v. University of South Carolina*, the most highly anticipated civil rights case in a generation.

Westfall returned to his chair. "So you were only allowed to nominate a bachelor? *Please*, Mr. President, you're blaming yourself for nothing."

"I guess you're right." Jackson rubbed his tired eyes. "I guess risk just comes with the territory. But that doesn't make me worry any less about Professor McDonald's health."

The Oval Office became surprisingly quiet. Usually there was a constant hum of activity in the nation's most important room. Now it felt like a church on a Monday.

Finally, Westfall said, "I don't mean to sound insensitive, Mr. President, but have you thought about a replacement for Professor McDonald ... you know, in case he doesn't make it?"

Jackson's jaw tightened like that of the squirrel who had managed to pry the acorn free. "I refuse to think about that, Jim. Professor McDonald will pull through. I know he will. I just know it... ."

CHAPTER 22

Kelsi Shelton could barely concentrate on the lecture. She never had cared much for Corporate Tax, but that wasn't the reason she was having trouble paying attention on this particular morning. She was worried about Professor McDonald.

Kelsi still would have been waiting at the hospital if it hadn't been for her mother. Brian Neal, the Secret Service agent assigned to protect McDonald, hadn't been able to convince the strong-willed young woman to make the two-hour drive back to Charlottesville, and the doctors and nurses hadn't been able to convince her, either. But after a tear-filled conversation with her mother in the wee hours of the morning, Kelsi had decided to return to school. "It'll help take your mind off him for a while," Kelsi's mother had said. "Besides, there's nothing you can do for him at the hospital. You're a lawyer, not a doctor, and it's up to the doctors and nurses now."

Kelsi wasn't a lawyer *yet*, but she understood her mother's point. She drove back to Charlottesville and arrived just in time for her nine o'clock Corporate Tax class.

"We'll pick up here next time," the tax professor said.

Kelsi had no idea where "here" was. The entire class had passed in a blur.

Sue Plant, Kelsi's best friend since their first year at law school, realized that Kelsi was lost. She said, "He wants us to re-read the double taxation of dividends material."

Kelsi blushed. "Thanks, Sue." She tossed her casebook and statutory supplement into the daypack that seemed to accompany her everywhere she went. "I'm a bit out of it this morning. I didn't get enough sleep. Who am I kidding? I didn't get *any* sleep."

Sue switched off her laptop. She snapped the screen shut and returned the computer to its carrying case. "Any more news about Professor McDonald?"

The assassination attempt on the life of Professor Peter McDonald was about all anyone could talk about at UVA law school at the moment. After all, Professor McDonald was one of UVA's own. In fact, the dean had considered canceling classes for the day, and perhaps for the week, but he had decided against it because he wanted to try to maintain as much of a sense of normalcy in the law building as he possibly could. However, he had scheduled a meeting with the faculty, staff, and students for 10:00 A.M. Kelsi and Sue were on their way to the meeting now that Corporate Tax was done for the day.

CHAPTER 23

"No drinks in the library."

Clay Smith twisted in his seat, and his eyes met the eyes of an elderly woman pushing a cart full of law books. "Sorry," he said to her. He got out of his chair, walked to the end of the row of library carrels, drained the remnants of a Sprite, and tossed the soda can into the wastebasket.

He stopped for a minute and glanced out the window toward the Blue Ridge Mountains on the horizon. The morning fog blanketed the peaks like mist on a Scottish moor.

Clay Smith had mixed emotions about what he had been asked to do. On the one hand, his future looked bright. No other member of the Smith family had attended college, let alone law school. He also had a summer job lined up with the Charleston office of the largest law firm in South Carolina. On the other hand, his Uncle Earl had served as a surrogate father to him ever since his real father—Earl Smith's younger brother—had been shot and killed in a barroom brawl when Clay was seven. There also was the undeniable fact that the Smith men had always been active in the Ku Klux Klan. Always. Clay himself had been initiated into the brotherhood during his sophomore year of high school, and he attended Klan meetings whenever he was home on break. He might have been an honors student at a top-ranked law school, but he knew that niggers had to be kept in their place. His Uncle Earl had reminded him of that at six o'clock this very morning.

One of Clay's classmates walked by and tapped him on the shoulder. She said, "Stop daydreaming, Mr. Dershowitz." Alan Dershowitz was the most famous lawyer in the country. "It's time to get your butt out of the library for a change. The dean has called a meeting in the auditorium. It starts in five minutes." She smiled and added, "Kelsi will be there."

"I know," Clay said, blushing. "I know."

The law school was like high school as far as gossip was concerned, and seemingly every law student in the building knew that Clay had a crush on Kelsi Shelton. Unfortunately, Kelsi was now Clay's responsibility. That was what his uncle had called to tell him.

CHAPTER 24

Kelsi Shelton and Sue Plant spotted two seats in the rear of the auditorium. Almost everyone in the law school knew that Kelsi was Professor McDonald's research assistant. Consequently, words, looks, and hugs of support were in ample supply as she and Sue squeezed through the crowd. But just as Kelsi was about to take her seat, the assistant dean for student affairs asked her to step back out into the aisle for a moment.

Kelsi felt a knot in her stomach. The assistant dean was almost never the bearer of good news. Kelsi tripped over more than a few stray feet as she scrambled to the aisle. "Wh ... what is it?" she said. "Wh ... what's wrong? Is it about Professor McDonald?"

The assistant dean, a woman in her late fifties who looked an awful lot like Kelsi's favorite aunt—round face, pear-shaped build, constant smile, compassionate eyes—brushed a loose strand of hair from Kelsi's concerned face. She said, "Yes. But it's not what you think. The dean was hoping you would say a few words about the professor from a student's perspective."

Kelsi never had been one for speaking before large groups of people. In fact, she shared the preference for death over public speaking that opinion polls showed the majority of Americans favored. (*Death* over public speaking.) Her aversion to talking in front of crowds explained most of her curriculum choices; she tended to avoid, except for bar exam preparation purposes, courses that were courtroom-oriented (Evidence, Trial Advocacy,

Criminal Procedure, etc.). This time, though, she decided to face her fear. This time, it was about something—about some*one*—larger than herself. "I'd be honored to say a few words."

Dean Diego Rodriguez was addressing the audience of law faculty, staff, and students. Dean Rodriguez reflected the commitment—some called it an obsession—the nation's colleges and universities had to diversity. He was a competent man—he had done pretty well at a pretty good law school, his practice and clerkship experiences were respectable, and he had published two or three decent pieces of legal scholarship—but many of the candidates against whom he had competed for the deanship at the University of Virginia School of Law had accomplished more than he had. Much more. But they weren't Hispanic or gay. He was both. As a result, the other candidates hadn't had a chance against him in the hiring process, especially given that only 10 percent of the law professors in the United States identified themselves even in part as conservative. Indeed, as one lonely legal conservative had colorfully quipped, "Just as it was said in late-nineteenth-century England that the Anglican Church was the Conservative Party at prayer, American colleges and universities today were the Democratic Party at play." They weren't much interested in hiring straight WASP men to work at—let alone lead—their institutions of higher education.

The dean sang Peter McDonald's praises. He said that McDonald was what every law professor should aspire to be: a terrific colleague, a world-class scholar, and a teacher who actually cared about his students. Then he glanced over at Kelsi Shelton. Their eyes met, and she appeared ready to address her peers. The dean said, "I've asked Kelsi to say a few words to you about Professor McDonald. As most of you know, Kelsi is Professor McDonald's research assistant. She has been helping him prepare for his Supreme Court confirmation hearing. Few know him better than Kelsi does. I think it's more appropriate, particularly under current circumstances, for her to say a few words about Professor McDonald than it is for me to go on and on about him. And believe me, as a dean, I know how to go on and on."

Awkward laughter came from the audience.

Then Dean Rodriquez said, "Kelsi." The dean smiled warmly as Kelsi approached the podium.

Kelsi had received no advance warning that she would be speaking to an auditorium full of people. She certainly wasn't dressed for the occasion. She was wearing typical law student attire: jogging shoes, jeans, and an oversized sweatshirt with the school's logo embossed across the chest. Unlike most law students, however, she still looked like she had just stepped off the runway of a Paris fashion show. Only a handful of people could make a sweatshirt look like high style. Kelsi Shelton was one of them. And only a handful of people could address a standing-room-only crowd on a moment's notice. Unfortunately, Kelsi Shelton was *not* one of them.

She clutched the podium for support. Even then, her hands were quivering like a rabbit about to be slaughtered for stew. "H ... hi," she said.

Her classmates couldn't help but sense her discomfort. Many of them called out, "Hi, Kelsi!" It was like a greeting at an Al-Anon meeting.

A brief smile spread across Kelsi's beautiful face. "I only found out about five minutes ago that I was supposed to say something today. I haven't prepared anything, obviously." She glanced over at Dean Rodriguez and then returned her attention to the audience. "The dean asked me to say what it's like to work for Professor McDonald." She made sure to speak in the present tense. Professor McDonald wasn't dead... . "It's great. He's brilliant, hardworking, and very considerate. He always makes sure that I've got more to do than just xeroxing and filing. He says he wants me to learn something, not simply assist him with what he needs to get done. Even now, during his confirmation hearing, he's always talking to me about the process and about the Supreme Court's role in the justice system. Believe me, he's got plenty of things to worry about, but he worries about *me*, about whether *I'm* learning something. So, all I can really say is that Professor

McDonald is the best boss I've ever had, and the best teacher. It's been my privilege to work for him."

Clay Smith sat in the back of the auditorium and listened to Kelsi Shelton commend Professor McDonald to the UVA law school community. Clay, a first-year student at the law school, shared Kelsi's high regard for Professor McDonald, but he also shared his Uncle Earl's desire to see the professor's nomination to the Supreme Court go down in flames. Unfortunately, killing Kelsi was part of the plan to ensure it did.

CHAPTER 25

The doctors and nurses rushed around the emergency room as if someone's life depended on them. It did.

"Charge the paddles to two hundred!"

"Stat!"

"Clear!"

Dr. Morris Tanenbaum, the president's personal physician and the man trying to bring order to the chaos, applied the paddles to Professor Peter McDonald's chest in an effort to shock McDonald's heart back into rhythm. It didn't work.

"Charge to three hundred!" Nothing. No response. Still flat-line. "Four hundred!"

Perspiration dripped from underneath the doctor's surgical mask. The thought of losing any patient was nerve-wracking enough, but this patient was the president's choice for a seat on the most powerful court in the world.

Finally, a heartbeat. Finally, the monitor resembled a mountain range rather than a desert floor.

A spurt of applause filled the room. Everyone knew what was at stake.

Dr. Tanenbaum handed the paddles to the head nurse, pitched his soiled mask and gloves into the wastebasket in the corner, and headed for the waiting area to brief the president's chief of staff. "Good job," he said to the ER team as he exited the room.

Jim Westfall was popping a piece of nicotine gum into his mouth when the doctor arrived to update him.

Dr. Tanenbaum said, "I'm glad you're staying off the cancer sticks, Jim."

Cigarettes were every doctor's taboo. They were like going all in against the house at an Atlantic City casino.

Westfall said, "I'm trying, Doc. I'm trying. But I must be chewing two packs of this stuff a day." He held up the pack of nicotine gum. Only one stick remained.

"Better two packs of gum than two packs of cigarettes."

The president's chief of staff and the president's personal physician were both busy men. The former got straight to the point. "How's Professor McDonald? Is he going to pull through?"

Dr. Tanenbaum traced a long finger across his balding pate. "It's too early to tell. He went into cardiac arrest a few minutes ago, but we were able to get his heart back into a proper rhythm."

"Cardiac arrest! He was shot, not fat!"

"A lot of things can cause a heart attack, Jim. You're right. He was shot. But the gunshot put his system into shock, and that put too much stress on his heart. The result, unfortunately, was cardiac arrest. It's not uncommon."

Westfall popped the final piece of nicotine gum into his mouth. His jaw was as tight as a slingshot. "What's the prognosis? What should I tell the president?"

Doctors didn't like to be put on the spot, and Dr. Morris Tanenbaum was no different from any of the others. However, the person asking the question through his right-hand man, Jim Westfall, was *very* different: he was the president of the United States.

Dr. Tanenbaum said, "The prognosis isn't good, I'm sorry to say. The gunshot wound was bad enough, but a heart attack is always dangerous. On the plus side, Professor McDonald is a relatively young man, and he kept —*keeps*, sorry—himself in good shape. He looks more like thirty-five than forty-five."

"So you're saying that the president should find another nominee?" Westfall was devastated at the prospect. McDonald was the perfect nominee—until he got shot, that is.

"It's not my place to say that, obviously. But as a doctor, and as a friend to the president, it is my place to say that this particular nominee might not be alive to serve."

CHAPTER 26

The nurse studied the monitors above Peter McDonald's bed. She entered the data onto the patient's chart. She returned to her chair in the corner of the room.

Normally, the nurse would have left to check on her other patients. But McDonald wasn't a normal patient; he was her only patient. Nominees to powerful government posts always got special treatment. Dr. Tanenbaum had made that point clear beyond cavil at the beginning of her shift.

Peter McDonald had never wanted special treatment, though. All he had ever wanted was to be a teacher and scholar.

McDonald loved being a law professor. He loved almost everything about it. Sure, he disliked the infighting among many of his colleagues over petty issues such as who got which office or who stood before whom in the commencement processional, but the joy he felt working with bright young students and writing about legal issues that affected almost every facet of American society more than offset the bullshit that was faculty politics.

McDonald was often asked which he enjoyed more, teaching or writing. He always answered, "It's impossible to say. I love the give-and-take with my students in the classroom, but I also love to bury myself in the library to research and write." He would usually smile and add, "It's like being asked to choose between chocolate cake and apple pie. They're both delicious."

McDonald could still remember his first day in the classroom. He had always been a relatively shy person—that was one of the qualities that had endeared him to his wife—and he had spent the morning alternating between putting the finishing touches on his lecture notes in his office and kneeling over the toilet in the faculty bathroom. He didn't throw up, but he came close on more than a couple of his mad dashes down the hallway.

There wasn't a sound when he entered the classroom. Students with a new teacher were like the family dog with a new pet—suspicious and apprehensive but full of hope and wonder. There was plenty of poking and prodding in both scenarios.

"Good morning," McDonald could remember saying. At least he hadn't lost the use of his voice. "This is Constitutional Law. I'm Peter McDonald." He had his eyes glued to his notes for even that perfunctory introduction. "I'd like to begin this morning with Chief Justice John Marshall's opinion in *Marbury v. Madison*." He lifted his eyes from his notes to discover a roomful of students staring at him from behind their casebooks and coffee cups. His knees buckled a bit. He suddenly realized that he wasn't much older than most of his students. He suddenly remembered that he had graduated from law school himself only two years earlier. But given the fact that he had spent those intervening two years in prestigious clerkships—the first year with a judge on the U.S. Court of Appeals for the D.C. Circuit and the second with the chief justice of the United States—the appointments committee at the University of Virginia School of Law had deemed him qualified for the position. At the moment, McDonald couldn't have disagreed more with the committee's decision. It was almost as if the PGA Tour had declared him eligible to play in the Masters because he had once played a round of golf at Augusta National.

"Can anyone tell me the facts in *Marbury*?"

Dead silence.

McDonald could hear the proverbial pin drop.

A hand raised slowly from the back of the room.

It was like the sight of a pool of water to a man stranded alone in the desert.

McDonald—*Professor* McDonald—glanced down at his seating chart and called on the student by name.

CHAPTER 27

Peter McDonald survived that memorable first day in the classroom. In fact, he eventually became one of the most innovative and popular teachers on the UVA law faculty. It had taken a while, but he had gotten there. Writing had come quickly to him, however.

Most law professors were lawyers, not scholars. In other words, they didn't have advanced training in traditional academic fields such as history, political science, or economics, but they knew how to argue. And boy, did they like to argue. Most of them didn't care that they didn't know as much about a subject as they needed to know before they could comment on it intelligently: They could simply *assert* that they were an expert in the field.

The best example of this phenomenon was what was known in academic circles as "law office history." Law professors had spent an inordinate amount of time over the years writing about what the "framers" of the U.S. Constitution had thought about particular legal questions. The place of religion in public life was a frequent subject of debate. "The framers intended a strict 'wall of separation' between church and state," a noted Yale Law School professor had written in an article published in the *Yale Law Journal.* "Religious activities have no place in our public schools. Prayer certainly doesn't."

A Columbia Law School professor had countered that Thomas Jefferson, the author of the "wall of separation" metaphor, wasn't even in Philadelphia in 1787 when the Constitution was being drafted. He was serving as the U.S. ambassador to France. "Jefferson's absence aside," the Columbia professor had penned, "there is no single entity that can be called the 'framers' of the Constitution... . The 'framers' did not have a collective mind, think in one groove, or possess the same convictions."

Peter McDonald, in contrast, had tried to steer clear of debates among academic lawyers about the meaning of history, philosophy, and the like. "Law professors need to concentrate on the *law*," he had once said during a symposium about the state of legal scholarship. "We should leave history to the historians, economics to the economists, and philosophy to the philosophers. To make the point another way, although it makes perfect sense to ask Phil Mickelson how he hits such incredible golf shots, it seems like pure lunacy to care what he thinks about the Sixth Amendment right to counsel in a criminal trial. Believe it or not, I once heard a reporter ask him about the Sixth Amendment. It was during the time of the Michael Vick dog fighting trial. Phil stared at the reporter as if the reporter was crazy and moved on to the putting green. We should follow Phil Mickelson's example and stick to what we know best."

CHAPTER 28

Peter McDonald's scholarship had made him famous. He was frequently invited to lecture at law schools across the nation, his articles and books were cited by other scholars in his field, and he had won numerous awards for excellence in legal research. But what made the celebrated law professor most proud was the life he had shared with his family.

Jenny and Megan McDonald certainly had been aware of Peter's professional success—Jenny because she was a high powered intellect in her own right and Megan because her father often brought her along on his speaking engagements—but they much preferred spending private time with him at home. Their favorite family activity was tending the garden in their backyard. None of the McDonalds possessed what could be called a green thumb —Megan's thumb was usually *brown* from playing in the dirt—but there was something about trying to bring plants and flowers to life that appealed to them. Perhaps it was because both Peter and Jenny had grown up in an urban environment. Peter had been raised in Chicago, where his father was a senior vice president for a commodities firm and his mother a dentist with her own successful practice. Jenny had grown up in South Boston. Her father had worked for thirty years as a heating and cooling repairman. Her mother stayed home to raise the kids. About as close as either family had gotten to horticulture was a pair of flower boxes in the front windows of their respective residences.

Cooking dinner together was Peter, Jenny, and Megan's second favorite family activity. Cooking was something at which Peter's and Jenny's families *had* excelled growing up. Jenny's mom had been a wonder in the kitchen. In fact, she had been renowned throughout her South Boston neighborhood for her Irish stew: a delicious concoction of lamb, carrots, potatoes, and gentle spices from the Emerald Isle.

Peter's father had been the gourmet in their household. His specialty was marinated Chicago strips as thick as a suburban phonebook. He also could bake a cherry pie that put Rachel Ray to shame.

Culinary skills aside, what Peter, Jenny, and Megan enjoyed most about cooking was the time they got to spend together. Peter and Jenny were the copilots in the kitchen—they prepared the food and the table—while Megan was the gap-toothed navigator. She got to suggest the menu. Or at least Peter and Jenny liked her to believe she suggested it. They usually had to remind their young daughter that it might be nice to make something other than "humbragger and french frieds" for dinner.

The critical care nurse rose from her chair to check the monitors again. Professor McDonald was still alive... .

CHAPTER 29

The young black man tied to the tree thought of Denzel Washington in the whipping scene from the movie *Glory*. Denzel had won his first Academy Award for his portrayal of a proud former slave who fought for the Union army during the Civil War but refused to kowtow to the white officers who led the black brigade in which he served. The young black man remembered Denzel's character staring defiantly at his white commanding officer while being whipped for deserting his post to find shoes that didn't cut his feet. Tears clouded Denzel's character's eyes as both the pain of the whipping and the memories of a lifetime of whippings flooded over him. Denzel's character didn't scream, though. He refused to give the white man the satisfaction.

This wasn't a movie. No matter how hard he tried and no matter how much he wanted to deny the white men in white sheets the pleasure they obviously felt in watching him suffer, the young black man couldn't help but scream.

Billy Joe Collier said, "Scream, nigger. Go ahead and fuckin' scream. Your mama can't do nuthin' for you now." Collier spat in the young black man's face.

Several other members of the konklave hurled rocks at the young black man's naked body. "Bull's-eye!" one of them shouted when a particularly large rock hit the young black man in the head. A second rock to the head knocked the young black man unconscious.

"Wake him up," Collier said. "Wake the fuckin' nigger up." Collier wanted the young black man to *feel* what the konklave was about to do to him.

A hydra reached for a canteen and unscrewed the cap. He splashed water into the young black man's face. "Wake up, nigger! Wake the fuck up!"

The young black man began to cough and wheeze. He was regaining consciousness. He wished that he wasn't. His eyes opened to the sight of more than a dozen white men in white sheets glowering at him as if he had done something wrong... . The only thing he had done "wrong" was be born black.

But that was more than enough for Billy Joe Collier. "Give me a knife," Collier said. "Give me a fuckin' knife!"

The same hydra who had splashed water into the young black man's face reached into his pocket and pulled out a switchblade. He slapped the knife into Collier's palm like a nurse handing a surgeon a scalpel.

Collier snapped open the blade. *Thpp.* "Give me your hand, nigger. Give me your fuckin' hand."

The young black man was strong—he moved furniture for a living—but he couldn't overpower a dozen men, especially when he was tied to a tree. He tried, but it was pointless.

The hydra grabbed the young black man's hand and pried open his fingers.

The young black man knew what was coming. "Don't," he said. "*Please*, don't."

But a plea for mercy from a black man simply inspired Collier to press forward more vigorously. He kissed the blade for luck and began to saw off the young black man's forefinger.

Howls of pain echoed through the woods.

Collier smiled.

The konklave cheered and applauded.

Blood poured from the young black man's hand like water from a broken faucet.

Collier kept sawing.

The finger fell to the ground.

The young black man continued to scream and beg for mercy.

None was forthcoming.

Collier bent down to pick up the finger. The young black man kicked him in the head as he did. Collier grabbed the finger and then punched the young black man hard in the face.

"Fuck you, nigger," Collier said. He held up the severed finger so that the konklave could see it.

More cheers and applause rang out.

"Here," Collier said as he tossed the finger to the hydra who had lent him the knife.

The hydra pulled out a handkerchief, wrapped the bloody finger in it, and said, "Thanks, Billy Joe." He smiled. "I'll add it to my collection."

That drew laughter from the konklave.

One of the other klansmen said, "I've got dibbs on the next one."

Collier proceeded to saw off the young black man's middle finger. By this point, the young black man was in too much shock to feel the pain. When he began to pass out again, another canteen of water was splashed in his face.

Earl Smith approached the konklave. "What's going on here?"

Collier said, "Just cuttin' up another nigger, Earl."

Smith stared at the bloody young black man. "Can I see you for a minute, Billy Joe?"

"Give me a second, Earl. I've only got two fingers to go."

"Now, Billy Joe. *Now.*"

Earl Smith and Billy Joe Collier walked to a large oak tree about twenty-five yards from the rest of the konklave. The tree's branches hung long and loose from a thick trunk.

Smith said, "I thought we agreed to hold off on any more lynchings until after we'd done our favor for Senator Burton?"

Collier said, "'We'? ... 'Our'? ... *You're* the only one who gets to have any fun."

Smith glanced over at the young black man tied to the tree. Members of the konklave had started throwing rocks at him again. "We've had this conversation already,

Billy Joe. This is a really, really big favor we've been asked to do. We gotta do it right. And as the grand dragon of South Carolina, I get to decide what right is. You know that."

Collier shook his head. "I know ya do, Earl. I know it. But it's tough to hold back. There are so many niggers that need killin'. Shit, you shoulda seen what I done to that white whore we saw in the bar the other night. You know, the one with the nigger boyfriend. I opened their skulls with a golf club."

"What?!" Smith said. "Why'd you go and do that?"

"Because there ain't nuthin' more agin the Klan way than fuckin' a nigger."

Smith stared at Collier. He had hung around with him for so many years that he had become numb to the hatred that Collier had inside him. Then he thought about Cat ... about *him* and Cat.

CHAPTER 30

"What are you doin' here, suga? I thought you'd be in D.C. by now." Cat Wilson opened the door to her double-wide. She lived at the back end of a mobile home park on the west side of Charleston.

Earl Smith stepped over the threshold. He maneuvered passed a stack of ragged *People* magazines. His eyes surveyed the place. "This is nice," he said.

It wasn't. The thin metal walls were rusting, the carpet was stained, and only about half the light fixtures seemed to work. But the trailer had been in far worse condition when Cat had moved in. She had done her best to make it look like a home for her young daughter.

"I thought you said it weren't safe for you to come to my house—that that was why we kept meetin' at the motel?"

"It ain't safe, Cat. But ... but I needed to see you." Smith's eyes locked on Cat's.

"Why'd ya need to see me, suga?" Cat smiled. "You just can't get enough of your sweet chocolate, can ya?" She ran the tips of her fingers across Smith's chest.

His entire body tingled when she did. "That ain't it."

"Why, then? Why did ya need to see your Cat?"

Smith blushed. He was one of the toughest guys in Charleston, but Cat Wilson had made him blush. "I ... I just did, is all. I felt bad about what I said at the diner."

Cat smiled again. She took Smith by the hand and led him to the bedroom in the rear of the trailer.

"Where's your daughter?" Smith asked.

"Sleepin' at the neighbor's," Cat answered. She pushed Smith to the bed. She began to unbutton her shirt. It was just an old work shirt, but she filled it out nicely. She unbuttoned one button at a time.

Smith sat on the edge of the bed and took a deep breath. He couldn't take his eyes off Cat. He knew Cat was right about why he had come; he needed to be with her one last time before he left for D.C.

Cat finished unbuttoning her shirt and began working on her jeans. She slithered out of them like an exotic dancer at a downtown gentlemen's club.

Smith took another deep breath. His eyes remained transfixed on Cat's fabulous body. Her skin glistened in the moonlight shining through the window.

Cat leaned over and pulled Smith's face to her breast. He began to suckle like a baby thirsting for his mother. He moved to the other breast.

Cat joined him on the bed. "You gonna miss your Cat, ain't ya? You're gonna miss me when you're gone."

Earl Smith didn't say a word. He didn't need to. His answer was revealed in the heat of the moment.

CHAPTER 31

Billy Joe Collier dropped his beer in disgust. "I can't fuckin' believe it," he muttered. He drew closer to the window to make sure that his eyes weren't deceiving him. They weren't; Earl Smith, the grand dragon of the South Carolina Realm of the Ku Klux Klan, was having sex with a nigger woman.

Collier had decided to tail Smith after the evening's konklave had adjourned. The work of a klansman was almost always conducted in secret, and Collier had tailed many people over the years. But he had never tailed Smith before. He had never imagined that he would need to.

Billy Joe Collier and Earl Smith used to have a terrific relationship. They used to hunt and fish together almost every weekend, and best of all, they used to lynch a lot of what were, as far as Collier was concerned, worthless niggers.

But Smith had changed over the past several months. He kept canceling their hunting and fishing trips, and he seemed less enthusiastic about putting niggers in their place than a loyal klansman should be. Now Collier knew why: Smith was doing the horizontal mambo with a piece of nigger ass.

Collier would have kept watching Smith and his whore have sex—Collier was a big fan of porno movies—but the sight of a member of the brotherhood rolling around in the sheets with a nigger woman was too much for his stomach to take. Consequently, he stepped away from the window. He couldn't just leave, though. Instead, he searched the ground for some sticks. He found two sturdy ones. He tied them together with a thick weed that he had pulled from the side of the trailer. He had learned how to build a makeshift cross at a Klan Youth Corps meeting when he was a kid. It was at that meeting nearly forty years before where he had first met Earl Smith.

Collier stuck the cross into the ground. It stood about two feet high. He reached into his pocket for a pack of matches. Every good klansman carried matches. He had learned that at the junior Klan meeting, too. He struck a match against the metal trailer and lit the cross. He jogged toward his car. He stopped for a moment and picked up a rock. Every good klansman could hit a target with a rock from at least twenty-five yards away. Collier was no exception to this rule. He took dead aim at the trailer's bedroom window. He hurled the rock like the baseball pitcher he had wanted to be in high school.

Crssh. Bull's-eye! The glass shattered, sending shards falling to the ground and to the floor inside the trailer.

Earl Smith shot up from the bed in time to see Billy Joe Collier's Ford Monte Carlo speed off into the distance.

CHAPTER 32

Jim Westfall poured himself a cup of coffee while Cheryl Richards pulled a single sheet of paper from her briefcase.

Richards was White House counsel, which meant she was the president's lawyer. The sheet of paper was the list of potential candidates her office had compiled to replace Peter McDonald as the president's nominee to the Supreme Court of the United States.

Westfall returned to his seat at his cluttered desk in his tiny office. Space was at a premium in the West Wing. Only the president's office—the Oval Office—was large. As a result, the desks and offices of the president's staff—even the senior staff—became overwhelmed in a hurry. Westfall pushed aside a stack of memos and placed his coffee cup on a coaster emblazoned with the White House seal. "Are you sure you wouldn't like a cup?"

Richards said, "I'm sure, Jim. But thanks."

"You used to drink this stuff like it was water when we were in law school." Westfall took a slow sip from his steaming cup. It, too, was emblazoned with the White House seal.

Richards smiled. "That was a long time ago, Jim. My nerves can't handle the caffeine like they used to."

"Mine, either. But mine are already shot... . What a week." Westfall reached for his coffee again. He took another sip. "How does the list look?"

Richards focused her eyes on the sheet of paper she was clutching in her hand like a sacred scroll. "I think the staff came up with three excellent possibilities."

"Who are they?"

"Judge Joseph Saltzman, Judge Thomas Woodward, and Professor Barbara DeCew."

"Saltzman from the Ninth Circuit?"

"Yes."

"Woodward from the Fifth?"

"Yes."

"DeCew from Yale Law School?"

"Yes."

Westfall rocked forward in his seat. He braced himself against his desk. He looked like a lion about to leap. "Where's Richards from the White House counsel's office?"

Richards shook her head. "I've already said no, Jim. It wouldn't look good for the president to nominate someone from his own staff."

"Why the hell not?" Westfall got up from his seat and walked toward the window overlooking the presidential putting green. The president's teenage son was working on his short game. The young man was a scratch golfer. He hoped to play for Stanford after he graduated from high school. "Nixon nominated Rehnquist, and Rehnquist eventually became chief justice. And don't forget about the greatest chief justice of them all: John Marshall. He was secretary of state when John Adams nominated him to be chief. Besides, Cheryl, you're more than qualified for the job. You graduated at the top of our law school class, you clerked at the Court for Justice Ginsburg, you made partner at the most prestigious law firm in the city, and now you've got some government service under your belt."

Richards was watching Westfall watch the president's son practice putting. "Ten months, Jim. I've only been working at the White House for ten months."

Westfall turned from the window and met Richards's eyes. "But you've been *effective*, Cheryl. Shoot, you've been effective in every job you've ever had. And despite what Senator Burton might be telling the press, effectiveness—talent, competence, work ethic—is what the president cares most about."

Richards shifted in her seat. She smoothed the crease on her designer skirt. "What about Peter

McDonald?" she asked uncomfortably. "I thought the president hadn't given up hope for his recovery. I thought *you* hadn't."

"He hasn't. And I haven't, either." Westfall returned his attention to the putting green. The president's son continued to hole putt after putt. "But the attending physician told me that the prospects aren't good. Given who that doctor is—Morris Tanenbaum, the president's personal physician—I'm inclined to take his word for it. The president knows the facts. And he also knows that he owes it to the country to name a replacement if Professor McDonald doesn't take a turn for the better. A quick turn, I might add."

A long silence filled the room. The sound of golf balls popping off the president's son's putter seeped in through the windowpane.

"All right," Richards finally said. "You can add my name to the list."

CHAPTER 33

Jim Westfall entered the Oval Office as he had done virtually every day since Charles Jackson had taken the presidential oath. One of the perks of being White House chief of staff was that Westfall didn't need an appointment to see the president. He and the president's wife and children were the only people who didn't.

President Jackson was seated behind a desk that had once belonged to William Howard Taft. Jackson, like Taft, was a large man, although in Jackson's case his size was attributable to hours in the weight room rather than at the dinner table. The president said, "What's up?" He closed the CIA report he was reading.

Westfall continued his march toward the president's desk. He stopped directly in front of it. "I asked Cheryl Richards to prepare a list of replacements for Peter McDonald. I thought you should see it."

President Jackson shot up from his chair like a pilot from an ejection seat. "Who told you to do that?! Who told you to look for a replacement?!"

Luckily for Westfall, he had known Jackson for years. Consequently, he wasn't as taken aback by the president's outburst as he otherwise might have been. Although Jackson came across in public as laid-back and unflappable, Westfall knew that in private the president was capable of erupting like a volcano.

"Nobody told me to do it, Mr. President. But after talking to Morris Tanenbaum at the hospital, I thought it needed to be done. As you know, it's the chief of staff's job to try and anticipate what the president might need."

Jackson was circling the room. For once, it made sense that the Oval Office was round; pacing in large circles gave the most powerful man in the world a chance to cool down. The president collapsed onto a couch that Laura Bush had selected when she had refurbished the White House during her husband's second term. Jackson said, his voice dripping with concern, "What did Morris say about Professor McDonald's prospects?"

Westfall hadn't budged an inch during the entire time the president had been circling the Oval. However, when the president sat, Westfall sat. "He said that the professor's prospects aren't good. In fact, it was Morris who recommended that I start working on a list of possible substitutes." Westfall rubbed his hand across his whiskered chin. He was exhausted, and he knew he looked that way. "Morris is doing all he can to save Professor McDonald, Mr. President. But the gunshot wound went pretty deep."

The president studied the face of his chief of staff and longtime friend. He had known Westfall since college. They had been fraternity brothers at Yale. They had also played on the rugby team together. They had become best friends during countless hours in the whirlpool soothing their bruised bodies after rough matches. Most important of all, it was Jim Westfall who had devised the strategy that had turned the charismatic governor of a small New England state into the first African American president of the United States. Finally, the president said, "Let me see it."

Westfall stood up, walked to the couch, and handed the president the list. He felt like a jury foreman delivering a verdict form to a judge.

The president studied the list. Three of the names were typed. He smiled when he noticed that a fourth name had been penciled in. "You finally managed to twist Cheryl's arm, huh?"

Westfall returned the president's smile. It felt good to smile under the circumstances. Strange, but good.

"Yeah. It wasn't easy, but she finally agreed to let me throw her hat into the ring. I think she'd make a terrific choice."

The president folded the list and placed it in his pocket. "So do I. But not as terrific as Peter McDonald... . Pray for him, will you Jim?"

"Certainly, Mr. President."

The two old friends dropped to their knees and asked for God's mercy.

CHAPTER 34

Clay Smith had been tailing Kelsi Shelton for the better part of three miles. He had always liked Kelsi. Every first-year student at UVA law school was assigned an upper-class mentor—a more experienced classmate who could explain the ropes and who was available for questions during the daunting 1L experience—and Kelsi was his. Talk about serendipity, Clay said to himself as he made a left turn onto University Avenue. He knew the person that his uncle had told him to kill.

It wouldn't be easy. It wouldn't be easy for a couple of reasons. First, Clay had never killed a white person before. A nigger, yes. Clay had killed two niggers in his young life. But whites and niggers were different. Niggers weren't people. Every klansman knew that. Clay certainly did.

The second reason that he would have trouble killing Kelsi was because he liked her, and not merely in the sense that a new student liked a mentor. No, Clay had romantic feelings for Kelsi. He had had them for a long time.

Kelsi pulled onto Rugby Road and maneuvered her VW Beetle into a vacant parking space.

Clay whizzed past her and found a spot about two blocks down the street. He switched off the ignition, popped his keys into his pocket, and started to jog in Kelsi's direction.

Like most pretty girls, Kelsi walked quickly. It was almost as if she knew someone was after her.

Clay got to within a hundred yards of her. He said, "Kelsi! Hey, Kelsi!"

Kelsi stopped. She turned to identify the source of the interruption. A brief smile spread across her beautiful face. She waved and then waited for Clay to catch up with her.

"Hi," Clay said when he finally did. "I thought it was you." He was breathing heavily from the hundred-yard dash.

Kelsi glanced at her watch. "Don't you have Civil Procedure now?"

Clay grinned. "Always the big sister, huh?"

"Mentor," Kelsi said, smiling again. "Always the mentor. It's my job to give you grief."

They shared a laugh.

Clay said, "Where are you off to?"

Kelsi said, "I wanted to get Professor McDonald something from Mincer's."

Mincer's was one of Charlottesville's many souvenir shops. It sold almost every UVA memento imaginable; from sweatshirts to key chains, all manner of memorabilia was available for purchase at grossly inflated prices.

"Why?" Clay asked. He wiped a bead of sweat from his forehead with the back of his hand. "I would've thought that he already owns more than his fair share of UVA stuff."

Kelsi brushed a loose strand of hair from her face. "Believe it or not, he doesn't. And I was thinking that it might make him feel better if he could drink his juice or coffee from a UVA mug. You know, it might remind him of home... . Hospitals are lonely places."

Clay waved at a friend who rode by on a bicycle. His attention returned to Kelsi. "So he's feeling better? The dean didn't make it sound like he was doing too well."

"He's not." The color rushed from Kelsi's face. "But I thought a UVA mug might help."

"It might," Clay said, trying to sound supportive. He knew it wouldn't, though. And if it did, he knew his uncle would have something to say about it. "Would you like some help picking one out? I've got a pretty good eye for crap. You should see my collection of UVA stuff." He tugged on his UVA sweatshirt. "Besides, it'll give me an excuse for missing Torts."

The smile returned to Kelsi's beautiful face. "As your mentor, I shouldn't be contributing to your truancy. But, hey, I'd enjoy the company."

The problem was, so would Clay.

CHAPTER 35

Kelsi found a UVA mug that she liked. Actually, Clay was the one who discovered it. Much to Clay's surprise, the souvenir shops didn't only sell crap. This particular mug was made of bone china, and the UVA logo affixed to it didn't assault the senses like a neon sign on a skid row tavern.

Clay waited patiently at the front of the store while the cashier wrapped the mug in tissue paper and tied an orange and blue ribbon around it.

Kelsi signed the card that hung from the ribbon and then said, "Do you have time for lunch?"

Clay spun around to make sure that Kelsi was talking to him. "Me?"

Kelsi giggled. "Of course, you. I'll even pay. It's the least I can do after you spotted the perfect mug... . Professor McDonald will love it."

Clay recommended The White Spot for lunch. It wasn't a racial thing this time. He loved greasy spoons. That said, dining at a restaurant with "white" in the name wasn't lost on the young klansman.

Their orders arrived quickly.

Kelsi asked, "Where do you plan to practice when you're done?" She nibbled on a crouton.

Clay answered, "Charleston, I hope. But it all depends on whether I get an offer." He bit into his house special: a quarter-pound hamburger topped with cheese, chopped onions, and a fried egg called a Gusburger.

Frequent connoisseurs of this artery-clogging delicacy were lucky that UVA hospital was located across the street.

"Why wouldn't you get an offer? UVA's the best law school in the South, and as far as I can tell, most of our classmates are interested in working in D.C. or New York. Charleston should be wide open for you."

Clay wiped grease from his chin. "I hope so. My family's counting on it."

"Why? Is your dad a lawyer? My granduncle is, and he keeps dropping hints about wanting me to go back to Wisconsin when I graduate." Kelsi smiled. "They're not subtle hints, either. He sent me a mock set of business cards for my birthday that read, 'Shelton and Shelton, Attorneys-at-Law.'"

"That's funny." Clay popped a piece of stray egg into his mouth. "But my dad's not a lawyer. No one in my family is. In fact, I'm the first one to graduate from college, let alone go to law school."

Kelsi took a sip of Diet Pepsi and then plunged her fork into her tossed salad. She was trying her best to avoid the caloric train wreck that constituted The White Spot's menu. "Why do you have to go home then? With your grades and a UVA law degree, you can go pretty much wherever you want."

Clay fidgeted with a paper napkin. Clearly, he couldn't tell Kelsi the real reason he needed to go home: to continue his work with the Charleston den of the Ku Klux Klan. Instead, he chose, "Because my mom is sick."

Kelsi's eyes became as wide as the onion rings on Clay's plate. "That's terrible. Is she going to be OK?"

"We don't know yet. That's why I need to go home."

"What's wrong with her?"

"Cancer."

Clay Smith's sob story about his mother's illness had an unintended consequence: he ended up at Kelsi Shelton's apartment.

CHAPTER 36

After the third beer, Clay had convinced Kelsi to turn on some music. It had been Kelsi's idea to turn down the lights. It wasn't long afterward that the make-out session began.

"I feel like I'm in high school," Kelsi said as she came up for air. "Either that or in an episode of *Desperate Housewives*... . You should know that I usually don't make-out with my mentees."

Clay placed his hand on Kelsi's breast, French kissed her for what must have been the tenth time in the past twenty minutes, and then said, "I'm glad it's a standard, not a rule."

They both laughed. Law students were beaten over the head with the distinction between a "bright line rule" and a "flexible standard." The former permitted no exceptions. The latter was essentially nothing but exceptions.

"Can I see your bedroom?" Clay's hand slid to the inside of Kelsi's thigh.

"OK." Kelsi grabbed Clay's other hand and led him to the back of her apartment.

They stepped over a pile of casebooks. They maneuvered their way around a stack of commercial outlines. Kelsi was the first to drop to the bed. She unbuttoned Clay's shirt and ran her fingers across his chest. It was easy to see that he spent a fair amount of time working out at the North Grounds Recreation Center.

Clay sat on the bed. It was his turn to unbutton her shirt. For most guys, unbuttoning a woman's shirt for the first time was one of life's great experiences. This time was no different. Kelsi was wearing a black lace bra. Clay admired her breasts, moved his eyes from her chest to her face, and kissed her deeply yet again.

They rolled around the bed like animals during mating season. Kelsi pulled Clay on top of her. She tore at the zipper of his pants. He tugged on the waistband of hers. His pants came off first. Hers quickly followed. She reached for his penis and placed it inside of her. Yet another one of life's great experiences for a man: when the woman placed him inside of her.

The sex was fast and rough. Clay was working off instinct. Kelsi was trying to forget. He said he was about ready. She climaxed first. He immediately followed. They lay back on the bed and tried to catch their breath.

"Wow," Kelsi said.

"Ditto," Clay said. "And I thought Nancy Ellsworth was good."

Kelsi elbowed Clay in the ribs. "Nancy Ellsworth, huh? I knew there was something going on between you two."

Clay rolled onto his side and pinched Kelsi's button nose. It was his favorite part of her perfect face. "I'm just kidding. I've never been with Nancy Ellsworth... . She only dates law review types."

"OK. I guess I believe you... . *Not.*" Kelsi giggled and then said, "Would you like something to drink? There's more beer, and I've also got 7UP and Dr. Pepper."

"A 7UP would be great, thanks."

Kelsi pecked Clay on the cheek, shot up from the bed, and headed for the refrigerator.

"Are you coming?" Kelsi shouted from the kitchen. She placed two cans of 7UP on the counter. She popped the tab on one and took a long drink. "Hey, lazybones, are you coming or not?" She opened a cabinet and scavenged for some chips. Sex always made her hungry, especially good sex. She spun around and saw Clay standing in front of her. "You scared me half to death," she said.

Clay said, “Sorry. I didn’t mean to. I guess I’m just light on my feet.”

They both laughed again.

“Here... . Your 7UP.” Kelsi tried to hand Clay the can. “Take it, lazybones. Take it.”

But the reason Clay wouldn’t take the soda can wasn’t because he was lazy. It was because he was holding a knife.

CHAPTER 37

A fiery summons had been issued. The brothers had once again gathered around a bonfire deep in the woods on the outskirts of Charleston. The burning cross signified that there was a konklave underway. This time, there hadn't been time to string a nigger from a tree. This was an emergency meeting called on an hour's notice.

Billy Joe Collier was the one who had called it. That wasn't unusual. The Charleston den often met on short notice. What was unusual was that Collier had called the meeting on his own initiative rather than at the behest of Earl Smith, the grand dragon of South Carolina. The explanation for this breach of protocol? The meeting was *about* Earl Smith.

Kludd Johnny Bates opened the ritual book and said, "The sacred altar of the Klan is prepared; the fiery cross illumines the konklave."

The konklave said, "We serve and sacrifice for the right."

Collier said, "Klansmen all: you will gather for our opening devotions."

Those words were usually spoken by Smith, but Collier had heard them often enough that he knew them by heart.

The konklave sang the Klan's sacred song. The chorus rang out:

Home, home, country and home,
Klansmen we'll live and die

For our country and home.

Kludd Bates read more from the Kloran.

When Bates had finished, Collier said, "Amen." He rubbed his hand across his whiskered face. He almost always sported a three-day beard, and this day was no exception. Being well groomed wasn't a prerequisite for working on the assembly line at the tire factory.

Earl Smith stood straight, like a soldier. He knew what was coming, but that didn't make it any easier to take. Being romantically linked to a black woman was tantamount to treason in the Ku Klux Klan. In fact, it was listed among the offenses against the order in the original Ku-Klux Prescript of Reconstruction, the Klan's original constitution.

Collier said, "Hydra Cain, please bring Grand Dragon Smith to the front of the konklave."

Cain did.

Collier said next, "Nighthawk Wallace, are you ready to proceed?"

A nighthawk was a sort of investigator and watchdog who checked the character of prospective Klan members and their later conduct. Each local unit of the Klan had one.

Wallace said, "Yes, Klaliff Collier." Wallace stepped away from Smith and faced the konklave—the jury for all intents and purposes.

"Proceed." Collier was serving as the de facto judge.

"Kigy." Wallace nodded to the konklave. "My report'll be brief and to the point. Grand Dragon Smith stands accused of datin' a nigger woman."

"What's the name of this nigger woman?" a member of the konklave shouted out.

Unlike courthouse juries, the members of a konklave were permitted to ask questions about the defendant.

"Cat Wilson," Wallace said. "She works at the Waffle House down by exit 39."

Smith flinched when he heard Cat's name uttered in public. He had known all along that his relationship with her would probably come back to haunt him, but he was too hooked on her to end it. She was like a drug—intoxicating but potentially lethal.

"How do you know that Earl's datin' her?" another member of the konklave asked.

"Because I've seen them together."

"Why? When?" These particular questions were phrased skeptically. Smith had a lot of friends in the konklave. He had been an effective leader for years.

"'Why?' Because it's my job to investigate problems like this. I am the den's nighthawk. 'When?' On several occasions over the past couple of weeks. I started watching Earl after the incident involving him and Buck."

Wallace was referring to the fight that had broken out at the Waffle House when Buck Jansen had accused Smith of sticking up for Cat.

"Where did you see them together?" The questioner remained skeptical.

"Out at the Interstate 26 Motor Inn."

"They were at the motel together?"

"Yep."

A gasp from the konklave.

"I still don't believe it," the skeptical klansman said. "Earl's too loyal to the cause."

"Believe it," Collier interrupted, with an edge to his voice. "I saw Earl fuckin' the nigger woman with my own two eyes."

"Nigger lover!" a member of the konklave shouted out.

Smith's eyes danced with fear.

Collier held up his hand to calm the crowd. "Quiet, brothers. Quiet." It worked. "Why would Earl do it, Nighthawk Wallace?" Collier might have seen it with his own two eyes, but he didn't want to believe it was true. Earl Smith was his best friend.

Wallace said, "I didn't know why at first. I mean, I *suspected* why, but I didn't *know* why."

Collier asked next, "So what did you do?"

"I followed them. I couldn't follow them for long, though."

"Why not?"

"Because they went into a motel room and closed the shades."

"String him up!" a member of the konklave said.

About a dozen klansmen rushed at Smith. Collier tried to calm the crowd again, but this time it was to no avail. The klansman who had called Smith a "nigger lover" took two wild swipes at him. But before anyone else could take a swing, another member of the konklave called out, "Sanbog! Sanbog!" It was a warning between klansmen. It meant, Strangers are near. Be on guard.

The moment that was said, a dozen FBI agents came bursting from the bushes. The klansmen scattered as they had been trained to do since they were kids. This wasn't the first time the authorities had come after the Charleston den, although it was the first time the Feds had done so.

"Stop!" the FBI agent in charge shouted. "Federal officers!"

The command caused the klansmen to run faster. They rushed through the brush like escaped convicts in a low-budget prison movie.

Earl Smith stood frozen in place, though. He didn't know why, but he did. Perhaps it was because he knew he had violated one of the cardinal tenets of the brotherhood and felt he deserved to be punished. Then he heard, "Run, Earl! Run!"

It was Billy Joe Collier who was shouting his name —the same man who had convened the trial in the first place.

So Earl Smith ran ... and ran ... and ran.

CHAPTER 38

Clay Smith made himself comfortable on the couch. Well, not *comfortable...* . He knew he wouldn't enjoy what he was about to do. He should have done it when they were in the kitchen. He was still half asleep then, and he would have been acting on instinct.

Kelsi Shelton entered the room. She was wearing an oversized sweatshirt and nothing else. She made her way to the stereo and put on the new James Taylor CD. "He's an old fart, but he's dreamy," she said.

"He's frickin' bald, girl. Are you nuts?" Clay's eyes were locked on Kelsi's.

Kelsi smiled. "His voice is like maple syrup." She sat on the couch. "Oh. I forgot. You're from South Carolina. You use molasses down there." She leaned over and kissed Clay on the cheek.

Shit, Clay said to himself. This is going to be even more difficult than I thought.

The first cut was the deepest. Sheryl Crow had sung that line in a pop hit once, but she surely had something else in mind when she did.

Kelsi was too stunned to scream. Instead, she gasped and slid off the couch. Blood spotted the rug like a bug against a trucker's windshield.

Clay said, "Sorry" and raced from the room. So much for earning a law degree from UVA, he said to himself. But his loyalty to the Klan came first. "Akia," he said as he slammed shut the door to Kelsi's apartment. A klansman I am.

Minutes passed like hours as Kelsi Shelton struggled for her life. She now knew what Professor McDonald must have felt like. Professor McDonald ...

She should have been dead already. Clay certainly thought she was. Why would he do it? Why would he stab her?

Kelsi had known ever since the first time she had met Clay at a 1L orientation that he had a crush on her. She had finally given him what he wanted—herself—and this was how he responded? It didn't make sense. Yes, she had heard the rumors about Clay and the Ku Klux Klan, but she had never believed them. Nobody did. But were they true? Could Clay Smith really be a member of the most hate-filled organization in U.S. history?

Kelsi knew she would never know the answer. She knew she would never know anything ever again.

She closed her eyes. For forever, she thought.

CHAPTER 39

The Ku Klux Klan had entered the twenty-first century; most klansmen now carried cell phones or Blackberries. Earl Smith certainly did, and he had forgotten to turn his off. It started ringing—an old Hank Williams Jr. hit served as the ring tone—and that stopped the FBI agents who were chasing him dead in their tracks.

"What's that?" one of the agents asked.

"It sounds like a cell phone," another one answered. "Is it yours?"

"No," the first agent said. "It's coming from over there." He pointed to a large oak tree a hundred feet to the left of where the agents were standing.

But Earl Smith was already gone.

"Answer the phone, Uncle Earl," Clay Smith said. "Answer your goddamn cell phone."

Clay was driving down Emmet Street on his way to who knew where. He passed several of the local haunts he had grown to know and love: John Paul Jones Arena, where the men's and women's basketball teams played to capacity crowds; China Dragon, the best Chinese buffet in town; and the Emmet Street Apartments, where he shared a room with a graduate student in the American history department. Clay wondered how long it would be before his roommate—a quiet, socially awkward guy from Vermont—would notice he was missing.

He turned onto University Avenue and headed toward the Corner, the part of town where his day with

Kelsi Shelton had begun. His stomach felt as if it were being attacked by fire ants as he realized that Kelsi had probably bled to death by now.

He pressed the speed dial on his cell phone again. This time, all he got was his uncle's voicemail.

Earl Smith pushed through the brush. Vines and branches snapped against his face like switches to the bottom of a spoiled child. If he hadn't traversed the terrain hundreds of times during his youth, he never would have made it. He knew that the Feds were probably having all sorts of difficulty keeping pace with him.

He made his way toward an abandoned moonshiner's shack. He had frequented the shack many times over the years. He used to play hooky there as a kid. More recently, the shack had served as a hideout for when the local cops decided to make their annual raid on one of his Klan meetings. Billy Joe Collier was the only other member of the Charleston den who knew about the place. Smith could only hope that Collier hadn't decided to make his escape there, too.

Clay Smith flipped on the radio. He tuned the dial to 93.7. He figured that the college station would be the best place to learn whether the cops had discovered Kelsi's body.

Clay's car sounded older than the DJ did. She said, "This is Annie Paulsen, and you're listening to WUVA in Charlottesville. I'd like to send a shout out to the brothers at Kappa Sig. That was a slammin' rave last night, fellas. I sure hope that Kenny Watts managed to pull his head out of the toilet!" She giggled like the sorority girl she undoubtedly was. Then, she paused. Her tone changed 180 degrees. "I've just been handed a bulletin," she said, her voice cracking. "Campus police are reporting that Kelsi Shelton, a third-year law student, has been stabbed."

"But is she dead?!" Clay shouted. "Is she *dead?!*" He was confused about what he wanted the answer to be.

The student DJ continued, "She's being rushed to UVA hospital. No word yet on whether her injuries are life-threatening. No word on who her attacker was, either."

After another pause, she said, "Please say a prayer for Kelsi, people. And please be careful out there."

Earl Smith struck a match. He lit the kerosene lamp he kept behind the door. He was pleased to see that the cabin was just as he had left it. A week's supply of canned food, crackers, and bottled water was stacked in the corner. A tattered but functional army cot—Smith had done a tour in Iraq during the second Gulf War—looked particularly inviting at the rear of the room. Most important of all, there was no sign of Billy Joe Collier ... or of anyone else.

Smith removed his left boot and shook a stone loose. It had been irritating his foot for a good quarter mile, but he couldn't risk slowing down to get rid of it. He wiped his face dry with the blanket that covered the cot, grabbed a bottle of water from the stack in the corner, and took a long drink. He had forgotten how good water could taste.

He remembered his voicemail. He plopped down on the cot and checked it. There was a message from Clay. His nephew sounded frantic. Smith could understand why: It was the first time that Clay had been asked to kill a white person.

Clay said, "It's me, Uncle Earl. I did it. I killed Kelsi Shelton... . At least I think I did."

Shit, Smith said to himself. Clay "thinks" he killed her? He better have succeeded. Smith was in enough trouble as it was with the Klan. He didn't need to piss off Senator Burton, too.

Earl Smith had never understood why Senator Burton had wanted Kelsi Shelton dead. Burton had said that it was to throw people off track. "Folks'll think it was some love triangle gone bad," Burton had told Smith over a secure phone line. "Everybody already thinks that McDonald is sleeping with the girl. This'll just add more fuel to the fire. Especially if that pretty boy nephew of yours is involved."

Of course Smith had never told his nephew that he was just a pawn in Senator Burton's chess game. He should have told him, but he didn't. Some things were thicker than blood.

CHAPTER 40

Senator Alexandra Burton rushed into her suite of offices.

"Good morning, Senator," one of her legislative aides said. The aide pushed aside some draft legislation and stood to his feet.

The senator kept walking.

"Coffee?" Burton's secretary asked. She smiled politely at her boss.

"No," Burton answered. "And no interruptions."

The senator entered her private office and closed the door. She flipped on all four of the television sets, which filled a space formerly occupied by books. Burton's books—thousands of them—had been relocated to her home library.

Unlike most Americans living in the age of digital this and electronic that, Alexandra Burton still read books. But her literary sensibilities weren't dictated by Oprah Winfrey, *The Today Show*, or the *New York Times*. She had never read a James Patterson suspense novel, let alone a self-help book by Dr. Phil. She didn't have a clue who Stephanie Meyer was. No, Burton preferred the great works of political philosophy. Her favorite—her bible—was *The Prince* by Niccolo Machiavelli.

The Prince, written in 1513 but not published until after Machiavelli's death in 1532, was one of the most significant books ever written about the art of politics. Its essential contribution rested in Machiavelli's assertion of the then revolutionary idea that theological and moral imperatives had no place in the political arena. "It must be understood," Machiavelli had written, "that a prince cannot observe all of those virtues for which men are reputed good, because it is often necessary to act against mercy, against faith, against humanity, against frankness, against religion, in order to preserve the state."

That was precisely what Burton was trying to do: "preserve the state." Or at least that was what she kept telling herself when she arranged Ku Klux Klan hits on innocent people who got in her way.

The senator sat back in her captain's chair. Her eyes scanned the four television screens in front of her. CNN was in the midst of what was likely its tenth story of the day about the "crisis in North Korea." MSNBC was broadcasting some sort of political talk show hosted by a former legislative aide to a backbench congressman. CNBC was squawking about the latest insider trading scandal rocking Wall Street. Last but far from least, FOX News was busy spinning out conspiracy theories against the "liberal establishment" in general and the "liberal media" in particular.

But then everything changed in the blink of a digital eye. All four twenty-four-hour news networks cut to an anchorperson for "breaking news." Burton turned up the volume on the television tuned to CNN. She muted the other three. She leaned forward in her chair. She cupped her chin in her hand.

"This is Marie Gonzalez in Washington," the anchorwoman said. "CNN is reporting that Kelsi Shelton, a student assistant to Supreme Court nominee Peter McDonald, has been wounded at her apartment in Charlottesville, Virginia." The anchorwoman, who barely looked old enough to have graduated from law school herself and who undoubtedly had landed her plum assignment as part of CNN's diversity initiative, continued. "There's no word yet about whether Ms. Shelton has survived the attack... . Stay tuned to CNN throughout the day for updates on this developing story."

Burton switched off the TVs and smiled. She opened *The Prince* and began rereading her favorite passage. For the first time since her grandson's suicide, she thought that her plan to capture the presidency might actually work. Burton loved her grandson, and she was being sincere when she had stated publicly that she supported her daughter and son-in-law's lawsuit against the University of South Carolina "one hundred percent." But she loved power more and realized soon after her grandson's death that she might be able to parlay that tragedy into the most powerful office in the world ... an office currently occupied by a black man.

CHAPTER 41

The University of Virginia Medical Center had received a fifty-million-dollar upgrade two years earlier. It was a good thing, too. Otherwise, Kelsi Shelton wouldn't have stood a chance.

The EMT burst through the emergency room door. "Laceration to the abdomen! Massive blood loss! Patient isn't conscious! Stat! Stat, goddamn it! Stat!" The EMT maneuvered the stretcher down the congested corridor like Jeff Gordon on a NASCAR track.

The ER doctor came running. "Excuse me!" she said as she weaved through a sea of nurses, orderlies, and hospital staff. "Excuse me, please!"

The UVA Medical Center usually wasn't this busy. However, a school bus had slid off the road in Albemarle County, and dozens of injured teenagers were in need of medical attention.

"Geez, Doc," the EMT said. "It's like Foxfield in here."

Foxfield was the annual steeplechase that drew thousands of people to the Charlottesville area every spring. That was a happy day. This wasn't.

"I know. It's nuts." The ER doctor directed her attention to Kelsi Shelton. "What happened?"

"Campus police said that somebody stabbed her. Can you imagine such a thing? This is a university town, for God's sake." The EMT was still pushing the stretcher down the corridor. "Lucky for her, a friend came in and found her. Lucky for her, her friend had decided to skip class this afternoon."

The ER doctor was eyeballing the location and depth of the stab wound. "Bring her to trauma five. I just hope we're not too late."

Dr. Morris Tanenbaum appeared on the scene almost the instant he was paged. Normally, the pressure of prior commitments would have made it difficult for him to answer a page in less than fifteen minutes, but this page concerned a nominee to the Supreme Court of the United States.

"Welcome back," Dr. Tanenbaum said to his patient. "We were worried there for a while." The doctor couldn't hide his joy.

Peter McDonald stared up at Tanenbaum. He rubbed the sleep from his eyes. He said, "Where am I? Wh... what happened?"

Tanenbaum said, "You're at Bethesda Naval Hospital. You got shot. I'm Morris Tanenbaum, the doctor in charge of your case."

McDonald's eyes searched the room. He still didn't appear to know what was going on or where he was. "What do you mean, I got shot? Who would want to shoot me?"

Tanenbaum inched closer to the bed. He checked the IV bag and the heart monitor. Both were in good shape. He entered these facts onto McDonald's chart. "The police said that it was probably someone who wanted to keep you off the Court."

The mention of the Court snapped McDonald back to coherence. "Where's Kelsi? Is she all right?"

Tanenbaum swallowed. "We don't know yet. She wasn't hurt when she was with you, but she got stabbed earlier today."

"Stabbed! I need to see her!" McDonald swung his legs over the side of the bed and tried to struggle to his feet.

"Don't, Professor. You need to stay put. Besides, Kelsi's not here. She's down in Charlottesville at the UVA Medical Center."

"Then that's where I'm going." McDonald pulled the tubes from his arm and scavenged through the closet for his clothes.

CHAPTER 42

The stabbing of Kelsi Shelton was receiving major play in the national media. CNN, MSNBC, CNBC, and FOX News had been focusing exclusively on the story for the better part of the afternoon, while ABC, NBC, and CBS were devoting special reports to it during breaks in their regular programming. Even E! and MTV were covering the story. People got attacked every day in the United States, but they usually weren't beautiful research assistants to telegenic Supreme Court nominees. TV journalists lived for stories such as this one.

The ER team was working feverishly to save Kelsi's life. A doctor applied compression to try to stop the bleeding. A nurse attached an IV bag and a heart monitor. A second nurse watched Kelsi's breathing. Both her heart and breathing were extremely weak.

"We're losing her," the first nurse said.

"*Come on*, Kelsi," the doctor said. "Stay with us. Stay with us!"

Kelsi wasn't responding.

The second nurse handed the doctor the defibrillator. The doctor hadn't asked for it, but this particular ER team had worked together long enough that each member anticipated what the others needed.

"Clear!" the doctor said. She applied the paddles to Kelsi's chest and administered a two-hundred-volt shock.

The first nurse said, "Still falling."

"Give me three hundred." The doctor administered another shock.

"Still falling."

"Four hundred... . Clear!"

"Got it," the nurse said.

The ER team issued a collective sigh of relief as the patient's vital signs began to stabilize.

The doctor pulled her surgical mask from her face, wiped the sweat from her brow with the sleeve of her scrubs, and said, "Any word on Professor McDonald?"

The second nurse said, "The news said he's going to make it."

The first nurse said, "They called from Bethesda to let us know that he's on his way."

"Here? To the hospital?" The doctor pitched her surgical mask into the wastebasket. "Tell them to stop him. Kelsi's not ready for visitors. Kelsi's not out of the woods."

CHAPTER 43

"Please, get back in bed." Secret Service Agent Brian Neal watched helplessly while his body—Supreme Court nominee Peter McDonald—struggled to pull on pants. "You're not well enough to travel."

Dr. Morris Tanenbaum said, "He's right, Professor." Dr. Tanenbaum sounded more helpless than Agent Neal did. But the doctor was hoping to play a trump card. *Please*, he said to himself. Ring. *Ring.* He stared at the telephone on the nightstand next to McDonald's bed. Unlike the proverbial watched pot, this phone did ring.

Tanenbaum sprang across the room to answer it. "Mr. President," he said. "Thanks for calling."

McDonald and Neal both froze. Mere mention that the president—*any* president—was on the phone tended to elicit that sort of reaction. It always had, and almost certainly always would.

Tanenbaum next said, "Yes, Mr. President. He's here."

The doctor handed the telephone to McDonald.

The professor said, "Good afternoon, sir."

Peter McDonald had spoken to Charles Jackson on only one prior occasion. But he would never forget that conversation because of where it had occurred and what they had discussed. The place: the Oval Office. The topic: filling a vacancy on the nation's highest court.

That particular week had started out innocently enough. McDonald had faced the usual crush of publishing deadlines, teaching preparations, and law school committee meetings. However, on Tuesday, February 5—McDonald would never forget the day—he returned to his office to find a telephone message taped to his computer screen. The note, written in his secretary's familiar succinct style, read:

> *PM:*
> *Call Jim Westfall at the White House ASAP.*
> *MJ (2:47 p.m.)*

Speculation about who would be nominated to replace Edwin Crandall on the Supreme Court had dominated the blogosphere that week, and any law professor with even a pea-sized brain would know what the message from Jim Westfall meant. McDonald certainly did. But before he returned Westfall's call, he wanted to talk to Jenny about it.

McDonald could have contacted his wife on her cell phone, but this news was too important for anything except a face-to-face conversation. The principal reason that Peter and Jenny McDonald's marriage had stayed so strong for so long was communication. At least that was what Jenny would remind McDonald of every time he reverted to the tight-lipped behavior that John Gray had described so vividly in his mega-selling book *Men are from Mars, Women are from Venus.* Jenny had bought her husband the book on CD so that he would have no excuse not to read it.

"What are you doing home?" Jenny said when her husband strode through the back door of their four-bedroom colonial on the south end of Charlottesville. She was folding laundry on the kitchen table. "I thought you had office hours this afternoon."

McDonald smiled at his wife and kissed her on the forehead. Twenty years into their marriage, he still got chills when he saw her. "I canceled them. Where's June Bug?"

"She's taking a timeout in her bedroom. She's been a little cranky this afternoon. She threw a tantrum when I told her to stop wiping her muddy paws on her new outfit."

Jenny reached into the laundry basket for another batch of clean clothes to fold. "Why did you cancel your office hours? Unlike most of the prima donnas over there, you never do that."

McDonald chuckled at his wife's perceptive remark about his law faculty colleagues' dislike for holding office hours. Meeting with students took time away from research and writing, they insisted. He said, "You might want to sit down for this one, Jen."

Jenny's brows furrowed. "Did something bad happen?"

"No." He pulled out a chair for his wife. "Please, Jen. Sit."

Jenny sat. She rested an elbow on a pile of laundry. "What is it, Peter? The suspense is killing me."

McDonald rubbed the heel of his hand across his cheek to erase any trace of the powdered donut he had eaten on the ride home. He was supposed to be dieting. "I got a call from Jim Westfall today."

"President Jackson's chief of staff?" Even housewives with small children to raise knew who Jim Westfall was. Or at least Harvard-educated ones did. "It's about the vacancy on the Court, isn't it?"

"Probably."

"'Probably?' You mean you haven't called him back?"

McDonald blushed. "Not yet."

"Why not?"

"Because I wanted to discuss it with you first. It's not like I'm being asked to deliver a paper in San Diego over the weekend. It's a lifetime commitment. And not just for me. Do you really want your life to change that much, Jen? And what about Megan's? Wherever she goes, she'll be known as the daughter of a Supreme Court justice. Is that fair to her? She's a little kid."

As if on cue from Steven Spielberg, Megan Mallory McDonald came skipping into the kitchen. "Daddy!" She raced to her father and wrapped her tiny arms around his waist.

McDonald lifted his daughter into the air, smothered her with kisses, and said, "Hi June Bug."

"Did you bwing me a prethent?"

McDonald always brought something for Megan when he came home from work. Jenny said he was spoiling her, but given the difficulty they'd had becoming pregnant, she never discouraged the practice.

McDonald searched through his pockets and retrieved an individually-wrapped Lifesaver he had snatched from his secretary's candy dish. "Here, June Bug." He handed his daughter the candy.

"Yippee! ... A Lifethaver!"

Jenny beamed at what was transpiring in front her: pure, unadulterated love between a father and daughter. She said, "Obviously, Megan will go anywhere you need her to go, Peter. So will I." She rose from her seat, ran her fingers through her daughter's tussled hair, and kissed her husband softly on the mouth. "Accept the nomination, Peter. You've earned it."

CHAPTER 44

Peter McDonald snapped back to the moment. "Good afternoon, Mr. President."

The president said, "How are you feeling?"

"Fine, sir. Fine. Thanks for asking."

"That's not what Morris is telling me."

So much for doctor-patient confidentiality, McDonald said to himself. Aloud to the president, he said, "You know how doctors are, sir—always viewing the glass as half empty ... always making things sound worse than they are ... always wanting to be overly cautious."

"But in your case, you need to be 'overly cautious.' *I* need for you to be 'overly cautious.' The *American people* need for you to be. Believe me, Peter,"—the president had never called McDonald by his first name before—"I know how worried you are about Kelsi Shelton. We're all worried about her. But you're not out of the woods yet. Morris tells me that you're not strong enough to travel, even if it is only two or three hours from D.C. to Charlottesville. Besides, there's nothing you can do for Kelsi right now. Morris says that you couldn't get in to see her even if you wanted to, which I know you do. But it's up to the doctors now. You need to let them do their job. You need to let Morris do his job. And his job is to help you. His job is to make sure you get well so that you can serve the country for decades to come. Like it or not, those of us called to public service sometimes must make decisions that, at least in the short term, run contrary to what we think we need and what we think our friends and family need."

McDonald sat back on the bed. He closed his eyes for a moment to allow the president's words—the president's *plea*—to wash over him. "OK," he finally said. "I'll stay in the hospital. But only for a little while longer. I know it's up to the doctors now, sir, but I disagree that there's nothing I can do for Kelsi. I can be there for her as a friend. I can be there like I wasn't for my family." He hung up the phone, took a sip from the cup of water on his lunch tray, and turned to Morris Tanenbaum. "I assume you heard that, Doctor."

Tanenbaum nodded that he had. "I think you're making the right decision."

McDonald held up his hand to signal that he had said all he planned to say about the matter. He settled back into his bed.

Tanenbaum got the hint. "Come on," he said to Secret Service Agent Brian Neal. "Let's let the professor get some rest."

CHAPTER 45

Senator Alexandra Burton switched off the evening news with the flick of an angry thumb. She yanked open the bottom drawer of her desk and retrieved the bottle of Wild Turkey to which she often turned to take the edge off a stressful day. She poured two fingers into a tumbler with the Clemson University logo stenciled across the front. The glass had been a gift from an influential constituent who wanted the senator to remember the university during a recent debate about an appropriations amendment to an education bill. The senator had fought hard for Clemson during that debate, and she had won. The senator always fought hard, and she almost always won.

Burton got out of her chair and made her way through the suite of staff offices. It was twenty minutes past seven on a Friday evening, and her staff was long gone for the weekend. There was one notable holdover: Jeffrey Oates. Burton had to give Oates credit. The chief of staff certainly worked his ass off. Unfortunately, he wasn't very effective ... and not simply with respect to legislative matters. The evening news had reminded Burton of Oates's inefficiencies.

"Senator," Oates said when Burton appeared in the doorway. "I thought you had left for the day." Oates began to stand, but Burton signaled that it was unnecessary.

"I got lost in the news."

"What happened?" Oates's question dripped with concern that he may have missed something important.

He had.

"CBS News is reporting that Peter McDonald is alive and kicking."

All the color rushed from Oates's face. "S ... sorry, ma'am. It looks like I let you down again."

Burton offered no response. She didn't need to. Oates knew what this meant.

Oates added, "I'll try again."

Burton shook her head. "You've had your chances, Jeff. It's up to some of my other friends now."

Why was Senator Burton telling him this? Oates wondered. Perhaps she wasn't going to show him the door. Aloud to the senator, he said, "Is there something else you would like me to do?"

"Yes."

A reprieve! Oates sang to himself. "Anything, ma'am. Just name it and I'll do it."

"I'd like you to touch base with Senator Carpenter's office about the possibility of reconvening Professor McDonald's confirmation hearings. My guess is that McDonald is too sick to appear. We've already postponed the hearings once at his request. You know, when his wife and daughter got killed." Burton shot Oates a look that Oates had never seen before—a strange combination of pain and pleasure.

Surely, no one but the most extreme of psychopaths could fail to feel bad about the tragic deaths of Jenny and Megan McDonald. Alexandra Burton was no psychopath. But the senator clearly couldn't hide the pleasure she felt from wielding power to its maximum degree—taking human life.

Oates said, "But he's in the hospital. Won't it look bad for us if we put pressure on him while he's recovering?"

"It won't be *us* pressuring him. It'll be Senator Carpenter's office. Besides, postponing the confirmation hearing once was unusual enough. Postponing it twice is asking too much."

"I'll get right on it, ma'am. Is there anything else?"

There was, but Burton had assigned the additional task to someone else.

CHAPTER 46

Earl Smith was gnawing his way through yet another packet of Saltine crackers. What he wouldn't give for a hamburger, a piece of chicken, a hot dog ... anything that wasn't ninety-nine percent flour and salt. He couldn't afford to stop by a Burger King for a Whopper yet, though. He couldn't afford to venture more than a few hundred yards from the moonshiner's shack. It had been only three days since he had fled from the Klan meeting ... and from the FBI. The FBI was notorious for its willingness to keep searching until it got its man. The Klan was even more dedicated to that task. Smith should know; he had led dozens of Klan search parties over the years.

Although Smith was dying for something substantial to eat, he was sort of enjoying the time alone that hiding out in the shack was affording him. He *needed* some time to himself. He needed some time to *think*. What was he doing with his life? What was he doing *to* his life? He was the grand dragon of the South Carolina Realm of the Ku Klux Klan. He had no business falling in love with a black woman.

The course of Earl Smith's life had been set by his father. Theodore Smith—"Big Ted" to his friends—was a legend in South Carolina Klan circles. It was Big Ted who had revived the long dormant Charleston den, and it was Big Ted who reminded Klan members across the state at konklave after konklave what the Klan was all about: protecting the white race from Catholics, Jews, and especially blacks.

Earl Smith could still remember sneaking out of bed as a boy to wait by the kitchen door on the nights of his father's Klan meetings. His father would arrive home beaming with pride about the course of the evening's events. Big Ted would regale his young son about the power and glory of the brotherhood. "We are the law itself," the father would tell the son. "We are patriots dedicated to what is fair and just... . Akia."

By the time the son had reached adolescence, he had fully committed himself to the Klan way of thinking and to the Klan way of life. His friends were the sons of klansmen. His nights, like those of his father, were spent fighting for what was fair and just. In Earl Smith's case, as in the cases of most junior klansmen, "fighting" meant beating up Catholics, Jews, and especially blacks. There was nothing subtle about the mindset of a klansman-in-the-making committed to the cause.

Eventually, though, Smith began to question the Klan way. He remembered the day he did as if it were yesterday. It was his third meeting as a full member of the Charleston den. He was eighteen years old. He was deep in the woods on the outskirts of the city. A fiery cross was ignited. A young black man was dragged kicking and screaming before the konklave. The sack was removed from the black man's head. His eyes, as wide as Carolina crab cakes, locked on Smith's. The young black man's name was Tim Anderson. He was the starting tailback on the South Charleston High School football team. Smith was Anderson's blocking back. In short, they were teammates. They didn't speak much during practices or games, but they were teammates. That was supposed to mean something to Smith. And it did.

"Please, Earl," Anderson had said shortly after the sack had been removed from his head. "Don't let them do this. Don't let them kill me. Please, Earl. *Please.*"

But Smith had to ignore his teammate's plea. If he hadn't, he would have been next. In fact, he took the lead in Anderson's lynching. He tied the noose. He cut the rope. He led the konklave in the singing of the Klan's sacred song.

CHAPTER 47

Billy Joe Collier had just finished his shift at the Taylor Tires plant. Earl Smith hadn't shown up... . Smith hadn't shown up in three days. Collier wasn't surprised. Indeed, he would have been stunned if Smith had dared to come to work. After all, Smith knew what was waiting for him if he did.

One of Collier's coworkers passed by on the way to the soda machine and said, "What'ya got planned for the weekend, Billy Joe?"

Collier said, "I think I'm gonna do me some huntin'."

"Huntin'?" The coworker slid a tattered dollar bill into the soda machine. "It ain't deer season no more. And the ducks've already flied south for the winter."

"Don't worry." Collier watched his coworker struggle to persuade the soda machine to accept the dollar. It finally did. The coworker punched the Coke button. Collier continued: "I'll find me somethin' to shoot at."

"What about your knee? How ya gonna hunt when you can barely walk?" The coworker drained the soda in three large gulps and pitched the empty can into the recycling bin. Even rednecks had gone green.

Collier had wrenched his knee when his foot had gotten snagged in a stack of tires that had come off the assembly line too quickly.

"It don't hurt too bad." The pained expression on Collier's face suggested otherwise.

"Is Earl goin'?"

Everybody at the plant knew how close Collier and Smith were.

Collier didn't answer his coworker's final question. He was already out the door.

Billy Joe Collier limped into his rusty Ford Monte Carlo and exited the parking lot of the tire plant where he had worked ever since he had dropped out of high school when he was sixteen. His guidance counselor had tried to convince him that he should stay in school—that he had only three more semesters until he graduated and that a high school diploma was a prerequisite for a successful life in this day and age—but Collier had told the man to fuck off. Literally.

But as Collier wended down one back road after another in his search for Earl Smith, he had to admit that perhaps the guidance counselor had been right. What kind of life had Collier led during the twenty-five years since he had walked away from South Charleston High School in the middle of his junior year? He had no wife. He had no kids. He had no house. Shit, he hadn't been promoted from the minimum wage job he had accepted the week after he quit school.

Collier did have one thing going for him: the Klan. The brotherhood. The fiery cross.

Collier might not have been anyone in the work-a-day world that his guidance counselor had been preaching to him about, but he was someone in the South Carolina Realm of the Ku Klux Klan: the klaliff—the second highest-ranking member of the organization.

After he got through with Smith, he would be number one. Then his guidance counselor and everyone else who had doubted him throughout the course of his sorry life could go fuck themselves for real.

CHAPTER 48

Billy Joe Collier pulled his car off the road and locked it into low gear. He spotted a large oak tree with a V-shaped trunk and maneuvered the car across the path to the left of it. His head nearly hit the roof as the car bounced through one hole after another. The path was bumpier and more difficult to traverse than he remembered. But he had never tried to drive it before. He had always walked it in the past. He was tempted to hop out and finish the trip by foot. His aching knee wouldn't permit it, though. Now he finally appreciated the sense of physical pain that Earl Smith had been trying to convey to him during one of the many hunting trips they had enjoyed together over the years.

Smith used to love to entertain Collier with stories about what it was like to play high school football back in the day. The thrill of competition. The adrenalin rush of throwing the perfect block. The deafening cheers from the crowd when the team scored a touchdown. The post-game parties at the coach's house. The cheerleaders ... ah, the cheerleaders. That was the part that Collier liked to hear about the most. Hooking up with a cheerleader was every man's fantasy, and Billy Joe Collier definitely liked to fantasize.

His fantasy had once become a reality. He didn't remember her name, and he never saw her again after that night. But it was a night he would never forget. She was tall, blonde, and had legs sculpted by years of cartwheels and backflips. She was from out of town ... a cheerleader for the visiting team. She said she would go all the way, and she did.

Bam! Collier's car crashed into a large rock.

"Shit! *Shit*!" he said, jolted back to the present. The rock was covered by a thick patch of weeds, and he hadn't seen it. He popped the car into reverse and tried to back up around the rock. The car wouldn't budge. He shifted the car into low gear again. Still nothing. It still wouldn't budge. Next, he tried to sway it back and forth by quickly alternating between reverse and drive. Still nothing but spinning wheels and flying dirt.

Collier switched off the ignition, threw open the door, and squeezed out of the car. "Shit," he said again. "A fuckin' flat." He retrieved the spare and the jack from behind the passenger's seat. He kneeled to the ground to get a better look at where he should attach the jack. He couldn't find a stable place. The combination of the flat tire, the slope of the terrain, and the rock itself had caused the car to lean too far forward for anything but a wrecker to be of use.

Collier hobbled to his feet, using the jack as a crutch as he did. He wiped dirt from his face with his shirt sleeve. He surveyed the area. He hadn't been to this part of the woods for about a year—since the last time he and Smith had gone deer hunting—but he figured that he was about three-quarters of a mile west of the moonshiner's shack.

Could he do it? he asked himself. He wasn't wondering whether he could make the walk. No, he was wondering whether he would really be able to kill his best friend.

"Akia," he said as he began to limp toward the shack. A klansman I am.

CHAPTER 49

Earl Smith reached into his pocket and pulled out a cross. At first glance, the cross appeared to be an ordinary Christian cross. But upon closer inspection it was more than that. Much more.

The Sacred Cross of the Kloncilium was three inches high, two inches wide, and forged from twenty-four karat gold. It was conferred upon only seven klansmen in the United States: the imperial wizard and the six members of his executive council. These seven men set Klan policy for every Klan chapter and den in the nation. The Klan was an oligarchy—some said it was a monarchy—and membership on the kloncilium brought both power and privilege to those fortunate enough to serve.

Earl Smith had been called to service after ten years of loyal and effective stewardship of the South Carolina Realm. His brothers in the Charleston den had been telling him for years that his time would come—that he would be bestowed the honor that had eluded his late father—but he didn't believe them. It happened, however. *How* it happened was something that Smith would never forget.

Smith had been summoned to Washington, D.C. on what he was told was important business concerning the brotherhood. He had no idea what that business might be. He did know that if the location of the meeting was the nation's capital, the imperial wizard—the Klan's top official—almost certainly would be in attendance. Although the Klan's national headquarters had long been located in

Atlanta, the current imperial wizard lived and worked in D.C.

For the first time in the history of the Klan, the name and identity of the imperial wizard were unknown to anyone but the kloncilium. The reason for this was never conveyed to the brotherhood—again, the Klan was an oligarchy, which meant that ordinary members did as they were told without questioning why and what for—but speculation centered around the possibility that the imperial wizard was a high-ranking official in the government of the United States. If true, the argument went, his effectiveness would be reduced to zero if the nation's movers and shakers knew that they were dealing with the head of a so-called terrorist organization.

Smith had never been to Washington, D.C. before. Night-shift foremen at regional tire plants didn't have much occasion to hobnob in the epicenter of American politics. He was excited about the trip, though, both because he had always wanted to spit on the Lincoln Memorial and because the imperial wizard was reputed to be a truly impressive man. A holy man ...

The meeting was being held at a Reconstruction-era Masonic temple about three blocks west of the Capitol building. Smith arrived by Greyhound bus, his Klan regalia packed neatly inside a Wal-Mart bag that he had brought with him from Charleston. He located the entrance to the temple, ducked inside a bathroom, changed into his white robe and pasteboard, and made his way to the ceremonial meeting room at the rear of the temple.

Smith was the first person to arrive. He inspected the room for security as every good klansman had been taught to do. His eyes danced from one sacred ornament to another: a china vase adorned with the symbols of the brotherhood, a golden chalice from which the sacrament would be served, a leather-bound copy of the Kloran, and a small wooden cross encased in a glass box that would be ignited to signify the commencement of the ceremony. The fiery cross ... always and forever, the fiery cross.

Five men entered the room. They, too, were dressed in white robes and pasteboards. "Ayak," they said in unison. Are you a klansman?

"Akia," Smith said. A klansman I am.

"Kigy," the tallest of the five men said. Klansman, I greet you.

A klonversation ensued.

"You must be Grand Dragon Smith," the tall man said next.

"That's right," Smith said.

"Welcome to the Temple of the Kloncilium."

The sign on the front of the building said it was the Masonic Temple of Capitol Hill, but the Klan had their own names for things.

"The kloncilium?" Smith asked. "The imperial wizard's executive council?" His voice cracked. His knees buckled a bit.

The five men nodded.

Smith knew what this meant, but he asked the question anyway. "Is he here?" His voice cracked again.

"Yes."

Out from behind a velvet curtain strode the Honorable Alexandra Rutledge Burton, the senior U.S. senator from the great state of South Carolina.

CHAPTER 50

Earl Smith didn't care much about politics. He wasn't even registered to vote. But he knew who Alexandra Burton was.

Burton had represented Smith's home state of South Carolina in the U.S. Senate ever since Smith was a boy. He had seen Burton's campaign ads on TV—a shrewd politician, Burton had been the first elected official in the nation to run ads during NASCAR telecasts—and he had met Burton once before when the senator had made a campaign stop at the Taylor Tires plant in Charleston. However, never in a million years could Smith have imagined that Senator Burton was a member of the Ku Klux Klan, let alone the imperial wizard of the exalted brotherhood. After all, Burton was a United States senator. She was also a woman.

There was some precedent for klansmen in the federal government. The most famous was the late Robert C. Byrd of West Virginia, the longest-serving U.S. senator in American history. Senator Byrd had once been an active member of the KKK—rising to the office of kleagle, which meant he was his den's official recruiter. In 1944 a young Robert Byrd had written to segregationist Mississippi Senator Rhett Henderson, "I shall never fight in the armed forces with a Negro by my side. Rather I should die a thousand times, and see Old Glory trampled in the dirt never to rise again, than to see this beloved land of ours become degraded by race mongrels, a throwback to the blackest specimen from the wilds."

Byrd later stated publicly that he regretted joining the Klan, but klansmen everywhere knew that the senator had to say that to rescue his political career. He had learned that lesson after Hugo L. Black had saved his Supreme Court nomination from going down in flames with a similar public statement of amends.

The fact that Senator Burton was a woman shouldn't have surprised Smith as much as it did. It was true that, historically, most women committed to the Klan way simply supported the men in their lives from a distance, but records uncovered by Klan historians in recent years revealed that some women were official members of the sacred order as early as the mid-1860s. A century later—by the 1980s, to be precise—women became eligible to serve in leadership roles. But it was Alexandra Burton who, in 2005, had broken the glass ceiling when she was elected by the kloncilium imperial wizard of the brotherhood, and now, sisterhood.

Earl Smith noticed that, at first, Burton didn't say a word. She simply took her seat on a gold-leafed throne in the center of the dais.

The tall man who had greeted Smith opened the glass case that contained the small wooden cross. He lit the cross and then said to Burton, "Your Excellency, the sacred altar of the Klan is prepared; the fiery cross illumines the konklave."

Burton said, "Faithful kludd, why the fiery cross?"

The tall man said, "Ma'am, it is the emblem of that sincere, unselfish devotedness of all klansmen to the sacred purpose and principles we have espoused."

Burton said, "My terrors and klansmen, what means the fiery cross?"

The konklave of a half dozen men said, "We serve and sacrifice for the right."

Burton said, "Klansmen all: you will gather for our opening devotions."

The konklave sang the Klan's sacred song.

Burton said, "Amen." Then she added, "Kludd Watson, please escort our honored guest to the dais."

Watson was the tall man. He said, "Grand Dragon Smith, please follow me to the sacred altar."

Smith's knees began to shake again. He managed to conceal his nervousness. He knew what was about to happen.

Kludd Watson retrieved the leather-bound copy of the Kloran from the table on the dais. Legend had it that the copy had once belonged to William J. Simmons, the most powerful imperial wizard of the twentieth century.

Simmons had been known as "Doc," in reference to fictitiously claimed medical training. He dedicated himself to rebuilding the Klan after viewing the film *The Birth of a Nation.* He obtained a copy of the Reconstruction Klan's Precept and used it to write his own prospectus for a reincarnation of the organization. However, he delayed his plans until the media-inspired lynching of Leo Frank, the accused murderer of thirteen-year-old Mary Phagan. This horrific incident became a flash point for anti-Semitic feeling in Georgia. Frank was taken from prison and lynched by a mob on August 16, 1915. The lynch mob called themselves the Knights of Mary Phagan, and on October 16 they climbed Stone Mountain and burned a giant cross that was visible throughout Atlanta. The imagery of the burning cross, which hadn't existed in the original Klan, had been introduced via *The Birth of a Nation.* The film, in turn, had borrowed the idea from the works of Thomas Dixon. He had taken his inspiration from Scottish clans, who had burned crosses as a method of signaling from one hilltop to the next.

Doc Simmons organized a group of thirty-four men as the nucleus of his revived Klan. The group included many of the Knights of Mary Phagan, in addition to two elderly men who had been members of the original Klan. Fifteen of them went to Stone Mountain with Simmons to burn a second cross and inaugurate the new Klan. Simmons's later retelling of the founding included "a temperature far below freezing," although weather records revealed that the temperature had never fallen below forty-five degrees that night. The actual date of the founding was also in dispute, as some sources cited Thanksgiving Day,

1915. Simmons declared himself the imperial wizard of the new Klan. He died in Atlanta on May 18, 1945.

Alexandra Burton, who worshiped Doc Simmons, owed her own success to a Simmons-like knack for mythmaking.

CHAPTER 51

Kludd Watson opened the Kloran to page 3 and read, "The kloncilium is the sacred order's executive body. It is responsible for setting policy for every realm in the nation. It is to be comprised of seven men: the imperial wizard and six kloncilmen. Whenever a vacancy occurs on the kloncilium, the imperial wizard shall promptly appoint a replacement." Watson closed the Kloran—the ritual book contained various administrative details, in addition to songs and prayers—and looked at Earl Smith. "Imperial Wizard Burton has selected you to fill that vacancy."

Smith said, simply, "Thank you." He turned to Burton, who remained seated on her gold-leafed throne. "And thank you, Your Excellency."

Burton nodded and said, "I will now administer the oath. Please raise your right hand, Kloncilman Smith, and place your left hand on the Kloran."

Smith did as he was told. It was as if he was being sworn in as a member of the U.S. president's cabinet. In a sense, he was.

Burton said, "Repeat after me. I hereby pledge my life and honor to my sacred service on the kloncilium."

Smith repeated what Burton had said.

Burton continued: "I vow to serve with the best interests of the sacred order in mind, never deviating from my pledge and never failing in my duties."

Smith repeated that part of the oath as well.

Burton extended her hand to Smith and said, "Kigy."

Smith said, "Akia."

Burton turned to Kludd Watson. "Are we ready for the final ritual of the sacred ceremony?"

Watson said, "Yes, Your Excellency."

Smith watched Watson walk to a closet in the rear of the room. Watson opened the closet's door. What was inside was briefly obscured by Watson's large body. Watson stepped aside. Smith wasn't surprised by what he then saw: a middle-aged black man tied to a chair with packing tape across his mouth.

Smith might not have been surprised by what he saw—this was a Klan ceremony, after all—but he was disappointed. He was growing tired of lynching black men for the sole reason that they were black. Smith was still a klansman, and he was about to become one of the most powerful klansmen in the nation, but he was beginning to question the Klan's knee-jerk hatred of any person who wasn't white. Like it or not, what he had done to his high school football teammate years earlier had changed him forever.

Burton said, "Deliver the sacrifice, Kludd Watson."

Watson bowed to the imperial wizard. He returned his attention to the black man in the closet. "Stand, nigger."

The black man struggled to his feet. Muffled screams—pleas for mercy, no doubt—sounded from his tape-filled mouth.

"Walk, nigger," Watson said next.

Hop was more like it. The black man stumbled to the front of the room. He stopped short of the dais. His bound feet made it impossible for him to elevate the distance necessary to reach the podium.

"Jump, nigger," Watson said this time. "Like you do in basketball. Ain't that all you niggers do all day? ... Play basketball? You sure don't work." Watson punched the black man in the back of the head. He obviously didn't know, or care, that the man worked two full-time jobs to support his wife and three children.

The black man jumped, but he couldn't jump high enough. He lost his balance and crashed to the floor.

The konklave laughed—everyone but Smith, that is.

Burton seemed to pick up on Smith's sympathy for the black man's plight. "Kludd Watson, present the klonknife to Kloncilman Smith."

The klonknife was the antique, pearl-handled blade that had been used at kloncilium initiations for more than 150 years. It had once belonged to Nathan Bedford Forrest, the original Klan's first imperial wizard. Watson removed the klonknife from its sterling silver sheath, wiped the blade clean with a silk cloth, and handed it to Smith.

By this point, the black man had been delivered to the dais by two members of the kloncilium. His eyes were locked on Smith's.

"Complete the sacrifice," Burton said, with an edge to her voice. "Show yourself committed to the cause."

Earl Smith took a deep breath, glanced briefly at the black man trembling in front of him, and cut the man's throat.

CHAPTER 52

Clay Smith had been driving all night. He had spent the previous two days holed up in a budget motel on the east side of Charlottesville. He knew it wasn't smart to stick around for so long, but he wanted to know how Kelsi Shelton was doing and he felt that the best way to find out was by staying within earshot of the local television and radio stations. Unfortunately, the reports he had heard stated that it would be several more days before the doctors could say whether Kelsi was going to make it or not. Clay couldn't afford to hang around Charlottesville that long. In fact, he noticed a police car pulling into the parking lot of the motel he had been staying at only moments before he had decided to leave.

Clay had driven Interstate 95 many times over the years. But this was the first time he had done so since law school had started in late August. First-year law students barely had time to come up for air. Road trips home were unthinkable—unless, that is, you were fleeing the scene of a homicide.

Clay arrived in Charleston at 9:15 A.M. Twenty minutes later, he reached his desired destination. He pulled his car off the road and headed for the V-shaped tree that marked the path leading to the moonshiner's shack. His Uncle Earl didn't know that he knew about the shack, but he did. He used to follow his uncle from a distance when he was a boy. He always wondered what the shack looked like from the inside. Now he would get to see for himself.

Clay switched off the ignition, yanked the parking brake up, and exited the car. He began the trek to the shack. He hadn't walked more than a hundred yards before he spotted Billy Joe Collier's rusty Ford Monte Carlo stuck against a large rock several hundred yards ahead. Clay had never cared much for Collier—he was too moody and unpredictable for Clay's cerebral tastes—but he knew that Collier was his uncle's best friend and top lieutenant.

Clay jogged to Collier's car. Collier wasn't inside. Clay scanned the area. He didn't see him. He hurried toward the moonshiner's shack, figuring that Collier must have been headed there, too. And if he was, that probably meant that Clay's Uncle Earl was there. Clay certainly hoped that was the case. He needed all the help he could get.

Clay continued his march to the shack. He passed a tall ash tree that marked the spot where he was supposed to turn left. He did. Then, about seventy-five yards in front of him, he spied a man limping down the path. "Billy Joe!" Clay called out. "Wait up!"

Collier flinched. He spun on his heel. He tried to pick up his pace, but his aching knee made it difficult to do.

"Billy Joe!" Clay said again. "It's me, Clay! Clay Smith!"

Collier stopped. He glanced down the path. It was Clay. He waited while Clay jogged to catch up to him.

"Hey, Billy Joe." Clay was breathing heavily from the run ... and the stress of recent events.

"What the fuck are you doing here, kid?" Collier rubbed his knee to try to ease the pain. It wasn't working.

"You didn't hear?"

"About what?"

"About what happened in Charlottesville?"

"No. What happened? Did you flunk outta school?"

"No," Clay said. "I killed that girl." His voice caught. "Or at least I tried to."

"What girl?" Collier leaned on the tire jack he was using as a cane.

"The one Uncle Earl told me to kill. You know, Professor McDonald's research assistant."

The blank expression on Collier's face suggested that Clay had spoken out of turn.

"Shit," Collier said, shaking his head. "I didn't know nuthin' about it. That don't surprise me, though. Earl's been freelancin' a lot lately. That's what I'm on my way to talk to him about."

That wasn't true. Collier was on his way to "talk" to Smith about hooking up with a nigger woman, but the less Clay knew about it the better.

"So he's at the shack?"

"Yeah, but you don't wanna go there. Trust me, kid. You're better off headin' back to school."

"School? Did you hear what I said, Billy Joe? I can't go back to school. I'm running from the cops."

Collier studied Clay's face. The kid sure looked scared. He couldn't afford to have Clay around when he confronted Earl, though. He reached into his pocket and pulled out his keys. "Here," he said as he tossed his keys to Clay. "Wait for us at my place. 544 Crane Road, Apartment 3. It's across from Lee's Chicken. I'll bring your uncle with me."

In a body bag ...

CHAPTER 53

Clay Smith was halfway back to his car when the feeling that his uncle was in trouble rushed over him. It was one of those feelings—a knot in the stomach, neck hairs standing on end, a chill down the spine—that most people experienced at least once in their lives.

Clay stopped walking. The air was thick with humidity, which was typical for Charleston. The wind whistled through the trees. Crows cackled and cawed like a hostile crowd urging an athlete to change direction.

Clay began to walk back toward the moonshiner's shack. His pace went from a brisk walk to a full-blown sprint as the feeling of concern for his uncle's safety engulfed him. He thought more about Billy Joe Collier ... and about what he knew Collier was capable of. He had heard the stories. He had even witnessed several displays of Collier's coldhearted brutality.

Clay reached the shack in two and a half minutes. It was the fastest half mile he had ever run.

"Don't!" he heard from inside. "Don't, Billy Joe!"

It was his Uncle Earl shouting. His uncle's daydream about being inducted into the kloncilium had turned into a nightmare.

Next, Clay heard a loud bang. It must have been the tire jack smashing against the wall.

Clay pushed open the door. His eyes met Collier's. Pure hatred, Clay said to himself. Collier's eyes were small slits of pure hatred.

Clay said, "Stop, Billy Joe! He's your friend! He's your coworker! He's the grand dragon!"

But Collier wouldn't stop. He raised the tire jack and took another violent swing at Earl Smith's head. He missed again.

Clay rushed toward him.

Collier spat, "Stay away, kid! This ain't got nuthin' to do with you!" Collier stood over Smith like a large dog over a cornered cat.

"Of course it has something to do with me, Billy Joe. He's my uncle. He's my leader. He's *your* leader."

Clay hoped that he had learned enough about the art of persuasion after only one and a half semesters at UVA law school to help his uncle. He had won the 1L moot court competition, so that was a good sign. But the situation unfolding before him with Collier wasn't an academic competition. It was real life—his uncle's *life* ... and perhaps his own.

Clay inched forward, hoping that Collier wouldn't notice.

He did. "I said stay away! I've always liked you, kid. But I'll kill you, too, if I have to. This is Klan business."

"Come on, Billy Joe," Clay said. "You're acting crazy. What on earth could my uncle have done to justify trying to treat his head like a baseball at a batting cage?"

"He violated a fundamental tenet of the brotherhood."

At least Billy Joe had stopped swinging the tire jack for a moment, Clay said to himself. He said to Collier, "What are you talking about? Uncle Earl's the grand dragon of the South Carolina Realm and a member of the kloncilium. He would never violate a fundamental tenet." Clay's attention switched from Collier to his uncle. The expression on the older Smith's face—shame? guilt? sorrow?—wasn't reassuring. "Which tenet?" Clay asked softly. "Which?"

"The one about sleepin' with a nigger woman," Collier answered.

Conventional wisdom notwithstanding, there wasn't actually a formal tenet against having sex with a black woman. But given that the Klan was dedicated to the supremacy and purity of the white race, Clay knew that Collier was on solid ground if his uncle had in fact done so. *If* ...

Clay looked at his uncle again. "Is it true, Uncle Earl? Are you having sex with a nigger woman?"

Earl Smith still had his arms in front of his face in case Collier decided to start swinging the tire jack again. He dropped them long enough to look his nephew in the eyes. He said, "I ... I can explain."

Clay held up his hand to signal for his uncle to say nothing more. He walked over to Collier and snatched the tire jack from Collier's grasp. He turned back to his uncle and smashed the tire jack against his uncle's skull. Pieces of brain splattered against the wall of the moonshiner's shack.

CHAPTER 54

Senator Alexandra Burton pulled her cell phone from her pocketbook. It was one of two cell phones that she owned. One was for official government business. Although that cell phone's number wasn't listed in the Congressional Directory, the number was well known by her Senate colleagues and by her personal Senate staff. The second of the cell phones was for her Klan business. Only members of the kloncilium had access to that number. It was the second of the cell phones that Burton had retrieved from her pocketbook.

She scanned the cell phone's contacts list of preprogrammed numbers. She had entered the cell phone numbers of all the members of the kloncilium. She stopped when she reached *SC*. *SC* was short for *South Carolina*. *South Carolina* meant *Earl Smith*.

There was a knock on the senator's door. She tucked the cell phone back into her pocketbook. "Yes?" she said, in her most senatorial tone.

Jeffrey Oates pushed open the door. "Sorry to disturb you, Senator. But I thought I should remind you that you've got a Judiciary Committee meeting at ten."

Burton glanced at the antique grandfather clock in the west corner of her office. The clock had been a gift from a grateful constituent. It read 9:44. "I remember," Burton said. "I called the meeting. As I mentioned to you earlier, we've got to do something about the McDonald confirmation process. We've already given the nominee one lengthy delay when his family died. The nation can't afford another one. The Supreme Court is too important not to be operating at full strength."

The grandfather clock chimed on the three-quarter hour.

Oates said, "I'll see you in a few minutes then, ma'am."

"Ass-kisser," Burton muttered as she watched Oates disappear behind the closing door. The senator retrieved her cell phone from her pocketbook. She highlighted Earl Smith's phone number—SC—on the contacts list and punched the send button with the top of a well-manicured thumb. The phone rang and rang and rang.

Finally, she heard, "Hello?"

"Who is this?" Burton said. She knew the sound of Earl Smith's voice, and what she heard emanating from the other end of her cell phone wasn't it.

"Who's calling?" Clay Smith said.

Billy Joe Collier said, "Who is it, kid?"

Clay cupped his hand over the mouthpiece of his uncle's cell phone. "I don't know."

Burton said, "This is a friend of Earl Smith's." She obviously wasn't going to tell a total stranger that she was the chairwoman of the Senate Judiciary Committee and the imperial wizard of the Ku Klux Klan.

Clay glanced at the cell phone's display and saw a number with the area code 202. The call was coming from Washington, he said to himself. Clay knew that his uncle knew Alexandra Burton—that the senator sometimes helped the Charleston den raise cash for local Klan activities. He took a shot: "Senator Burton?"

"Er ... Yes. Who's this?" It was the first time in years that Burton could remember being surprised. Successful politicians—and Burton was certainly that—didn't get surprised often.

"It's Clay Smith, ma'am. Earl Smith's nephew."

Collier said, "Is it Burton?"

Clay nodded.

Burton said, "Where's Earl? I'm calling for Earl."

Silence came from Clay's end of the line. Then he said, "He's dead, ma'am. My uncle is dead."

"*Dead?!* ... How?! When?!"

"I don't know how he died, ma'am. And I don't know when. I just found out myself." Clay was lying, of course. He was the one who had killed him. His cause was just, though. Any klansman would agree. But Clay didn't know that Burton was in the Klan, let alone that the senator was the imperial wizard.

"Can you find out for me, son? Your uncle was a friend of mine. I need to know how he died. I need to know *why* he died."

There was another knock on the senator's door.

Jeffrey Oates pushed open the door again.

The grandfather clock chimed ten times.

Burton said into the cell phone, "I'm late for a meeting. But please get me that information. I'll be in your debt if you do." She pressed the END button.

"What information, ma'am? I ... I can get you any information you need. That's my job."

Burton ignored Oates's question, not to mention the anguished expression on Oates's face. "Where's the meeting?" she said.

Clay Smith switched off his uncle's cell phone and rolled it between his fingers. He was smiling for the first time in weeks—for the first time since his uncle had asked him to kill Kelsi Shelton.

Billy Joe Collier asked, "What did Senator Burton say?"

Clay answered, "That we need to dispose of Uncle Earl's body. And that we need to do so ASAP."

"Then what?"

"I don't know."

Clay knew. But he didn't want to tell Collier.

CHAPTER 55

Alexandra Burton burst through the committee room door. "Sorry I'm late," she said. "My AA forgot to remind me about the meeting."

Jeffrey Oates, who, as usual, was walking three paces behind his boss, reddened when she faulted him for her own tardiness. He was used to taking the blame, however. Politicians never liked to admit they were wrong. Their egos wouldn't permit it.

"I'm surprised that you needed reminding, Alexandra. Professor McDonald's fate seems to be about all that you think about these days." Jonathan Wells sat back in his leather captain's chair and chuckled. Wells was the senior Democrat on the Judiciary Committee. His job was to see to it that Peter McDonald got confirmed to the Supreme Court. Burton, of course, had other ideas.

Burton snapped, "Some of us have to work for a living, Jonathan... . How is Kate, by the way?"

Kate Wennington Wells was Jonathan Wells's wife of two years. She was his third wife, and by far the wealthiest of the three. Her father had made a fortune on the commodities market during the height of the stock market run-up in the mid-1990s.

Wells said, "She's fine, Alexandra. She'll be pleased to know that you were asking about her. Now, can we get to the business at hand? I've got an Armed Services meeting at eleven."

Burton took her seat at the head of the conference table. She reached for a pitcher of ice water and poured herself a glass. She took a long sip and then said, "I'm concerned about how long Professor McDonald's confirmation hearing is taking. As members well know, the Court's docket is chock-full of important cases this term."

Wells interjected, "Including one in which you've got a particular interest. Right, Alexandra?"

Of course Senator Wells was referring to *Tucker v. University of South Carolina.*

Senator Gregory Carpenter rocked forward in his chair and pounded his fist on the table. "I resent that remark, Senator Wells! The entire committee should resent it! It's the chairwoman's responsibility to see to it that these hearings proceed in an expeditious fashion!" Carpenter glanced at the senior senator from South Carolina ... at the woman to whom he owed his own Senate seat. "The honorable chairwoman should be commended for her concern, not criticized for it."

Wells said, "What a load of horse manure, Gregory. Don't you think it's about time you removed your nose from Alexandra's butt?"

Burton struck her gavel. It sounded like machine gun fire in a Hollywood war epic. "Enough! Enough! We're *United States senators,* for God's sake, not high school bullies!" She struck her gavel again. The committee room grew as quiet as a classroom during final exams. "Believe me, I know that many members of this committee think that I'm only interested in helping my daughter and son-in-law win their case, but that's not true. It's simply not true. Sure, I want them to win. Alexander was my grandson—my namesake. Any grandparent would feel the same. But this process is about more than my family. It's about more than any of us. It's about making sure that the Supreme Court—the nation's highest court; the most powerful court in the world—is operating at full capacity. It's about making sure that the justice system in this country isn't shortchanged because one man is either too sad or too sick to go through the confirmation process. I know this seems harsh, but it's time to put the nation's interests ahead of Peter McDonald's. The Court got along fine without him in the past, and it'll get along fine without him in the future."

Wells said, "What are you suggesting, Alexandra? That the president withdraw Professor McDonald's nomination?"

"I'm afraid that might be best, Jonathan."

"Best for you, maybe. But not best for the American people."

Carpenter again came to Burton's defense. "I agree with Alexandra. Professor McDonald is a very smart man; there's no question about that. He's also been through a lot recently, what with his wife and daughter getting murdered and a second attempt on his own life. But this process is bigger than he is. Shoot, this process is bigger than any of us in this room. It's even bigger than the president himself. We can't wait anymore, Jonathan. I wish we could, but we can't. I know you don't believe me. I know you think I'm saying what I'm saying because it's what Alexandra wants to hear. I'm not, though. I've sworn an oath to protect the Constitution. I take that oath seriously. And at this point, that oath requires me to think that the committee should recommend to the president that he find someone who is physically able to serve. Unfortunately, Professor McDonald doesn't appear to be that person."

Wells rocked back in his chair.

Print journalists scribbled feverishly in their notepads. One of them said to another, "I didn't think Carpenter had it in him. I didn't think Carpenter could make so much sense."

"Have you discussed this with the president?" Wells finally said. He wasn't addressing his question to anyone in particular, but everyone knew who was supposed to answer it.

Burton said, "Not yet. I wanted to get the sense of the committee first. What does everybody think?"

A Republican senator from New Mexico said, "I think the president needs to find another nominee. Professor McDonald impresses the hell out of me, but Alexandra and Greg are right. The Supreme Court is too important not to be operating at full strength."

A Democratic senator from Iowa said, "I hate to say it, but I agree with my colleagues from the other side of the aisle. It pains me to say that—it pains me more than you can ever know—but the committee has been more than generous in accommodating Professor McDonald during this process. Don't get me wrong; we did the right thing—the *moral* thing—in delaying the hearing both times the White House asked us to. But, as others have already said, the nation can't afford to let this process drag out forever ... . I think it's time the chair notify the president to that effect."

Burton tried her best to suppress a smile. It was difficult for her to do. Her plan was progressing better than she could have anticipated.

Then ...

"Why can't we question Professor McDonald via video hookup?" the senior senator from Virginia said. He was a Republican, but he clearly felt territorial about a Supreme Court nominee from his home state. He knew that his constituents would accept nothing less than a full-throated defense of the nominee.

"That's a terrific idea!" Wells said. "I knew all this newfangled technology was good for something. I can't figure out how to send an e-mail, but I've got to believe that someone in the building can make a video hookup happen. If they can't, I'll ask my granddaughter. She knows more about computers than Bill Gates does."

Wells's reference to his granddaughter drew smiles from his colleagues. The little girl was only seven years old. Wells had introduced her to the members of the Judiciary Committee on several occasions in the past.

Burton said, "I'm not so sure conducting the hearing by video is such a good idea. I've never heard of such a thing."

"This is the twenty-first century, Alexandra. I think we should give it a try." The Republican senator from New Mexico had done a 180 in his stance about whether the committee should continue to press forward with Peter McDonald's confirmation hearing.

Senator Burton—*Imperial Wizard* Burton—knew that sealed the deal.

CHAPTER 56

Cat Wilson pulled her cell phone from her purse. She had the ringtone set to Willie Nelson's *On the Road Again.* She hated the song, but it was Earl Smith's favorite. She had never heard it before she met him. She downloaded it at his insistence as a remembrance of him. "What do ya got to remember me by?" she had said at the time. Smith had smiled and grabbed her ass.

"Hello," Cat said as she snapped open the phone. Smith had promised to call when he reached D.C. and Cat was hoping it was him. It wasn't. It was her manager at the Waffle House. He wanted to know whether she could come in at midnight to work an extra shift. She said she would let him know after she tried to find a babysitter.

Cat normally tried to avoid babysitters, both because they were expensive and because she had seen an episode of the Tyra Banks Show a couple of months earlier entitled *Babysitters Who Kill.* The program had scared her to death. She was grateful to Tyra for airing it, though. Tyra cared about regular folks like Cat. Oprah only talked about things rich women liked.

Cat's dislike of babysitters notwithstanding, she needed to figure out a way to work the extra shift. She was desperate for money. Kids were expensive. And even though Cat avoided buying her daughter fancy toys, the child needed to be clothed and fed. Cat pushed the button for her contacts list and dialed her mom.

Cat hadn't been on speaking terms with her mom for years. Her mom seemed to resent the fact that Cat—an unexpected pregnancy from an unexpected man—had disrupted her dreams of becoming a nurse. High school students with a baby on the way weren't attractive candidates to college admissions officers—at least not in South Carolina. So Cat's mom, Beth, had foregone college for a life as a chambermaid at the Charleston Holiday Inn. Beth loved her daughter, obviously, but it was too much to bear when Cat repeated her own mistake: an unexpected pregnancy from an unexpected man. But all was forgiven when Isabel Tamara Wilson entered the world on a sun-splashed Tuesday in March at 9:22 A.M.

"Hi, Momma, it's me," Cat said into the phone.

"What's wrong?" Beth Wilson said. "Is Bella all right?"

Bella was Isabel's nickname.

"Bella's fine, Momma. But she is why I'm callin'."

"Let me guess," Beth said next. "You need me to babysit, and you need me to babysit *now*."

"Yes, Momma. Sorry I didn't give you more notice, but my manager just called. He needs for me to pick up an extra shift at the diner. I need the money, but I don't need to tell you that."

Indeed, Cat didn't need to tell her mother about how short she was on cash at the moment. She was *always* short on cash. And that was why Beth Wilson had hoped that Cat Wilson would go back to school—so her daughter, and granddaughter, could stop the cycle of poverty.

Beth said, "You know how much I love that baby doll. Of course I'll babysit Bella. But don't forget to bring me a couple of them waffles when you come to pick her up after your shift's over. I love them things, too."

Cat said, smiling, "I'll remember. I always do." She terminated the phone call by snapping her cell phone shut and headed to Bella's room to get her daughter ready for yet another night at grandma's house. She called her manager to tell him she was on her way.

Cat turned into the Waffle House's parking lot. A knot formed in her stomach, as it always did when she arrived. Working a dead-end job in a decaying part of town in the middle of the night wasn't how she expected her life to turn out. But after Bella was born, she had to put food in her daughter's mouth, and waitressing was the only job she could get with a GED.

She parked her car in her usual spot next to the newspaper boxes. She exited her car and pushed open the door to the diner. Her manager said hello to her. He was a nice man, but she froze. Fear washed over her. "I gotta go," she said to him. "Sorry, but I gotta go."

She jumped back into her car and headed north to the nation's capital.

CHAPTER 57

"The senator will see you now," the heavyset secretary said with a cheerful smile.

Clay Smith returned the copy of *The Washington Times* that he was reading to the coffee table in front of him, straightened his tie, and stood.

The secretary escorted Clay to the private office in the corner of the suite, knocked lightly on the door, and turned the knob.

Senator Alexandra Burton greeted Clay with a warm handshake.

The secretary exited the room.

Burton said, "It's nice to finally meet you, young man. Your uncle was very proud of you. You'll have the world at your feet after you graduate from law school."

"Thank you, Senator. But that's what I needed to talk to you about."

Burton motioned for Clay to take a seat on the couch behind them. Clay did. Burton sat in the chair across from Clay. "So this isn't a courtesy call from a grateful constituent?" Burton knew it wasn't.

Clay shook his head. He studied the scuffs on his shoes. "May I speak freely? I mean, is there anyone listening?"

"Of course there's no one listening. You've seen too many movies, son. Hidden tape recorders went out the window when Richard Nixon was forced from office."

Well, not really. But Burton didn't think that Clay needed to know about *her* recording system.

"Thank you, Senator," Clay said. Then, without a moment's hesitation, he added, "Akia. Kigy."

Burton smiled and nodded. "Akia. Kigy."

"Is it true, Senator? Are you who my uncle said you are?"

For some reason, Burton had let her guard down with Clay Smith. Perhaps it was because Clay reminded her of her grandson; they were both tall, dark, and irresistibly handsome, as the cliché went. She knew what Clay was asking her. "Yes, it's true."

Clay dropped to his knees and kissed the imperial wizard's ring.

"Come on, son. Let's go somewhere we can really talk." Burton stood and walked toward the bookcase. She removed a two-volume set of David Duncan Wallace's *The History of South Carolina* from the shelf and pressed her palm against the marble block behind the books. The bookcase swung open and revealed a secret room.

Clay felt as if he were witnessing an episode of *24*, the over-the-top spy show that most UVA law students watched as a guilty pleasure to break the monotony of studying contracts law and the like. He glanced around the room to see if Kiefer Sutherland had somehow appeared out of nowhere, as he so often did on the TV show. Obviously, Mr. Sutherland was nowhere to be found.

"Come on," Burton said again.

Clay followed the imperial wizard into the secret room behind the bookcase.

CHAPTER 58

Clay took a quick inventory of the room. He estimated the room's dimensions at twelve feet by twelve feet with a ten-foot ceiling. Its walls were white marble, as were the walls in most of the rooms in the U.S. Capitol. But unlike the other rooms in the Capitol building, this particular room had a large cross in the west corner. No American flag. No South Carolina flag. Just a large wooden cross. The cross ... always and forever ... the fiery cross.

Burton directed Clay to the two chairs next to the cross.

Clay sat in the chair closest to the entryway. He noticed that both chairs were embossed with the seal of the U.S. Senate. The Senate's seal, based on the Great Seal of the United States, included a scroll inscribed with the words *E Pluribus Unum* floating across a shield with thirteen stars on top and thirteen vertical stripes on the bottom. Olive and oak branches symbolizing peace and strength graced the sides of the shield, and a red liberty cap and crossed fasces represented freedom and authority. Blue beams of light emanated from the shield. Surrounding the seal was a legend that read, *United States Senate.*

This is surreal, Clay thought. He turned to Burton but was at a loss for words.

"What is it, son?" Burton said. "What did you need to talk to me about?" She placed her hand on Clay's shoulder the way she used to do with her grandson.

"It's about my uncle."

"What about him?" Burton straightened in her chair. After all, Earl Smith was a member of the kloncilium, he was dead, and Burton had asked Clay to find out how he died. "Did you find out who killed him?"

Klansmen didn't die. They were killed.

"Ye ... yes ..."

"Who was it, son? Who was it?"

"Me... . It ... it was me." Clay started to cry.

"*What*? You killed your uncle? *Why*, son? Why?"

"Because he was sleeping with a nigger woman." The mere thought of such an unforgivable act had changed Clay's demeanor from sorrow to shame. Earl Smith was Clay's blood.

The secret room filled with silence, although if Clay listened closely enough he could swear that he heard the wheels in Burton's head turning. Clay was no dummy—a student didn't get admitted to the University of Virginia School of Law unless he was at the top of his college class and scored in the ninetieth percentile or better on the Law School Admissions Test—but he knew that Burton was operating at a different level. Only a truly brilliant woman could have had the kind of career that Burton had enjoyed: sitting U.S. senator, likely Republican candidate for president, and most important of all as far as Clay was concerned, imperial wizard of the Ku Klux Klan.

Burton said, "You did the right thing, son. I'm proud of you. Sleeping with a nigger is a sin. It's an insult to the sacred order and a betrayal of everything that's just and right."

"But he was my uncle ... my blood."

"The Klan is your blood, son. When your uncle slept with a nigger woman, *her* blood became *his* blood. He ceased being *your* blood then. He ceased being your family."

"Thank you for saying that, Your Excellency. That makes me feel a lot better." Clay had stopped crying. "Is there anything you need me to do? I'm here to serve. I'm here to fight for what's just and right."

It took Alexandra Burton merely a moment to realize that someone as bright as Clay Smith, and someone who was willing to kill a member of his own family, could be of tremendous value to her. The senator—the imperial wizard—explained to Clay what she wanted him to do.

CHAPTER 59

Cat Wilson exited Interstate 95 about two miles north of Richmond and searched for somewhere to eat. She spotted the familiar yellow Scrabble-like letters and parked her dilapidated Chevy in the space closest to the door. The irony wasn't lost on her: She had selected a Waffle House as her lunch venue. But she had never traveled outside of South Carolina before, she was nervous, and she wanted to eat at someplace she knew. Besides, she said to herself as she entered the diner, it would be fun to see how her colleagues did their jobs.

"Sit anywhere you like, hon," a waitress said when Cat crossed the threshold.

"Thanks." Cat grabbed a corner booth.

A different waitress approached. She looked like she was in high school. "Do you need a menu?"

Cat smiled and shook her head. "No, thanks. I work at a Waffle House in Charleston."

The waitress returned Cat's smile. "You've got the menu memorized then, huh?"

"Yep."

"What would you like? Get whatever you want. This one's on the house."

Cat choked up a bit. She wasn't used to people being nice to her... . Only Earl Smith was. Earl ... "Thanks. That's sweet of you. Since it's free, I'll have the All-Star Special!"

"A little thing like you?" The waitress was one to talk; she was as tiny as a teapot.

"Yep. I haven't eaten a thing since yesterday mornin'."

It took less than ten minutes for Cat's meal to arrive, but she took her time eating it. She didn't eat out much. She couldn't afford to. Almost every dollar she earned she spent on her daughter. She wanted to savor the moment, even if the moment involved a couple of eggs over easy, hash browns, two slices of bacon, and a waffle.

Fifteen minutes later, the waitress topped off Cat's coffee. "How's everything?"

"Wonderful. Everything's just wonderful."

"Glad to hear it." The waitress wiped the lip of the coffeepot with the spare napkin she kept tucked in her apron. "You never mentioned why you're in our neck of the woods. Richmond isn't exactly Atlantic City in the fun department."

Cat took a sip of coffee. "Richmond's just a pit stop on my way to D.C."

"D.C., huh? What are you gonna do there? Are you on vacation?"

"Kind of." Cat salted her eggs. "I'm hoping to surprise my boyfriend. He's in D.C. on business. I haven't heard from him in a while, and I miss him."

"I love that sort of thing." The waitress returned the spare napkin to her apron's pocket. "It's romantic. It's like one of those old Meg Ryan movies my mom is always watching."

Cat thought it was romantic, too. She could only hope that Earl agreed.

CHAPTER 60

Peter McDonald struggled to put on his shirt and tie. It still hurt when he moved. He planned to wait until the last possible moment to twist into his jacket.

Jim Westfall entered the room. He said, "Good morning, Professor. How are you feeling?"

McDonald had grown tired of that question. He was asked it seemingly every hour on the hour. He understood why: he had been nominated to the Supreme Court of the United States and he had been shot. He answered as he always did: "Fine, thanks." Then, he said something new: "I'm just looking forward to getting these hearings over with. They make a Dickens plot look simplistic. It's *Bleak House* all over again."

Westfall said, "I know. We're looking forward to the end zone, too. The president wanted me to pass along his best wishes. He also wanted me to say that he appreciates your continued willingness to serve our great country. He has complete confidence that you'll be confirmed and that you'll eventually go down in history as one of the finest justices to ever serve on the Supreme Court."

McDonald wiggled out of his hospital bed and inched his way to a chair in a corner of the room. "Tell the president I'm grateful for his kind words." McDonald sat. He grimaced when he did. "Is this where I'm supposed to be?"

"Yes. The camera's up there." Westfall pointed to a small TV camera hanging from a cord on the ceiling.

McDonald combed his hair with his fingers. "Obviously, the committee will be able to see me. But how will I see them?"

"Through the television. As you know, your hearings are being broadcast live on all the major networks. You'll see what the nation sees."

The nation saw a close-up of Senator Alexandra Burton.

The FOX News reporter said, "Good morning, America." The reporter used to be a news reader for ABC and he often forgot that "Good morning, America" was a registered trademark of a rival television network. "After much delay, the Senate Judiciary Committee's confirmation hearings for Supreme Court nominee Peter McDonald are about to resume. It looks like Senator Alexandra Burton, the committee's chairwoman, is reaching for her gavel as I speak."

Burton sounded her gavel. "Order. Order. The hearing room will please come to order. I hereby reconvene the confirmation hearings of Peter McDonald to be an associate justice of the Supreme Court of the United States."

The crowded hearing room became so quiet that Jim Westfall double-checked to make sure the volume on the TV was still on. It was.

The FOX News reporter said, "I feel like I'm back in constitutional law class. Boy, was my professor strict."

McDonald smiled at the comment. He wasn't a "strict" classroom teacher, but several of his colleagues were. They weren't particularly popular with the students. If a student was caught instant-messaging or surfing the Web during class, he or she was booted unceremoniously from the room.

The camera panned from Burton's regal profile down the dais of her fellow Judiciary Committee members. All were sporting expressions that bespoke the solemnity of the occasion.

Burton said, "Good morning, Professor. I was pleased to learn that you were feeling well enough to resume your confirmation hearings."

Of course that wasn't true, and McDonald knew it. But the nominee merely said, "Thank you."

Burton said, "If memory serves, it's Senator Foley's turn to question you. Senator Foley ..."

CHAPTER 61

"Thank you, Madam Chairwoman."

Frank Foley was a freshman senator from Massachusetts, and he was gay. He had already had several skirmishes with Alexandra Burton. None were major. They involved matters such as where Foley sat on the dais (Burton placed him on the end), whether Foley was entitled to an extra staff member to assist him with his Judiciary Committee responsibilities (Burton had said no), and whether Foley could participate by conference call in committee meetings when he was out of town (Burton had again said no). Foley could see the logic in Burton's decisions about those protocols, but he resented the fact that the senior senator from South Carolina tried to lord over him like, say, a master over a slave, especially given who Foley was: the rising star of the Democratic Party and, probably sooner rather than later, perhaps the first openly gay president of the United States. He was so popular that Ellen DeGeneres often raised money for him.

Frank Foley had been swept into office after delivering a stirring keynote address to the Democratic National Convention, the same convention that had selected Charles Jackson as the Democratic nominee for president. Foley wasn't merely a charismatic speaker; he was also a profound intellect and a dedicated public servant. He had graduated at the top of his class from Yale Law School but opted to work as a poverty lawyer in the rough-and-tumble Roxbury neighborhood of Boston rather than as a mergers and acquisitions attorney in the velvet-draped offices of the financial district. It didn't hurt his political prospects that his husband, whom he had met during a fundraising trip to California, was a beloved Hollywood actor.

Senator Foley said, "Welcome back, Professor."

Peter McDonald said, "Thank you, Senator."

McDonald knew all about Foley's past and probable future—the White House had made certain that the nominee knew everything they knew about every member of the Judiciary Committee—and he had been looking forward to being questioned by the senator. McDonald recognized a brilliant mind when he saw one. He was surrounded by them every day as a law professor at an elite law school.

"I've got a number of questions that I'd like to ask, but insufficient time in which to ask them." Foley shot a quick glare in Burton's direction. "Given the constraints of time, I'd like to focus my questions on gay rights." Foley reached for the sheet of paper that contained the list of queries he planned to ask the nominee. "I trust you're not surprised that I'm intrigued by what you've written on the subject."

McDonald said, "No, I'm not surprised."

Foley continued, "Is it fair to say that your approach to gay rights is closely related to your widely known interest in substantive due process?"

"You're being far too generous in your definition of 'widely known,' Senator. My colleagues in the legal academy are familiar with my views, but I can't say that the American people know anything about them."

"That's precisely why I'm asking about them, Professor. Please explain those views."

McDonald had to admit—to himself at least—that he was surprised by the confrontational nature of Senator Foley's line of inquiry. He expected Foley to be a certain vote for confirmation. They were both highly successful professionals ... They were both Democrats ... They were both Ivy League liberals. In a way, though, McDonald admired Foley's integrity. Apparently, not every politician was a partisan hack.

"I'd be happy to explain my views," McDonald said. He straightened in his chair. He did his best to suppress another grimace. "I became interested in substantive due process as a law student years ago when we were reading the *Dred Scott* case in con law class."

Foley leaned forward. "By 'con law,' you mean constitutional law?"

McDonald said, "Correct. Sorry for defaulting so quickly to code. And by the '*Dred Scott* case' I mean *Dred Scott v. Sanford*, the 1857 decision in which the Supreme Court held that no African American, slave or free, was a citizen of the United States. The case involved a claim by a black man born into slavery that his subsequent residence in a state and a territory that prohibited slavery made him free. By a seven-to-two vote the high Court, speaking through Chief Justice Roger Taney, disagreed and went so far as to strike down the Missouri Compromise, a set of federal laws adopted in 1820 to maintain the balance between slave and non-slave states, on the ground that the Compromise violated the Fifth Amendment property rights of slave owners."

Foley said, "The Court's 'self-inflicted wound,' as my constitutional law professor called it."

Alexandra Burton tightened her grip on the gavel. She was seething inside. The Ku Klux Klan considered the *Dred Scott* case the Supreme Court's greatest decision. They celebrated it every year with an extravagant party ... and with the lynching of a black man dressed to look like Scott.

McDonald said, "Precisely. Indeed, the Court's decision helped spark the Civil War. It was overturned after the war by the Thirteenth Amendment, which abolished slavery, and by the Fourteenth Amendment, which guarantees to everyone the equal protection of the law."

Foley said, "Amendments—together with the Fifteenth, conferring the right to vote upon African Americans—that allowed Charles Jackson to become president more than a century later. But what's the connection to substantive due process? ... What's the connection to gay rights?"

McDonald said, "Critics of substantive due process insist that the due process clause is about fair legal *procedures*—the right to a hearing before having your disability benefits cut off; the right to know the charges against you in a criminal case; et cetera—rather than a mechanism by which judges can make social policy that the Constitution reserves for legislators to make. *Dred Scott* is generally regarded as the Court's first substantive due process decision. So that's the connection to substantive due process. Chief Justice Taney held that an act of Congress that deprived a citizen of his liberty or property merely because he had come himself or brought his property into a particular territory of the United States, and who had committed no offence against the laws, 'could hardly be dignified with the name of due process of law.'"

Foley's face tensed. The TV cameras zoomed in for a close-up. "Are you suggesting that the Massachusetts Supreme Court was legislating from the bench when it ruled five years ago that my husband and I had a constitutional right to marry? Because if you are, I can tell you that Senator Burton won't be the only member of this committee opposing your confirmation to the U.S. Supreme Court."

Foley and his Hollywood partner had been the lead plaintiffs in the landmark decision by the Massachusetts Supreme Judicial Court holding that a Massachusetts statute barring gay marriage was unconstitutional... . Not all transformations in American law were launched from Washington.

McDonald stiffened in his chair. "I'm not saying that, Senator. But I'm not saying the opposite, either. As you know, the lower courts are divided at the moment about whether state legislatures can outlaw gay marriage. But as you also know, it's a virtual certainty that the question will soon find its way to the Supreme Court of the United States." The professor paused and cleared his throat. "I'll close by saying to you what I said to Senator Carpenter several weeks ago in response to his question about my views about affirmative action: It would be inappropriate for me to comment on a matter that will come before the Court." McDonald leaned forward. This time, there wasn't a hint of a grimace. "I'm sorry if that costs me your vote, but the Court would be ill-served by any nominee who felt otherwise. The *American people* would be ill-served."

The hearing room erupted into a spontaneous round of applause.

Senator Alexandra Burton tried to gavel it to order but couldn't.

CHAPTER 62

Secret Service Agent Brian Neal switched off the television with a pinch of the remote. He glanced over at Kelsi Shelton just as he had done dozens of times during the past week. This time, she was awake. This time, she was smiling.

Kelsi said, "I told you Professor McDonald would run circles around those Senate windbags." She coughed ... and coughed again.

Agent Neal quickly filled a cup with cold water and presented it to Kelsi. His hand was shaking. He hoped she didn't notice. "Drink this," he said to her. "It's great to see you up and about."

Kelsi took several small sips of water. "It's great to be up. I can't say that I'm 'about' yet."

Neal laughed. "Soon—very soon." He retrieved the water glass from Kelsi's hand and placed it on the nightstand next to her bed. "How are you feeling?"

"Tired. Sore. Angry... . Take your pick, Dr. Phil."

Neal laughed again. "So you noticed I'm a closet Dr. Phil fan, huh? ... A 'Phanatic,' as they say."

"How could I not? You've watched his show every day I can remember. Granted, I don't remember everything, but I do remember *that*."

Neal blushed. "What can I say? I've got a weakness for tall bald men from Texas. My dad was one."

"So what you're telling me is that you're going to be bald in a few years?"

"No. No. Absolutely not. The baldness gene comes from the mother's side, Einstein. My grandfather on my mom's side would've made Ronald Reagan jealous."

"Good."

Neal blushed again. He changed the subject. He never had been good at flirting. Shoot, he didn't even know whether Kelsi *was* flirting. "Do you think Professor McDonald will be confirmed?"

"It's difficult for me to say with a hundred percent confidence. I missed most of his testimony, what with me being in a coma and all. But from what I saw, and from what I know about him, he's a lock."

Neal was pleased to see that Kelsi was feeling well enough to make light of her recent brush with death. He now felt free to ask the question he had been dying to ask: "Do you remember what happened? I mean, how you got hurt? The police are gonna want to know. In fact, they've called the hospital every day to find out when you'll be strong enough to talk to them about it."

The smile that had spread across Kelsi's beautiful face quickly vanished. She traced her fingers across the brim of the water glass she had rescued from the nightstand. She was lost in thought, sort of like the way she got before a law school exam. She lifted her eyes to Neal's. "Of course I remember." Her eyes returned to the water glass.

"How?" Neal said in barely more than a whisper. He sat in the chair next to Kelsi's bed. He wanted to take her hands in his, but he knew their relationship hadn't evolved to that point—at least from Kelsi's perspective.

"One of the guys from school stabbed me."

"From UVA? Why on earth would he do that? Was he"—Neal struggled to say the words—"trying to rape you?"

Kelsi shook her head. She lifted her eyes to Neal's again, this time even more briefly than the first time. "He stabbed me af ... after ... "

"'After' what?" Neal said. "'After' *what*?"

"After we slept together."

The pained expression on Brian Neal's face made it obvious, if it hadn't been already—who spent a week sitting in a hospital room with an acquaintance?—that the Secret

Service agent's interest in Kelsi Shelton wasn't simply that of a bodyguard for a body. After all, Peter McDonald was Neal's real body, but the agent had somehow managed to convince his superiors at the Treasury Department that Kelsi needed around-the-clock protection, too ... and that he was the agent who should provide it.

"Sorry," was all Kelsi could think of to say.

CHAPTER 63

Clay Smith was sitting quietly in the back row of the Senate Judiciary Committee's ornate hearing room. The room was open to the public—it was public property, in fact—but securing a seat for a Supreme Court confirmation hearing was almost as difficult as winning the Powerball lottery. Just ask the hundreds of people who had stood in line for more than twenty-four hours only to get turned away in the end. Clay hadn't merely been fortunate in snagging a seat; one had been reserved for him in advance by Senator Burton.

Clay waited patiently, alone with his thoughts, while a sea of people cleared the room. He had to admit that he took pride in Professor McDonald's performance, even if that performance had been relayed via big-screen TV from a hospital room in Bethesda, Maryland. The University of Virginia law professor had represented the school well. And as far as Clay knew, he was still a law student at UVA. He had been following the news surrounding the assault on Kelsi Shelton, and no suspects had been named. It was only a matter of time, though. CNN had reported earlier in the day that Kelsi was awake, conscious, and almost ready to talk with the police.

A Capitol cop tapped Clay on the shoulder. Clay jumped, figuring that his luck had run out and Kelsi had identified him. "Ye ... yes, Officer?"

"Are you Clay Smith?"

"Ye ... yes. I was just leaving, though. I was waiting for the crowd to thin. I've never been in the Capitol building before. I wanted to soak up as much of it as I could."

The officer smiled. "It's not that. You're welcome to stay as long as you wish. The reason I'm asking is because Senator Burton would like to see you. She said she reserved a seat for one of her home state constituents, a bright young man who attends the law school that Professor McDonald teaches at. I trust that's you."

"It is." Clay's heartbeat had returned to normal. He checked his attire. He wasn't wearing a sport coat, let alone a tie. "I really don't think I'm dressed appropriately to meet with the senator."

"Don't worry about it. You look fine. You're in law school. Haven't you learned that you have a constitutional right *not* to wear a jacket and tie?"

Clay smiled. Apparently, *everyone* thought that lawyers were full of shit.

The Capitol cop escorted Clay to Senator Burton's office. The senator greeted Clay with a warm smile and a firm handshake. "Thanks," Burton said to the officer.

"You're welcome, ma'am." The officer returned to his post at the south entrance of the building.

Burton directed Clay to her private office.

Clay said, "Thanks for reserving a seat for me at the hearing, but I assume it wasn't simply an exercise in constituent relations."

The fish-out-of-water routine that Clay had pulled with the Capitol cop wasn't necessary with Burton.

Burton said, "Correct. The sacred order needs your service again. *I* need your service. Can I count on you, Brother Smith?"

"Yes, Your Excellency." Clay dropped to his knees and prepared to kiss Burton's ring.

At precisely that moment, Jeffrey Oates entered the room.

CHAPTER 64

Jeffrey Oates finally had the evidence to confirm his biggest fear: Senator Alexandra Burton, his boss for three decades, was the imperial wizard of the Ku Klux Klan. Oates had done enough reading about the Klan to know that only the imperial wizard was entitled to have her ring kissed by her followers. The Klan had borrowed that tradition from the papacy and the mob. What Oates had witnessed reminded him of the final scene in *The Godfather* when Michael Corleone had become the new don.

Of course, Oates hadn't uttered a word about the matter to the senator during the awkward moment when he had watched the young man—Clay Smith, Oates recalled his name being—kissing the senator's ring. He had simply apologized for interrupting, excused himself from the senator's office, and pretended as if he hadn't seen anything.

But Oates knew that both the senator and her young visitor were aware that Oates had seen *everything*. What concerned Oates was what Senator Burton—*Imperial Wizard* Burton—would do about it.

Oates exited Capitol Hill a bit earlier than usual. He was known as a hard worker—even Senator Burton would concede that much—but after seeing what he had seen, he wanted to go home and figure out what he was going to do next. It was bad enough that Oates had agreed to try to kill Peter McDonald in the first place when Oates had thought that he needed to do so in order to stay in Senator Burton's good graces. However, the longtime Senate aide drew the line when it came to advancing an agenda of racial hatred. Oates might have been a Republican—and a *southern* Republican at that—but he was adamantly opposed to discriminating against people, let alone *killing* them, because of the color of their skin.

Oates walked the length of the Mall. He smiled, like he always did, as he enjoyed the sights and sounds of the city. He passed the Smithsonian Institution on his left, a place where he had spent many pleasant weekend afternoons. Yes, he said to himself, he was going to miss the nation's capital. He knew he had no choice but to leave, though. Senator Burton couldn't afford to risk word spreading around town, and then around the nation, that she was rumored to be the imperial wizard of the Ku Klux Klan. No senator could afford it. No *president* could.

CHAPTER 65

Oates arrived at the studio apartment he rented in Georgetown. It was nothing more than a glorified closet, but it was all he could afford on his congressional aide's salary. People didn't work on Capitol Hill for the money. They did it because politics was in their blood. Most had resumes virtually identical to that of Oates—bachelor's degree in political science; leadership position in their college's student Republican or Democrat club; extensive volunteer service with local political campaigns. Unlike most of his congressional staff colleagues, however, Oates still enjoyed the give-and-take of the legislative process. At least he had enjoyed it until he was asked to murder a nominee to the Supreme Court of the United States. He didn't remember *that* being mentioned in the job description.

Oates searched his refrigerator for something to eat. He didn't find much. He tended to "dine" on the fly after work. In fact, he couldn't recall the last time he had eaten dinner at home. He opened the cupboard and discovered an ancient jar of peanut butter and a box of crackers. Supper. He slapped together a stack of peanut butter crackers, filled a tall glass with tap water, and marched the four short steps from the "kitchen" to the "dining room."

He switched on FOX News. The talking heads were opining about Peter McDonald's performance during the morning's confirmation hearing.

The blowhard who had reported live from the hearing room said, "I was there this morning, gang, and I can report that you could've cut the tension with a knife."

A pretty blonde who used to clerk for the chief justice and now hosted her own syndicated radio show chirped, "Thanks for the cliché, but Professor McDonald wasn't even in the room. The hearing was about as exciting as a Washington Redskins game."

The Redskins were suffering through yet another dismal football season. The Daniel Snyder Era was a disaster: one disappointing year after another.

The token former federal prosecutor—every law and courts TV roundtable was apparently required by statute to include one—said, "I agree."

The pretty blonde said, "With whom?"

"Er ... you."

This guy's fifteen minutes were up, Oates said to himself. He would never get invited back on the show. The key to being an effective talking head was *sounding* as if you knew what you were talking about. You didn't actually have to *know* what you were talking about. The pretty blonde had made it seem as if the former federal prosecutor didn't have a clue. He was toast on the talking head circuit.

Oates began to flip through the channels as quickly as he was popping peanut butter crackers into his mouth. He wasn't used to being home in the afternoon and he was horrified to see what passed for entertainment these days. Apparently, Dr. Phil knockoffs were the trend of the moment. A Dr. Margaret was advising a teenage girl to listen to her mother—"She loves you, Amanda; she cares what happens to you"—and stop dating the forty-year-old man who lived across the street. A Dr. Indra was telling a couple of newlyweds to "communicate better" and to "hug at least three times a day."

Mental health in thirty minutes or less, including commercial interruptions. Oates couldn't stand it anymore. He also couldn't stand another peanut butter cracker. He switched off the TV, tossed the remaining stack of crackers into the wastebasket, and headed out the door to grab a meatball sandwich at the Subway shop on the corner.

Clay Smith was waiting for him when he opened the door.

CHAPTER 66

Oates said, "Aren't you the guy who was meeting with Senator Burton a few hours ago?"

Clay said, "Yeah."

"Do you live in the building?"

"No."

"Do you know someone in the building?"

"No."

Silence filled the corridor.

Oates fidgeted with his keys.

Clay didn't move a muscle or blink an eye.

"Why are you here, then?"

Clay reached into his pocket and pulled out a knife. It was the same knife he had used to stab Kelsi Shelton. He lunged at Oates.

Oates managed to avoid the first thrust. "Hey!" he said. "What are you doing?!"

Clay said, "Akia." A klansman I am. He lunged again at Oates. This time, he got him. Blood started to pour from underneath Oates's shirt at a pace that would have made a surgeon squeamish. Clay had stabbed Oates in the side, just above his kidney.

Oates folded in agony, placing his hand over the wound to try to stop the bleeding. It wasn't working. He struggled to maintain consciousness. Everything appeared to be moving in slow motion. He lifted his head to see the knife coming at him again. This time, he managed to take a step to the left, like a quarterback adjusting in the pocket to avoid an oncoming rush.

"Fuck! Hold still! Let's get this over with."

Oates tried to push his attacker away. He was fighting for his life. He wasn't strong, though, and the blood he had lost because of the initial wound had drained his already marginal strength. But it was amazing the reserves human beings could draw upon when their lives depended on it. He gathered all the power that remained in his body and launched himself at his attacker.

Clay was caught by surprise. He had thought that Oates was only moments from death. Pints of blood had poured out of Oates's wound. The jolt Oates gave Clay knocked Clay back into the wall. The impact from the wall loosened Clay's grip on the knife. Oates noticed and swatted the knife to the ground. Oates tried to kick the knife down the stairs but missed. Clay held Oates by the neck with one hand and tried to reach down to pick up the knife with his other hand. It was just out of reach. Fortunately for Clay, Oates's earlier attempt to fend off Clay had sapped Oates's blood-depleted body of all its strength. Clay was able to drag Oates a few feet closer to the knife, snatch the knife from the floor, and thrust the weapon once more into Oates's side. Oates wailed in pain and then quickly grew silent. He collapsed to the floor.

Clay dropped to his knees. He wiped sweat from his brow. He glanced over at Oates, who wasn't moving. Clay placed his fingers on Oates's neck to ascertain whether Oates had a pulse. He didn't. Clay placed his fingers under Oates's nostrils to determine if Oates was breathing. He wasn't.

Clay raced from the apartment building to inform the imperial wizard that the deed had been done. Clay had now killed three people in the span of two weeks.

It was time to make it four.

CHAPTER 67

Kelsi Shelton peeked out from behind her hospital room door to ascertain whether Brian Neal was nearby. She smiled. She felt like she used to feel when she was a little girl trying to sneak off to somewhere her mother had told her not to go. Kelsi could hear her mother's voice: "Mommy needs to go downstairs for a few minutes, sweetheart. Be a good girl and play with your dolls. Stay in your bedroom, please."

Kelsi would always say, "I will, Mommy." And she had meant it when she said it. But hers was a soul filled with wanderlust, and she would manage to stay put for only a couple minutes before the urge to explore got the better of her.

Kelsi remained a little girl at heart as far as curiosity was concerned. She noticed that no nurse was in view, let alone a government agent with smoldering brown eyes and the cutest butt this side of a Rugby Road fraternity party. She stepped over the threshold and proceeded to saunter down the hallway as if she were a visitor on her way to check on the status of a sick aunt. There were two problems with her plan, though. First, she was wearing her hospital gown. Second, Brian Neal had been watching her the entire time.

Neal allowed Kelsi to drift about a hundred feet from her room before he said, "And where do you think you're going, young lady?"

Kelsi's mother used to ask her the same question... . Kelsi knew it wasn't really a question.

She answered, "I'm stretching my legs. I'm going stir-crazy in my room. Besides, I feel fine."

Neal smiled and shook his head. "You'll feel fine only if the doctor says you feel fine. You don't want to pop your stitches, do you?"

Stitches, Kelsi said to herself. She had almost forgotten about her stitches. There went swimsuit season. "Maybe if I pop them they'll disappear," she said to Neal. "I'm scarred for life now."

"You're being ridiculous. Your wound is only an inch long. It was deep, not long. You're also forgetting that doctors are very careful these days to minimize scarring. We're well past the era of the zipper scar."

Kelsi reached for her injury. "How do you know all that?"

"Because I asked the doctor."

"Why would you ask the doctor?"

Neal didn't answer the *why* question. But Kelsi already knew why: he was smitten with her.

Neal changed the subject. "Did you hear?"

"Hear what?"

"The Judiciary Committee voted to confirm Professor McDonald's nomination to the Supreme Court. The full Senate will vote on it early next week."

Kelsi smiled.

Neal felt himself getting weak in the knees. He had never seen such a beautiful sight. Kelsi's smile shone like a new moon on a dark night. "Good news, huh?"

"*Great* news." Kelsi began to hop up and down like a kid in a candy store. "What was the vote?"

"Ten to nine. Burton just missed. Apparently, Senator Foley voted to confirm after all."

Kelsi's mood switched from ecstasy to outrage. "I've got a question for you: why is Senator Burton participating in the confirmation process at all, let alone chairing the Judiciary Committee's hearing about a nominee who everyone knows holds the key to her daughter's lawsuit that's on the fast track to the Supreme Court?"

Kelsi's question wasn't really for Neal, but he happened to be in her line of sight at the moment.

"I don't know," Neal said. "I'm not a political scientist or a constitutional lawyer. But I *do* know that it's probably not a good idea for you to be standing around in your hospital gown. Your little adventure is over, young lady."

Kelsi smiled again. She thought again of her mother, who used to say the same thing about Kelsi's "adventures" when Kelsi was caught wandering from her bedroom. Kelsi responded to Neal as she had responded to her mom: "*This* adventure might be over. But there are plenty more to come."

CHAPTER 68

Peter McDonald listened patiently while Jim Westfall congratulated him on the Judiciary Committee's vote to send his nomination to the full Senate with a positive recommendation. McDonald was less patient when the conversation turned to his decision to return to Charlottesville to watch the Senate debate from the comfort of his home.

Westfall said, "Dr. Tanenbaum said that you're still not out of the woods. He recommends that you remain at Bethesda for another week or so."

McDonald said, "I feel fine, Jim. Not a hundred percent, but fine. I haven't been home in weeks. I need to make sure my house is still standing and that my office hasn't burned to the ground."

"We can have someone check on those things for you. With all due respect, Professor, Morris Tanenbaum is one of the best doctors in the country. He's the *president's* doctor. I think you should defer to his judgment."

McDonald walked to the closet. He tried to disguise how painful even that minor activity was. He bent down to retrieve the suitcase that the Secret Service had purchased for him for precisely this occasion. He winced in pain and let out an audible "*Sss.*"

Westfall shook his head. "Jiminy Cricket, Professor, it's still difficult for you to bend over."

McDonald smiled. "Painful, not difficult." He placed the suitcase on the bed and opened it. "I appreciate your concern, Jim, but my mind is made up."

Westfall watched helplessly as McDonald packed his bag with the items he had managed to accumulate during two weeks in the hospital. Most of what the professor was placing into the suitcase was books. Westfall hadn't read that many books during his entire lifetime, let alone in the span of two weeks. The president's chief of staff was even more in awe when he remembered that the professor had spent a large portion of those two weeks unconscious. "Why so many books?" Westfall finally asked.

McDonald answered, "I'm an academic. I read and write for a living."

"How do you find the time to read all of them? I mean, I barely have time to read the newspaper."

McDonald smiled again. "In here, I have nothing but time. At work, I make the time. It's part of my job... . The most important part."

"Will you miss it when you're on the Court?"

"No, because I'll still make the time."

"Why?"

McDonald chuckled. "Wow, Jim. I thought you vetted my nomination. I'd make the time because I think the nature of our Constitution requires me to. One of my most recent articles maintains that the founders of the American regime were steeped in the history of ideas, and the Constitution they created expressed their commitment to the power of ideas. Anyone who takes the Constitution seriously is *required* to take ideas seriously. You can't do that by simply watching the evening news or skimming the daily paper."

Westfall felt as if he had been scolded by his father, albeit more politely than his father used to do. He raked his hands through his hair. "You've just demonstrated why we nominated you."

"Thanks." McDonald zipped his suitcase shut. He yanked it from the bed. "Now, if you don't mind, can you please tell the Secret Service that I'm ready for my ride to Charlottesville?"

CHAPTER 69

McDonald asked the Secret Service agent whether he would like anything to eat or drink. The agent said he was all set and then assured McDonald that he would be fine waiting outside. It was forty-five degrees.

"Are you sure?" McDonald said. "I've got plenty of soft drinks and snacks in the house, and the house is certainly big enough for the both of us. It's also nice and warm. Or at least it will be once I turn the heat back on."

The agent said, "I'm sure, Mr. Justice. I'm supposed to wait outside. I do it all the time. I can sit in the car if I get cold. I've got a couple of sandwiches and a thermos of coffee in there."

Mr. Justice, McDonald said to himself. It's got a nice ring to it. It's a bit premature, but it sounds good. He said to the agent, "Well, come on in if you change your mind. I've got the NFL package from DirecTV if you feel the urge to see how the Redskins are doing. I think they're playing the Cowboys today."

The agent had confided on the drive from Bethesda that he was a diehard Redskins fan. "Thanks. But I've got Sirius in the car. My wife gave it to me for my birthday. It's great."

McDonald entered the house. The agent's comment about the present his wife had given to him made McDonald think of all the presents *his* wife had given to him over the years. Jenny's greatest gift had been Megan. Sweet, freckle-faced Megan. McDonald stopped in the middle of the entryway, closed his eyes, and thought of his beloved wife and daughter. His confirmation to the highest court in the land was all but certain, but sadness rushed over him like a cold breeze through a broken window.

Snap out of it, Peter, McDonald said to himself. Move on. You've *got* to move on. He wandered into the living room and flipped on the lights. Everything was as he remembered it being, albeit dustier after his two-week absence. In fact, everything remained as it had been when Jenny and Megan were alive. McDonald had considered redecorating—a psychologist friend with whom he occasionally played tennis had encouraged him to do so as part of the healing process—but he couldn't bring himself to do it. He couldn't bear to do anything that might further remove Jenny and Megan from his memory. Time, cruel time, was doing that, no matter how hard McDonald fought against it.

McDonald removed a dated *Washington Post* from his favorite chair and sat. The chair, an antique rocker that had once belonged to James Madison, had been a gift from Jenny on their tenth wedding anniversary. It wasn't particularly comfortable, but McDonald always got tingles when he thought about sitting in a chair in which the principal architect of the U.S. Constitution used to sit. McDonald was also fond of the chair because Jenny had searched long and hard for it, a point about which she would remind him during one of their rare spats. "I practically had to pry that chair from James Madison's dead hands!" she would exclaim in response to something her husband had said that she didn't appreciate. Her retort almost never had anything to do with what they were fighting about, but she seemed to think it was a conversation stopper. And it was. McDonald hated arguing with his wife.

After about ten minutes of rocking back and forth, McDonald stood and made his way—*willed* his way—to Megan's room. He hadn't visited his daughter's room since the morning of her death. His housekeeper had dusted and vacuumed the room every week, but he personally hadn't set foot in it. He couldn't bear to do so. He didn't want to do anything that might erase the last memory he had of the room. It wasn't a significant memory, but he wouldn't have traded it for anything in the world.

Megan, as usual, had overslept. Jenny, as usual, had asked her husband to wake their slumbering child. McDonald had entered Megan's room with a warm plate of pancakes and bacon, Megan's favorite breakfast. His daughter had rubbed the sleep from her eyes, sat up in her bed, and said, "Pancakes! Bacon!" It was amazing how she was able to go from zero to sixty in under ten seconds.

McDonald had said, "Correct, sweetheart. But you know Mommy's rule."

Megan repeated it by rote: "No eating in my bedroom."

"Correct again, sweetheart. How's this for a deal: I'll keep your breakfast warm in the oven and then you can enjoy it with *real* maple syrup—the bottle we bought in Vermont last summer—after you wash your face and dress."

"Hurray!" Megan had said. And she did what her father had asked. She always did.

CHAPTER 70

McDonald tossed his suitcase onto his bed. He didn't unpack it, though. Instead, he grabbed a REDSKINS FOOTBALL jacket from his closet, made sure that all the lights were off, and headed to the front porch.

The Secret Service agent was listening to the football game in his car. He was startled by the soft tap on the passenger's window. He spilled a bit of his coffee when he noticed it was McDonald. He quickly lowered the window. "Is everything OK, sir?"

McDonald said, "Yes. But how about taking a ride?"

"No problem, sir. Where to?"

"UVA hospital."

"You got it."

"Jay, isn't it?" McDonald said, buckling his seatbelt.

"Yes, sir. Jay Blakeman." The Secret Service agent kept his eyes riveted to the rural road in front of them. He didn't want to hit a deer. His cargo was too valuable.

"How long have you been with the service?"

"Ten years, sir. I joined right out of college."

"Where'd you go to school?" McDonald was an academic and always interested in where the people he met went to college.

The Secret Service agent smiled. "Tech."

"Virginia Tech?"

"Yes, sir."

"They assigned a Hokie to protect a Wahoo? No wonder the American people have such a low opinion of the government."

They both laughed. Virginia Tech and UVA were archrivals.

Twenty minutes later, they arrived at their destination. Agent Blakeman had never been to UVA hospital. McDonald had been several times. Megan, like most little kids, used to get sick a lot. And when she did, McDonald usually considered it an emergency. When it turned out to be nothing more than an upset stomach or some other minor ailment, Jenny would chastise him, albeit lovingly, for overreacting.

They approached the information desk. A white-haired man on the north side of eighty put down the Sunday paper and said, "May I help you?"

"Yes, please. What room is Kelsi Shelton in?"

The old man said, "You're Peter McDonald, aren't you? There was a big story about you in yesterday's paper. I recognize you from the picture. Congratulations on your appointment to the Supreme Court." The old man searched for a pen and paper. "May I trouble you for an autograph for my grandson? He wants to be a lawyer. He's applying to law schools this year. He's got very good grades and he sure can talk up a storm."

McDonald signed his name on the piece of paper and returned it to the old man. "Tell your grandson good luck. The law is a noble profession. As far as I'm concerned, though, there's still one more step in the process. The full Senate must vote to confirm my nomination. What happened yesterday was merely a committee vote."

The old man didn't appear to hear a word McDonald had said. He was too busy checking the computer for Kelsi Shelton's room number. "Room 512," he said. "The elevator's around the corner to the left."

McDonald could hear that the television was on in Kelsi's room. He knew they wouldn't be waking her. She was watching the Redskins game.

He said to Agent Blakeman, "I didn't even know she liked football."

She didn't. But Brian Neal did.

Agent Neal spun around in his chair when he heard the knock on the door. He stood the instant he realized it was Professor McDonald. "Good afternoon, sir," he said.

Kelsi said, "Who is it?"

McDonald said, "It's Peter."

Neal stepped out of Kelsi's line of sight.

Tears filled Kelsi's eyes. "It ... it's a good game. The Redskins just hit a home run."

McDonald smiled at Kelsi's malapropism, walked to her bed, and hugged her.

They hugged for five full minutes. It didn't seem long enough.

McDonald finally said, "How are you feeling, kiddo?"

Kelsi tried to answer but couldn't. Instead, she began to cry. "Sorry," she said, after she had regained her composure. She dabbed her eyes with the sleeves of her sweatshirt. She pulled her sleeves over her hands as makeshift mittens to comfort herself.

Megan used to do the same thing.

PART II

The Marble Temple

CHAPTER 71

Robert Johnson, the legendary African American blues musician, sung in one of his most famous songs:

I got to keep moving, I got to keep moving
blues falling down like hail
blues falling down like hail
Uumh, blues falling down like hail
blues falling down like hail
and the days keeps on worryin' me
there's a hellhound on my trail,
hellhound on my trail
hellhound on my trail.

Dontrelle Davis couldn't "keep moving" fast enough.

Davis, who was black, worked at an auto repair shop on the west side of Charleston. He had asked his employer for the day off to visit his sick mother in the hospital. His employer refused. A heated exchange of words ensued. The employer tried to hit Davis with a wrench, and Davis struck back in self-defense. The employer suffered a broken nose. Davis dislocated his shoulder. No charges were filed by either party—Davis, because he was too scared to do anything about it; the employer, because he had an alternative means of redress.

The Klan dragged Davis deep into the woods. They stripped him of his clothes and chained him to a tree. They stacked kerosene-soaked wood around him and saturated his body with motor oil. They cut off his ears, fingers, and genitals, and skinned his face. They plunged knives into his flesh, and cheered at the contortions of his body and the distortion of his features. Davis's eyes bulged out of their sockets and his veins ruptured.

Davis could be heard screaming, "Oh, my God! Oh, Jesus!" His blood sizzled in the fire. His heart and liver were removed and cut into several pieces, and his bones were crushed into small particles. The konklave scrummed for souvenirs.

One of the nighthawks handed Senator Alexandra Burton the largest portion of Davis's heart.

The Charleston den had been surprised to see a sitting United States senator at their konklave. They had long known that Senator Burton sometimes offered support for their activities—Earl Smith had mentioned it to them on several occasions over the years—but it nevertheless caught them off guard when Burton exited a car driven by Smith's nephew. They were speechless when the senator announced that she was the imperial wizard of the Knights of the Ku Klux Klan and that she felt compelled to deliver the news in person that both Earl Smith, the grand dragon of the South Carolina Realm, and Billy Joe Collier, the klailiff, were dead.

Burton then stated that she was proud to report that she had selected Clay Smith to replace his uncle as grand dragon. Scattered murmurs rippled through the konklave about Clay's age and inexperience, but there was nothing the brothers could do about Burton's choice. A hydra who foolishly uttered a derogatory remark about Burton's gender was pulled to the side and stoned.

Burton also said that she was sorry to report that Peter McDonald had been confirmed by the full Senate as an associate justice of the Supreme Court of the United States.

One of the nighthawks said, "You mean that nigger lover Earl was tellin' us about?"

"That's right." A warm sensation rushed over Burton's body. Although she was profoundly disappointed by the Senate's vote to confirm McDonald, she felt rejuvenated being in the company of her fellow patriots.

She also knew that there was still time to stop McDonald. It would be more difficult now that McDonald was a Supreme Court justice, but it wasn't impossible. After all, Burton said to herself as she joined in the singing of the Klan's sacred song, John Wilkes Booth had stopped Abraham Lincoln.

CHAPTER 72

It wasn't until 1935 that the U.S. Supreme Court got its own building. From 1800 until 1935, the Court was housed in cramped quarters in the U.S. Capitol. Prior to 1800, the Court sat in the Merchants Exchange Building in New York and Independence Hall and City Hall in Philadelphia. The Court finally received a home of its own after Chief Justice William Howard Taft lobbied for one in order to distance the Court from Congress as an independent branch of government.

Peter McDonald had served as a law clerk to Chief Justice William H. Rehnquist, argued more than a dozen cases before the nation's highest court after his clerkship had ended, and visited the Court many times over the years for his academic research. Nonetheless, his heart skipped a beat when he pulled his Volvo station wagon into the Court's underground parking lot on his first day as an associate justice.

"Good morning, Mr. Justice," the parking lot attendant said. "Where's your driver?"

"You're looking at him," McDonald said, smiling. He had declined the car and driver to which he was entitled by statute. He was a modest man, and just because he now occupied one of the most powerful positions in the federal government didn't mean he had forgotten how to drive.

McDonald went out of his way to chat for a few minutes with the parking lot attendant. He spoke with every Court employee he encountered on his way to his chambers, which explained why he was thirty minutes late by the time he arrived.

McDonald had convinced his longtime faculty secretary, Mildred Jacobs, to accompany him to the Court. Mrs. Jacobs—everyone, including McDonald, called her *Mrs.* Jacobs—was in her early seventies, comfortably married to *Mr.* Jacobs for the better part of four decades, and about as much fun as a root canal. But she also was as efficient as a Hollywood celebutante during a Rodeo Drive shopping spree. That's why the instant she saw McDonald burst through the chamber's door, she said, "You're late."

McDonald hung his trench coat on the coat rack next to Mrs. Jacobs's desk. He said, "I know."

"If you know, why are you late?"

McDonald smiled sheepishly and glanced at his watch. "Sorry about that, but I've got a few minutes yet before I'm scheduled to meet my clerks. I'll be in my office."

Mrs. Jacobs had made certain that McDonald's office was decorated how he would like it. She had secured for his use the desk once occupied by Felix Frankfurter, who, like McDonald himself, had worked as a law professor prior to being appointed to the Supreme Court. Sundry personal items were sprinkled throughout the room: a baseball autographed by Dustin Pedroia, McDonald's favorite player; a hole-in-one certificate from Birdwood Golf Course, McDonald's proudest athletic achievement; a copy of the first issue of the *Yale Law Journal* for which McDonald had acted as editor in chief; and a photograph of McDonald and former Chief Justice Rehnquist.

Mrs. Jacobs had taken special care with regard to McDonald's vast book collection. The complete series of the U.S. Reports was shelved in the bookcase closest to McDonald's desk. The U.S. Reports were the casebooks in which the official opinions of the Supreme Court were published. As of the current term, they consisted of 553 bound volumes and soft-cover preliminary prints of an additional three volumes. A final five volumes' worth of decisions also existed in individual slip-opinion form. Volumes were added to the set at the rate of three to five per term, and they were generally between eight hundred and twelve hundred pages long.

Likewise within reach of McDonald's desk were his favorite monographs on constitutional law. Mrs. Jacobs had been working for McDonald long enough to know what they were: John Hart Ely's *Democracy and Distrust: A Theory of Judicial Review*; Bruce A. Ackerman's *We the People: Foundations*; Larry D. Kramer's *The People Themselves: Popular Constitutionalism and Judicial Review*; and Ronald Dworkin's *Law's Empire*. All were penned by law professors who taught at elite law schools. But the book that Mrs. Jacobs had awarded prominence of place was Douglas Scott's *To Secure These Rights: The Declaration of Independence and Constitutional Interpretation*, which had been presented to McDonald by a colleague after a Federalist Society debate.

Professor Scott, who taught at a small law school in the Midwest that didn't have a trace of ivy on its walls or a single cabinet secretary on its governing board, argued in his book that the Constitution of the United States should be interpreted in light of the natural rights political philosophy of the Declaration of Independence and that the Supreme Court was the institution of American government that should be primarily responsible for identifying and applying that philosophy in American life.

McDonald wasn't completely convinced by Scott's book, preferring instead the conventional account that the Declaration of Independence had no *legal* significance—that it was merely an eloquent pronouncement to the world that the United States was a free and independent nation—but he had to admit that he found Scott's thesis difficult to resist. McDonald was particularly taken with Scott's claim that the theory advanced in the book—what Scott called "liberal originalism"—was neither consistently liberal nor consistently conservative in the modern conception of those terms. Rather, the theory was liberal in the classic sense of viewing the basic purpose of government to be safeguarding the natural rights of individuals. As Thomas Jefferson wrote in the Declaration itself, "To secure these rights, governments are instituted among men." In essence, Scott maintained that the Declaration articulated

the philosophical ends of our nation
Constitution embodied the means to effectu

McDonald had asked Mrs. Jacobs
lunch with the young professor just before
call from the White House nominating him
Court. Now that McDonald was on the Court, he still hoped to meet Professor Scott.

But the most important mementos in McDonald's Supreme Court office remained what they had been in his UVA faculty office: photographs of his family. A half dozen pictures of McDonald's wife and daughter were displayed on an antique table immediately behind his desk. McDonald leaned forward in his chair and studied each and every one—the wedding photo in which Jenny resembled a young Nicole Kidman; the picture of McDonald and Jenny on their honeymoon in Ireland; the smiling couple in front of their first home in Charlottesville; the photograph from the hospital on the morning that Megan was born; Megan's first day at school; and the family's most recent Christmas card in which McDonald was dressed as Santa Claus, Jenny as Mrs. Claus, and Megan as a tiny elf.

McDonald stared lovingly at the photographs and desperately missed the life he had led. However, before he had a chance to become too sentimental, Mrs. Jacobs buzzed him and said, "Your law clerks are waiting for you in the Harlan Room."

A law clerk was a recent law school graduate who provided assistance to a judge in researching and writing opinions. All federal judges were entitled to law clerks, and most state court judges were too. Being a law clerk to a U.S. Supreme Court justice was the most prestigious position a young lawyer could attain. Supreme Court clerks usually had graduated number one in their respective law school class, held a high-ranking position on the law review, and clerked for a year with a prominent U.S. court of appeals judge. McDonald had certainly done all of those things before he had clerked for Chief Justice Rehnquist. So, too, had the three young men and the one young woman who had agreed to clerk for him.

Technically, they had agreed to clerk for Justice Crandall, but McDonald had decided to retain Crandall's clerks, both as a courtesy to them—Supreme Court clerkships were difficult to get, and it would have been unfair to them to lose their positions after only three months on the job—and so he could benefit from their time at the Court. However, Justice McDonald already knew who his first pick would be for next year: Kelsi Shelton.

CHAPTER 73

The spring semester was already three weeks along by the time Kelsi Shelton was strong enough to return to school. Everyone at UVA had been wonderful during her time away. Her classmates had made sure that she received copies of the notes she needed, and her professors had taped the lectures she missed so that she could listen to them at her convenience.

Kelsi smiled and said hello to a steady stream of well-wishers as she scrambled for a seat in Federal Courts class. She spotted a familiar face waving her in like a flagman on an airport runway.

"Hi, gorgeous," Sue Plant said as Kelsi squeezed into the chair in the fourth row. "I missed you."

"I missed you, too." Kelsi wiped away a tear. "Thanks for the care packages. They always made my day."

Kelsi and Sue hugged for what seemed like forever.

"Get a room!" one of the class clowns said.

Kelsi laughed. It felt good to be one of the gang again.

She turned on her notebook computer, opened the file that contained her Fed Courts outline, and watched in wonder as her professor became animated about the *Pullman* abstention doctrine, arguably the dullest Supreme Court rule in the history of American law.

Kelsi's first day of classes passed in a blur. She had managed to discern that *Pullman* abstention permitted a federal court to stay a plaintiff's claim that a state law violated the U.S. Constitution until the state's judiciary had been afforded an opportunity to apply the law to the plaintiff's case. But she hadn't figured out why it had taken her professor fifty minutes to make that simple point, let alone why her professor seemed so enthralled by it. To each her own, as the saying went.

Employment Discrimination class was a different story altogether. Kelsi had no idea what her professor was talking about in there. The three-step burden-shifting framework of *McDonnell-Douglas* made her head spin. At least it was nice outside, which explained why she had decided to take a walk on the Lawn on an early February afternoon.

Throughout its history, the University of Virginia had won praise for Thomas Jefferson's architectural design. The American Institute of Architects, for one, called Jefferson's work "the proudest achievement of American architecture." Jefferson's plan revolved around the Lawn, a breathtaking terraced green space surrounded by residential and academic buildings. Technically, no one was supposed to walk on the Lawn, but that didn't stop students from doing so. In fact, rare was a sunny day *without* students studying under trees, sunbathing on towels, lunching from takeout diners, and playing ultimate Frisbee. The only activity in which students didn't engage was pitching golf balls. Some drunken fool had tried that once and was nearly expelled after the divots were discovered.

"A little help!" one of the ultimate Frisbee players called out. His disc had flown wildly off course and landed at Kelsi's feet.

Kelsi retrieved the Frisbee and executed a perfect scoober to the grateful player.

"Rad toss," the Frisbee player said, jogging toward her. "Wanna play?"

Newcomers were always welcome at pickup games or whenever people were throwing.

"I can't," Kelsi said. "I've got a lot of reading to do for tomorrow."

The Frisbee player—a freshman, or sophomore, tops —stared at Kelsi in disbelief. "Blow it off. I always do."

But before Kelsi could answer, the player was summoned back to the huddle.

Thirty seconds later, he called out, "Sorry! Game's called on account of darkness."

Kelsi waved and kept walking. The Lawn emptied. She enjoyed the solitude. She sat on the stairs of the Rotunda and thought about the last several months, especially about working for Professor McDonald and, of course, getting stabbed by Clay Smith. She tried to figure out why Clay had wanted to kill her, but before she could give it much consideration, he stepped out of the gloaming.

"Hello."

Kelsi stood and started to back away. "Wh ... what are you doing here? St ... stay away from me. St ... stay away."

"Relax," Clay said, with a reassuring smile. "I wanted to find out how you're feeling. You look good." He inched closer.

"I said stay away!" Kelsi's face tensed with fear.

"I'm sorry, you know. That's what I came to say—that I'm sorry." Clay flashed his soulful brown eyes. That had worked on Kelsi once; perhaps it would again.

It didn't. "Sorry?! *Sorry?!* You tried to kill me!"

"I know. Like I said, I'm sorry."

Resisting her better judgment—suppressing every lesson she had ever learned about human nature—Kelsi asked Clay the question that had occupied her mind since the day it had happened: "Why?" Simply, "Why?"

After a brief silence, Clay said, "I don't know. Believe me, a day hasn't gone by that I haven't asked myself that same question."

"I don't believe you. I mean, a person doesn't try to kill another person and not know why, especially after, you know ..."

"After we slept together."

"Y ... yes."

Clay said nothing.

Kelsi didn't either.

The Lawn grew eerily quiet. It was almost as if they had stepped back in time to the days when Edgar Allan Poe had been a student at the university.

Finally, Clay said, "I wish I could take it back. I wish I could undo what I did. But I can't."

Kelsi said, with tears streaking her cheeks, "I need to know why, Clay. I need to know *why*."

Clay stared into the darkness. The wind rustled the trees. Crickets began to sound. Then he said, as if reminding himself, "I'm not allowed to say."

CHAPTER 74

Clay Smith had been tempted to spend the night in Charlottesville, but he knew it would be unsafe for him to do so. Although his face wasn't plastered all over the news every hour on the hour as it had been during the first several days after Kelsi Shelton had identified him at UVA hospital as her attacker, he wasn't foolish enough to think that the police had abandoned their search for him. He also knew there was a good chance that Kelsi would report seeing him in town, which led him to chastise himself for making contact with her. But he was being honest when he had said that he wanted to see how she was doing. He liked her. He really did. He had tried to kill her only because his loyalty to the Klan had required it.

Clay drove the two and a half hours to D.C. Fortunately for him, by the time he reached the beltway the rush-hour gridlock for which the nation's capital was famous had dissipated.

He motored past the historical landmarks for which D.C. was also famous—the Jefferson Memorial, the Lincoln Memorial, the Washington Monument, the Mall—and located a parking spot on a side street near the Kennedy Center. He walked three short blocks to the Allen Lee Hotel on the corner of F and 23rd streets.

The proprietors of the Allen Lee described their establishment as an "old-fashioned hotel at old-fashioned prices." It was more accurate to call it a fleabag. It was cheap, though—fifty dollars per night in Foggy Bottom was a quarter of the price of its closest competitor—and Clay wasn't likely to run into anyone who might be able to identify him. Shoot, the hotel's clientele looked more like extras in a George Romero zombie flick than residents of one of the most significant neighborhoods in the world.

Clay paid cash for a three-night stay and then informed the desk clerk that he might stay longer. He traipsed up four narrow flights of stairs and located his room at the end of a musty hallway. He was stunned to see peeling paint, broken light fixtures, and all manner of abandoned maintenance equipment. Apparently, D.C.'s overworked building inspectors hadn't managed to fit the Allen Lee into their crowded schedules.

Clay tossed his suitcase onto the bed, which caused a cloud of dust to explode into the air. He searched in vain for a bathroom in his room. He remembered seeing a communal toilet next to the stairs and quickly headed in that direction to relieve himself after his long drive from central Virginia.

He tried to open the bathroom door. It was locked.

"Just a minute," said a female voice from inside.

Two minutes later, a light-skinned black woman who bore a striking resemblance to Halle Berry emerged with a towel wrapped around her head. "Sorry I took so long," she said, with a seductive smile. "I've been driving all night and I needed to wash the road off."

Clay said, "Don't worry about it. I'm in the same boat."

The beautiful black woman smiled again. "I'm Cat ... Cat Wilson."

CHAPTER 75

The water pressure was weak. Clay Smith didn't notice. He was preoccupied with fantasizing about Cat Wilson. As a klansman, Clay was supposed to detest black people. But Cat was so beautiful and sexy that she made his head spin. Moreover, his Uncle Earl had told him that every klansman was entitled to have sex once with a black woman, so that, as his uncle put it, "he can see what having sex with an animal is like."

Clay turned off the shower, reached for the thin cotton towel that came with his room, and dried himself. He put on the fresh set of clothes that he had purchased at the Target store in Georgetown and headed back to his room.

He spotted Cat exiting her room. He said, "Where are you off to?"

She said, "Sightseeing."

"Mind if I tag along? I'll go stir-crazy if I sit around here all day."

"I'll wait for you downstairs."

Clay hung his wet towel on the metal rack on the back of his door. He blow-dried his hair, snatched his jacket from his bed, and hurdled down the steps.

Cat lifted her eyes from the dated copy of *Time* magazine that she had found on the Formica coffee table in the lobby.

"Ready?" Clay said.

"Yes." Cat tossed the magazine onto the coffee table. "I didn't know that George Bush was running for reelection again. I didn't think three terms was allowed."

"According to the magazines in my room, Bill Clinton is running for a third term too."

They laughed.

"Where to?" Cat asked.

"I don't care," Clay answered. "Is this your first trip to D.C.?"

Cat nodded.

"Then I suggest we start at the White House. We can see if Bill and George are in."

Clay also wanted to get a sense of how difficult it would be to get a shot at President Jackson. A klansman's work is never done, Senator Burton had told him during a recent telephone conversation.

A chill wind typically blew in the nation's capital in mid-February, but this particular day was calm and pleasant. Clay and Cat seemed to enjoy the warmth of the sun as they made their way through the side streets of Washington toward 1600 Pennsylvania Avenue. They also seemed to enjoy one another's company.

Cat said, "You never said why you're in town."

Clay said, "I've got a meeting tomorrow." He did—with Senator Burton. But he didn't tell Cat that. "What about you? What brings you to our nation's capital?"

"I'm looking for a friend. Well, a boyfriend, actually."

"I knew it. A woman as beautiful as you couldn't be unattached... . Just my luck."

Cat blushed.

Dozens of protestors were picketing in Lafayette Park, as they usually did. The war in Afghanistan, the state of the economy, the health care crisis, ... even the president's decision to enroll his teenage son in an exclusive private school rather than in one of D.C.'s sub-par public schools. Nothing was off-limits, and no affront appeared to go unnoticed.

A protestor who looked as if he hadn't budged since the end of the Vietnam War said, "Now that's what I call a hot cup of cocoa." He was staring directly at Cat. His eyes traced the contours of her figure.

Clay said, "Shut up, old man." He had no idea why he was defending Cat. He had said much worse—he had *done* much worse—to blacks in the past.

But Cat had captured his imagination. It didn't matter that she was a few years older than he was. She didn't act like it, and she certainly didn't look like it.

She said, "Just ignore him, Clay. I'm much more interested in touring the White House than I am in letting some racist old fool spoil our day."

Clay and Cat made their way to the public entrance of the White House. Unfortunately, it was closed on Tuesdays.

"Now what?" Clay said.

"Is there something else you'd like to see?" Cat said.

"How about the Supreme Court building? I'm told they let the public listen to the lawyers' arguments. That might be interesting."

"*Lawyers* ... *arguments* ... can't we go to the dentist instead?"

"It's not as bad as all that. The Court has got more power than most people realize. It would be fascinating to see how they do their jobs, and to see the building."

Clay and Cat paused on the sidewalk in front of the Supreme Court building and admired the view.

"'Equal Justice Under Law.'" Cat was reading the motto carved into the Vermont marble used to construct the building.

"They don't mean it," Clay said. "It's all about money. If you've got money, you get all the justice you want. If you don't, you're shit out of luck."

They began to make their way up the steps toward the public entrance when Clay suddenly stopped.

"What is it?" Cat asked. "You look like you've seen a ghost."

But it wasn't a ghost. It was Kelsi Shelton.

CHAPTER 76

Kelsi Shelton's heart was beating a mile a minute. But it wasn't because she had sprinted up a mountain of marble steps. She was nervous. She hadn't told Professor McDonald—*Justice* McDonald—she was coming, and she didn't know what she was going to say to him when—if—she saw him.

She struggled to open the enormous bronze doors that greeted all visitors to the highest court in the land.

"Everyone has trouble with them," an elderly assistant U.S. marshal said when Kelsi finally managed to enter the building. "Each of the doors weighs a ton. I don't know why the chief justice keeps refusing to allow public access through one of the side doors."

Kelsi smiled. "Tradition, I imagine."

"Are you here for a tour or to watch the arguments?"

Kelsi wanted to say, "Neither." She wanted to say, "I'm here to see Justice McDonald. I'm here because I need his help." Instead, she said, "To watch the arguments."

The elderly marshal glanced at his watch. "They start in twenty minutes. The line's over there." He pointed to the sea of tourists crowded against the marble wall fifty yards down the corridor. He noticed the concerned look on Kelsi's face. "Don't worry," he said to her. "You'll get in. Visitors are permitted only fifteen minutes each when the line is as long as it is today."

Kelsi was among the last of the visitors seated in the courtroom during the morning's wave of tourists. The two people who made it in after her were newlyweds from Montana. Kelsi had asked them while they were standing in line why they had wanted to come to the Supreme Court on their honeymoon. They had answered that they had met in a civil liberties seminar at Montana State University and they thought it would be romantic. Kelsi said that was sweet and then proceeded to spend the rest of her wait reading the *Washington Post.*

She placed the newspaper in the recycling bin when she was escorted into the courtroom. The courtroom, known officially as the "court chamber," took her breath away. It rivaled a football field in length and width, and its ceiling seemed to reach to the sky. Kelsi counted twenty-four marble columns and more than fifteen separate sculptures on two magnificent friezes. She recognized most of them from her legal history seminar at UVA. The south wall frieze included lawgivers from B.C.: Menes, Hammurabi, Moses, Solomon, Lycurgus, Solon, Draco, Confucius, and Augustus. The north wall frieze was decorated with lawgivers from A.D.: Justinian, Muhammad, Charlemagne, King John of England, King Louis IX of France, Hugo Grotius, Sir William Blackstone, John Marshall, and Napoleon.

"All rise!" the clerk of court cried out.

Kelsi returned to the moment.

Everyone stood.

The chief justice and the two senior associate justices entered the bench from the center of an enormous ruby curtain. Three associate justices processed from one side and three others from the opposite side. They each took their respective places on the bench, with the chief justice in the center and the others alternating from left to right in order of seniority. Peter McDonald, being the most recently appointed justice, sat in the seat at the far right of the bench.

Kelsi got goose bumps at the sight of her professor in his black robe taking his seat on the most powerful court in the world.

The chief justice said, "Before we begin today's arguments, I'd like to take a moment to welcome our newest colleague, Justice Peter McDonald."

All the justices turned toward McDonald and beamed. The senior associate justice said, "Here, here!" He began to applaud.

The entire courtroom followed suit.

McDonald acknowledged the warm welcome with a polite "Thank you. Thank you very much."

The chief justice took that as a cue to gavel the proceedings to order and to call the first case.

CHAPTER 77

The case was *Tucker v. University of South Carolina*! Kelsi couldn't believe it. She was about to witness the oral arguments in the most highly anticipated civil rights case in a generation. The question presented to the Supreme Court was so important—whether the Court should reverse its 2003 decision in *Grutter v. Bollinger* that the nation's colleges and universities may take the race of applicants into account when deciding which students to admit—that, according to the morning's *Washington Post,* President Charles Jackson had instructed his White House counsel, Cheryl Richards, to file a friend-of-the-court brief on behalf of the university.

Kelsi was stunned that she had managed to find a seat in the courtroom, but the person sitting next to her said that the chief justice had instructed the clerk of court not to release the day's arguments list until fifteen minutes before the arguments were to commence. It was a highly questionable decision—the Court was a *public* institution—but the chief justified the secrecy on the grounds of national security: the president himself was in attendance.

Kelsi scanned the courtroom and discovered that Senator Alexandra Burton was sitting three seats to the right of the president. Kelsi recognized the senator from Professor McDonald's confirmation hearings. The president and the senator acknowledged one another with polite nods and handshakes.

The chief justice said, "We'll hear arguments now on number 11-426, Patricia and Michael Tucker versus the University of South Carolina."

Patricia and Michael Tucker were Alexander Tucker's parents. Alexander Tucker was Alexandra Burton's dead grandson.

The chief justice continued, "This matter is before the Court on the Tuckers' petition for expedited review. Before we begin, the Court wishes to commend the parties on their exemplary briefing under trying circumstances. We appreciate it ... Senator Burton."

Gasps filled the courtroom as Alexandra Burton stood from her seat in the gallery and made her way to the lectern. The fact that Senator Burton would be arguing her grandson's case was also kept secret from the press.

She said to the chief justice, "May it please the Court. I can tell from the gallery's reaction that many are surprised to see me at the lectern this morning. Well, they shouldn't be surprised. Alexander Tucker, God rest his soul, was my grandson ... and my daughter's only child. What kind of grandmother would I be if I didn't do everything in my power to see to it that Alexander didn't die in vain? What kind of mother would I be?"

The chief justice and the eight associate justices seated with him clearly understood, as did everyone else in the courtroom, that Senator Burton's powerful questions answered themselves.

But lawyers arguing before the nation's highest court rarely spoke for more than two minutes before getting peppered with queries from the bench. This case was no exception.

The chief justice said, "Senator Burton. I'm sorry for your family's tragic loss. I truly am. But, as you know, it's highly unusual for this Court to overrule one of its precedents so soon after deciding it. Why should we do so in this case? *Grutter* was decided less than ten years ago."

Senator Burton hadn't practiced law in thirty years, but she had done her homework on the issues that would likely determine how her grandson's case would come out. Stare decisis—the legal principle by which a court was obliged to respect a prior decision on the same question—

was perhaps the most important of those issues. The senator said, "I agree, Your Honor, that it's unusual for the Court to reverse itself so quickly. But it's not unheard of. The Court once overturned a precedent only one year after deciding it."

The chief justice, a large man with a large ego, leaned forward and said, "You're talking about *Booth v. Maryland.*"

Burton said, "That's correct, Your Honor."

A liberal associate justice seated on the left side of the bench interjected, "*Payne v. Tennessee,* the case that overturned *Booth v. Maryland,* was not one of our finest hours. Power, not reason, was the Court's currency in that decision. A number of my colleagues wanted to permit the use of victim impact statements during the sentencing phase of capital punishment trials and, after Justice Brennan's replacement by Justice Souter, they had the five votes they needed to do so. It's as simple as that."

Supreme Court justices often used oral argument to debate one another rather than to engage the lawyers, and that was what was occurring during Burton's presentation.

A conservative associate justice said, "I disagree with my honorable colleague that 'power, not reason' explains our decision in *Payne.* It was appropriate to overrule *Booth* in *Payne* because *Booth* was a constitutional case, which unlike cases interpreting statutes cannot be corrected by Congress if they are in error; it involved a rule of evidence in which no one had a vested economic interest; and the case had been decided by the narrowest of margins, over spirited dissents challenging the basic underpinnings of the precedent at issue."

The dozen or so journalists who happened to be in the right place at the right time—namely, in the courtroom of the Supreme Court of the United States during the unannounced oral arguments in *Tucker v. University of South Carolina*—were taking notes as quickly as they could.

A second conservative associate justice said, "Senator Burton, let's leave the debate over this Court's theory of precedent to our friends in the law professoriate."

The justice turned to her left and smiled at Peter McDonald. She continued, "What's your response to the university's argument on page 7 of its brief that a diverse student body benefits white students, not simply minority students?"

Senator Burton took a sip of water. She hadn't blinked in ten minutes. She said, "With all due respect, I don't buy that argument, Your Honor. Indeed, that argument goes to the heart of this Court's decision in *Grutter* in 2003, and it goes to the heart of my grandson's case today. The university is focusing on the wrong set of white students to be concerned about. Rather than focus on the white students who were fortunate enough to be admitted to the university, my daughter and son-in-law are asking this honorable Court to focus on the white students who were denied admission... . Students like their son ... students like my grandson. Succinctly put, the best way to stop discrimination on the basis of race is to stop discriminating on the basis of race. Justice requires nothing less."

The chief justice said, "Time."

CHAPTER 78

"Ms. Richards?"

Cheryl Richards approached the lectern. There had been a lot of discussion among the lawyers supporting the university's position as to whom should argue *Tucker v. University of South Carolina* on its behalf. The attorney general of South Carolina had suggested that the solicitor general of the United States present the case. The thinking there was that the solicitor general's job was to represent the United States in the Supreme Court, which meant that he appeared before the nation's highest court on a fairly regular basis ... and certainly more frequently than government lawyers from South Carolina did. Jim Westfall, the president's chief of staff, had countered that the United States wasn't a named party in the case. Charles Jackson was merely what was called an "interested party": a person with a recognizable stake in the outcome of a matter before the Court but not otherwise directly involved in the litigation of the dispute. Consequently, the decision was made that the White House counsel should present the case.

What precisely was President Jackson's stake in the outcome? The president decided that now was the time to explain it himself.

"Excuse me, Mr. Chief Justice," Jackson said as he stood to his feet. He turned to Richards, who was organizing her notes. "Sorry, Cheryl, but I think I should present the university's side."

President Jackson's unexpected entry of appearance in *Tucker v. University of South Carolina* made the commotion surrounding Senator Burton's entry of appearance seem like the height of normalcy by comparison.

The chief justice tried to gavel the courtroom to order. It took him a full ten minutes to do so. "Order!" he said, over and over again. "Order in the court! Order!"

Charles Jackson wasn't stupid. No one savvy enough to get elected president could be. He knew that he had to explain himself quickly. He pulled the microphone close to his mouth and said, "Please, everyone. Please. Five minutes. That's all I ask. Just five minutes."

It worked. Calm returned to the courtroom. The chief justice seemed grateful for that, but he was less than pleased about what had caused the commotion in the first place. He said, with a surprising edge to his voice, "You've got five minutes, Mr. President."

President Jackson said, "Thank you, Mr. Chief Justice, and may it please the Court."

The chief justice appeared surprised that the president—a politician, not a lawyer—was familiar with the proper salutation.

The president continued, "First, let me apologize for disturbing everyone. But I felt, in light of what Senator Burton said in her remarks, that I should say something too. Second, I'm not a lawyer, so please forgive me if I'm not as polished in my presentation as Senator Burton was in hers."

The president's first point was true: he was being a profound disturbance. His second point was a stretch: Charles Jackson was the most polished political orator since Bill Clinton and, although Supreme Court justices always denied it, the nation's highest court was a political institution.

The chief justice, a Republican appointee, said, "Four minutes, Mr. President. I suggest you get to the point."

"Certainly, Your Honor. Certainly." The president retrieved Cheryl Richards's notes from the podium and handed them back to her. He planned to speak from the heart. He said, "In case anyone failed to notice, I'm black."

Nervous laughter filled the gallery.

Even the chief justice smiled a bit.

The president continued, "I say that not to be funny, although I'm glad the tension in the room has dissipated a bit. I mention my race because, like it or not, race still matters in the United States. It doesn't matter as much as it used to matter—I was elected president, after all—but it still matters." Jackson turned and faced Alexandra Burton. "Senator Burton is simply wrong to suggest otherwise. Senator Burton is simply wrong to think, for example, that it's as easy for a black man to hail a cab in this country as it is for a white woman. It's not. It's simply not. In fact, before I became president—before anyone but the good people of Connecticut knew who I was —I often couldn't flag down a cab myself. Let me be clear, however: The case the Court has been asked to decide today isn't about me. It's about our future. We can't forget that during most of the past two hundred years, the Constitution as interpreted by this honorable Court didn't prohibit the most ingenious and pervasive forms of discrimination against blacks. As I've said, I'm not a lawyer. But I do know about *Dred Scott v. Sanford*, which relegated blacks to the status of property, and I do know about *Plessy v. Ferguson*, in which the Court endorsed racial segregation under the guise of 'separate but equal.'"

President Jackson reached for Cheryl Richards's water glass and took a slow sip. He held the glass high above his head and said, "Under separate but equal I would be subject to arrest for doing what I just did. Now when a state acts to remedy the effects of that legacy of discrimination—especially a former slave state such as South Carolina—I cannot believe that this same Constitution stands as a barrier. It doesn't. It *can't*."

The president returned the water glass to Richards, directed his attention back to the bench, and said, "Thank you, Mr. Chief Justice." He turned to the gallery. "And thank you, ladies and gentlemen."

CHAPTER 79

Cat Wilson said, "Why didn't we go in?"

Clay Smith searched for a plausible explanation about why they had walked twenty blocks from the White House to the Supreme Court and then immediately turned around and left. He knew the reason—because he didn't want Kelsi Shelton to see him—but he couldn't tell Cat that. He noticed they were standing in front of the Vietnam Veterans Memorial. He said, "Because I thought you should see this first. Isn't it amazing?"

No one could help but be impressed by the mirror-like surface of the polished black granite reflecting the images of the surrounding trees, lawns, and monuments. The walls seemed to stretch into the distance, directing visitors toward the Washington Monument in the east and the Lincoln Memorial to the west.

Cat certainly appeared impressed. "It's beautiful." However, she was poor, not stupid. "But why did we *really* leave the Court in such a rush? We could've stopped here on the way back."

Clay had to think fast. He couldn't afford to let Cat know the truth. "The truth?"

"Yes."

He lied. "Because I couldn't wait to be alone with you." Clay pulled Cat toward him and kissed her. It was the sort of kiss that signaled the climax of a Hollywood movie.

Cat didn't resist. In fact, she seemed to enjoy it. But after she had come up for air, she said, "I'm almost old enough to be your mother." That wasn't true. However, working full time while raising a child alone would make anyone feel old.

Clay said, "You're one sexy mama, then."

Cat giggled at Clay's pickup line. It was so lame that it worked.

Clay kissed her again. He whispered into her ear, "Let's go back to the hotel."

"To the fleabag, you mean."

"Yeah. To the fleabag."

Clay had a difficult time fitting his bent key into the rusty lock. By the time he did, Cat was undressed. Damn, Clay said to himself. She must have done this before. But he didn't care. Her body was flawless.

Cat *had* done this before. A lot. Her looks were her strongest asset. She didn't feel guilty about exploiting them, though. Life had dealt the poor, undereducated, unwed mother a bad hand, so she felt entitled to take advantage of the one thing that worked in her favor.

"Do you think the bed is strong enough to hold us?" Clay's hand was firmly attached to Cat's marvelous buttocks. "I thought it was gonna break when I rolled over last night... . I was by myself then."

"Who knows?" Cat reached her hand inside Clay's pants. "It's worth a try, don't you think?"

CHAPTER 80

Senator Alexandra Burton wasn't pleased with how the oral arguments had gone. She felt she had done well, but she didn't like the questions that some of the justices had asked. More importantly, she didn't like that Peter McDonald hadn't asked any questions. By not asking questions, the Supreme Court's newest member hadn't tipped his hand. Burton strongly suspected where McDonald stood on the case—where most academics stood: in favor of affirmative action—but he hadn't given Burton any ammunition to feed to the press by remaining silent during the hour-long argument. Consequently, Burton's legal team had to resort to asserting that Justice McDonald should have recused himself from the case, a technical claim about judicial protocol that most Americans wouldn't understand. Moreover, when the point about recusal had been floated to the reporter who covered the Court for *The Washington Times*, the reporter had reminded the Burton camp that many new justices sat on cases that were filed before they were appointed. "Don't forget," the reporter had said between puffs on a cigarette, "*Brown v. Board of Education*, the most famous civil rights decision in American history, was filed before Earl Warren had been appointed to the Court... . Warren ended up authoring the opinion." That fact was relayed to Burton, and Burton concluded that she needed to do something to relieve the stress of recent events.

She decided to do what she almost always did when she felt compelled to cheer herself up: attend a Ku Klux

Klan meeting. This particular meeting was being held in a large pasture on the outskirts of Spartanburg.

The exalted cyclops—the head—of the Spartanburg den said to the konklave, "Akia. Kigy. We are privileged to have with us this evening the imperial wizard herself."

The konklave said, "Akia. Kigy." The klansmen broke into a spontaneous round of applause. Many had tears in their eyes. This was the first time the imperial wizard had graced them with her presence. It was the highest honor any den could receive.

Burton said, "Akia. Kigy."

More applause.

Burton held up her hands to silence the konklave. As a U.S. senator, she was used to being fawned over. Those occasions were artificial, though. *This*—the reception from her compatriots in the sacred order—was sincere. She was glad she had come. She was warmed by the fiery cross, both literally and metaphorically.

The kludd read from the Kloran.

The exalted cyclops said, "My terrors and klansmen, what means the fiery cross?"

The konklave said, "We serve and sacrifice for the right." They sang the Klan's sacred song.

The kludd read several more passages from the Kloran.

When he had finished, the exalted cyclops said, "Amen."

The konklave said, "Amen!"

The exalted cyclops said, "Bring forth the sacrifice."

Klan protocol required that a sacrifice be offered the first time the imperial wizard visited a particular den. It was a sign of respect.

Two terrors—two members of the exalted cyclops's staff—dragged a middle-aged black man across the muddy ground. The black man had put up quite a fight thirty minutes before Burton had arrived, but the terrors had beaten the man into submission with a tree branch. They had to stop several times to make certain he wasn't dead. The sacrifice was required to be of a *living* black man.

The exalted cyclops said, "Tie the nigger to the tree."

Burton smiled at the spectacle. It was power in its ultimate form—the taking of human life. Burton loved power. That's why she originally ran for the U.S. Senate, that's why she became the imperial wizard of the Ku Klux Klan, ... and that's why she coveted the American presidency.

The next morning, smoldering ashes and a blackened tree were all that remained. A placard read, *We Must Protect Our Women.*

The local newspaper urged readers to "keep the facts in mind" when they judged the actions of the lynchers, whom everyone knew to be the local den of the KKK. This wasn't the first time a black man had been discovered hanging from a tree in Spartanburg. The newspaper's lead editorial insisted:

> *The people of Spartanburg are orderly and conservative, the descendants of ancestors who have been trained in America for more than two hundred years. They are a people intensely religious, home-loving, and just. There is among them no foreign or lawless element.*

The newspaper went on to provide the so-called facts of the black man's alleged offenses. They were implausible and untrue.

Alexandra Burton chuckled as she closed the local paper. She buttered a piece of toast and then swept the toast across the egg yolk that remained on her breakfast plate. Politicians needed to keep abreast of both local and national news, and Burton was no exception. She reached for *The Washington Times,* her national newspaper of choice. *The Washington Times* was founded in 1982 by the Reverend Sun Myung Moon. The paper was politically conservative, and most journalism scholars cited it, along with FOX News and radio host Rush Limbaugh, as epitomizing the conservative agenda. *The Washington Times* was Ronald Reagan's favorite newspaper. Burton liked to say, "If it was good enough for Reagan, it's good enough for me." That morning's edition included a clarion call against the "liberal activism of the politicians in robes." The editorial was referring to *Grutter v. Bollinger*. The piece concluded by urging the nation's highest court to overrule that precedent in *Tucker v. University of South Carolina*.

Burton had just poured herself a second cup of coffee when her secretary entered the room.

"Excuse me for interrupting your breakfast, Senator, but your nine o'clock appointment is here."

Burton checked her watch. Now we can end this matter once and for all, she said to herself.

She instructed her secretary to bring in Clay Smith.

CHAPTER 81

Peter McDonald said good morning to the parking garage attendant as he exited his car.

"You're here mighty early this mornin', Mr. Justice," the attendant said. He held the door of McDonald's car, the only one in the garage with a University of Virginia bumper sticker. Wahoo-wah.

McDonald smiled and said, "The chief has been asking about the status of my opinion in the South Carolina case. The arguments were a month ago. He's been polite about it—a brief e-mail here, a quick phone call there—but it's not difficult to tell that he wants to see a draft ... and pronto."

The attendant returned McDonald's smile. "I'm sure you're up to it, sir. I've been watchin' the news. Everyone says they expect great things from you."

McDonald arrived at his second floor office, unlocked the door, and switched on the lights. The silence was comforting. He wasn't used to the cacophony that had dominated both his nomination to the Court and the attempt on his life. Academics lived a quiet existence with their books and ideas. Judges usually did, too. He was glad the tumult had subsided ... at least a bit. Unfortunately, the media was having a field day with his failure to recuse himself from *Tucker v. University of South Carolina*. But the canons of judicial ethics were far from clear. Canon 3 was the only one plausibly at issue: "A judge shall perform the duties of judicial office impartially and diligently."

McDonald, being the former law professor that he was, researched the canon before deciding not to disqualify himself from the most important case of the decade. He had also discussed the matter with the chief justice.

The chief justice had demonstrated how comfortable he was with McDonald's participation in *Tucker v. University of South Carolina* by assigning McDonald the majority opinion in the case. It was unusual for a new justice to be assigned the opinion for the Court on such a significant matter, but McDonald was no ordinary junior justice. He was the Court's most sophisticated legal theorist since Oliver Wendell Holmes Jr.

The opinion for the Court was the most difficult opinion to write because it wasn't solely the opinion of the author. Justice Holmes had said that writing the Court's opinion required that the author "dance the sword dance." Justice Harry Blackmun had made the same point less poetically: "Other justices say that if you put in this kind of paragraph or say this, I'll join your opinion. So you put it in. And many times the final result is a compromise."

Compromise was difficult for law professors. Most professors had entered the cloistered walls of the academy because they wanted to express *their* ideas, not the ideas of a committee. McDonald was no different.

"Finally," McDonald said to his empty office. "A decent first draft."

He had been working on the opinion for fifteen hours straight, and he was exhausted. He saved the draft on his PC and on the thumb drive that accompanied him everywhere he went. He shut down his computer, stuffed the thumb drive into his pocket, and headed for the small apartment he rented in Georgetown.

McDonald had been encouraged to buy a home in the D.C. area. He declined. He couldn't bring himself to sell his house in Charlottesville. Jenny had loved that house, and so had Megan. He had promised them shortly after his nomination had been announced that he would never sell it. He wasn't about to break his word. His wife and daughter were dead, but they remained the two most important people in his life.

CHAPTER 82

Clay Smith waited for Peter McDonald to lock the door before he took his next breath. Clay was stunned that he had managed to sneak into the Supreme Court building after hours and he didn't want to spoil his good fortune by making a stupid mistake. He was torn, though. Should he kill McDonald immediately? He had a clear shot at him—probably the best shot he would ever get—and the imperial wizard had asked Clay to kill the Court's newest justice. Or should Clay first have a look around McDonald's office to see if there was something that might help Burton in the larger sense of the word, like, say, a draft opinion in *Tucker v. University of South Carolina*?

Clay chose the latter course. He was a klansman, and klansmen did what they were told, but he was also a law student—at least he had been until the week before when he had heard on the radio that he had been officially expelled in absentia—and curiosity required him to search for the draft opinion.

Many of the senior faculty at UVA law school continued to write their articles on legal pads for their secretaries to type. It was tough to teach an old dog a new trick, as the cliché went. But Kelsi Shelton had told Clay that McDonald did his own typing. That meant that Clay had to figure out how to access McDonald's computer.

Clay switched on the power, waited for the PC to boot, and took a few stabs at a security password. He first tried McDonald's wife's name. Next he tried McDonald's daughter's name. Then he tried WAHOO. Bingo! Clay said to himself. McDonald, whom everyone on campus had known as a sports nut, had used the nickname of UVA's sports teams as his password.

McDonald hadn't had a chance yet in his initial weeks on the bench to create many documents, which meant it didn't take Clay long to find the document for which he was searching. The file was entitled TuckerMajorityOpinion and, sure enough, McDonald had been assigned the opinion for the Court. There had been considerable speculation in the press about whether McDonald would get the plum assignment as his first opinion, and the document that Clay was reading as quickly as he could confirmed what the Washington whispers had suggested.

Nothing that Clay read surprised him. McDonald's draft was clear, thoroughly researched, and most important for present purposes, it came out in favor of the university.

McDonald took a different path than that suggested by President Jackson. Rather than emphasizing the president's point about making amends to minorities for previous discrimination against them—what civil rights activists called "reparations"—McDonald held that stare decisis mandated that *Grutter v. Bollinger* not be overturned by the Supreme Court. McDonald credited society's rejection of the "separate but equal" concept as a legitimate reason for the Court's rejection of *Plessy v. Ferguson* in *Brown v. Board of Education*, but he emphasized the need for the Court in the case at bar not to be seen as overruling a prior decision merely because the individual members of the Court had changed. Justice McDonald wrote:

> *Because neither the factual underpinnings of* Grutter's *central holding nor our understanding of it has changed, and because no other indication of weakened precedent has been shown, the Court could not pretend to be reexamining the prior law with any justification beyond a present doctrinal disposition to come out differently from the Court of 2003.*

Clay didn't know what to make of McDonald's argument. It was certainly original. McDonald had seemingly created a new theory of stare decisis, one that tried to reestablish the Supreme Court as a court of *law* rather than a *political* institution. But McDonald's approach was inconsistent with the vast majority of the Court's most recent decisions, including, most famously, *Bush v. Gore*, wherein the Court's five conservative justices essentially picked the president of the United States ... much to the chagrin of the Court's four liberals and to the Democratic Party writ large.

Although these shortcomings in McDonald's reasoning would probably occupy much time and attention in the nation's op-ed pages and law journals, they had no practical effect. In the immortal words of Justice Robert H. Jackson, Supreme Court judges "are not final because we are infallible, but we are infallible only because we are final."

Clay saved a copy of the draft to the thumb drive he had purchased for precisely this purpose and rushed off to share the news with the imperial wizard.

CHAPTER 83

Alexandra Burton poured a glass of wine. She was drinking a Mullet Hall Red from the Irvin House Vineyard in Charleston. Several of her U.S. Senate colleagues had been urging her for years to try a more expensive French wine, such as a Petrus or a Romanee Conti. Burton always declined. She was an American. She was a South Carolinian. She was a *klanswoman*. No foreign drink would ever touch her lips.

A soft breeze stirred the wind chime on Burton's porch. The setting sun painted a landscape above the tall oaks in her yard. A perfect Sunday afternoon, she thought. Almost ... Clay Smith had reported early on Saturday morning that the Supreme Court was poised to rule against her grandson. Burton knew that an opinion of that magnitude was unlikely to be released until the final day of the Court's term, so she still had time. Five weeks, to be precise. The Court always recessed during the last week of June.

Burton returned her attention to David M. Chalmer's *Hooded Americanism: The History of the Ku Klux Klan.* She was almost always reading two books at the same time: one—usually a biography of a famous politician —that related to her political career, and a second about the Klan. It was difficult to find unbiased treatments of the latter, but Chalmer's book was certainly one.

Burton turned to the chapter about South Carolina. Chalmers reported that the Palmetto state was the last of the realms chartered during the reign of Imperial Wizard William J. Simmons,

> *but there is scant detail of its history. This may well substantiate the general feeling on the part of historians that the Invisible Empire was of negligible force and importance in South Carolina.*

Burton knew otherwise. In the 1920s her grandfather had been one of the founding fathers of the South Carolina Realm. Hard times on the farm, an unexpected influx of Roman Catholics from above the Mason-Dixon line, and, of course, lingering racial unrest from the freeing of the slaves after the Civil War all provided fertile soil for the Invisible Empire. For example, when longtime congressman and future U.S. Supreme Court justice James F. Byrnes decided to run for the U.S. Senate in 1924, the South Carolina Realm flexed early political muscle and ensured his defeat by circulating thousands of copies of a petition the day before the election in which several of Byrnes's childhood friends had praised the candidate's efforts in saving the life of an African American playmate who had fallen into a local swimming hole.

By the time Burton had come of age, the South Carolina Realm was among the most vibrant in the nation. The Supreme Court's landmark 1954 public school desegregation decision, *Brown v. Board of Education*, had proved to be a powerful recruiting tool for the Klan throughout the country, especially in the South. The civil rights movement led by Martin Luther King Jr. in the 1960s had inspired thousands of white southerners to say that enough was enough. A young Alexandra Burton was among them, and with Burton's intelligence and work ethic, she quickly rose through the ranks of both the Klan leadership and state and national politics. At twenty-five, Burton was elected grand dragon of the South Carolina Realm. At thirty, she was a U.S. senator. At forty-five, she was the imperial wizard of the Ku Klux Klan. At sixty, she was poised to announce her candidacy for the Republican nomination for president of the United States.

Burton checked her watch. She couldn't afford to be late. She drained her glass of wine, stubbed out the one cigarette she permitted herself per day, and headed for her car. She wouldn't use a driver tonight.

CHAPTER 84

Burton had called an emergency meeting of the kloncilium to discuss Clay Smith's recent discovery that Peter McDonald was planning to rule in favor of affirmative action. A series of encrypted e-mails during the past couple of weeks suggested that the kloncilium had expected as much, but Clay's confirmation of their suspicions was important enough to merit a face-to-face discussion. They agreed to meet, as they almost always did, at The Sacred Temple of the Kloncilium.

The kloncilmen filed into the ceremonial room. The fiery summons had been issued only the day before. Burton apologized for the short notice. She said, "Akia. Kigy."

The other members of the kloncilium returned the imperial wizard's salutation.

The opening devotional was recited from the Kloran.

"I've called you here this evening to apprise you of some troubling news," Burton said. "The news was not unexpected, but it was nonetheless extremely disturbing when I received it. This young man to my right was the bearer of the bad news. I think it's best that he share it with you himself."

"Who is he, Your Excellency? It's unprecedented for a guest to attend a kloncilium meeting. Our meetings are sacred."

The kloncilman who had uttered the objection was the grand dragon of the Indiana Realm. The Hoosier state wasn't famous for basketball only. The Klan's presence in

Indiana was greater than that in any other state. It had been that way since the days of David C. Stephenson.

Stephenson had been one of the original backers of Hiram Evans's 1922 effort to unseat William Simmons as the imperial wizard of the Invisible Empire. When Evans's coup proved successful, he named Stephenson the grand dragon of Indiana and twenty-two other northern and midwestern states. Indiana was Stephenson's stronghold: at the height of Stephenson's power, nearly one-third of all adult white males in the state were members of the Indiana chapter. Although membership had waned over the years, Indiana still claimed more Klan members per capita than any other state.

Of course Burton knew this, and she handled the question from the current Indiana grand dragon with the kid gloves it required. She said, "This young man is the nephew of one of our fallen heroes."

"Which one?" the kloncilman from Ohio asked. Ohio was another legendary Klan stronghold.

"Earl Smith."

All six remaining members of the kloncilium stood as a sign of respect for their fallen colleague. "Akia! Kigy!" they said. They pounded the floor seven times with their feet... . Another Klan ritual.

Clay Smith didn't know how to react. He said, "Thank you" and added that he, too, was a klansman.

That drew a second chorus of the sacred Klan refrain.

Clay failed to mention that he was the one who had killed his uncle.

Burton stated that, in addition to being Earl Smith's nephew, Clay had been a law student at one of the top schools in the nation. "There's no one more qualified to explain what the Supreme Court is about to do than young Mr. Smith here." Burton patted Clay on the shoulder. "Clay, the floor is yours."

Clay proceeded to explain as simply as he could the gist of Peter McDonald's draft opinion in *Tucker v. University of South Carolina.* Most of the kloncil members seemed to understand what he was saying. The only exception was the grand dragon of Texas, the great grandson of Hiram Evans who owed his position on the kloncilium to his great grandfather's legacy rather than to any skill set, intellectual or otherwise, he personally possessed. But even that grand dragon appeared impressed when Clay described *how* he knew any of this: because he had broken into one of the most secure government buildings in the United States and stolen the draft.

After Clay had finished, he was instructed by a unanimous vote of the kloncilium to do anything he needed to do to make certain that McDonald's draft opinion didn't become the Court's published opinion. When Clay had asked for more specific guidance, Burton had said, "You know what to do."

Clay left the sacred temple more confident than ever that he did.

CHAPTER 85

Peter McDonald returned the vacuum to the closet and cleared the magazines from the coffee table. He was preparing for his first dinner guest since Jenny and Megan were murdered, and he was in over his head. Jenny had handled the lion's share of the party planning, not to mention the house cleaning. McDonald had been responsible for purchasing the wine and securing a babysitter. He had been given easy assignments; the Charlottesville area had several world-class vineyards and Megan had been adored by every babysitter who met her.

But now, it was different. Now Peter McDonald was alone.

McDonald had decided to spend the weekend in Charlottesville. He hadn't been back to his old stomping grounds since being sworn in to the Supreme Court, and he needed to check on his house. With the notable exception of dust and a musty smell, his house was in good order. He had opened the windows to solve the must problem, and he had vacuumed and swept to dispel the dust.

The grandfather clock next to the stairs struck seven o'clock. His dinner guest would be arriving momentarily. He stirred the chili simmering on the stove, uncorked a bottle of wine to allow it to breathe, and removed the cornbread from the oven.

The doorbell sounded. An unexpected sensation—nervousness coupled with excitement—coursed through his body. He opened the door.

"Hi, Justice McDonald," his dinner guest said.

"Hello," McDonald said. "But, please, you can still call me Peter."

"Thanks." Kelsi Shelton flashed a warm smile and stepped over the threshold.

McDonald led his dinner guest to the living room and offered her a glass of wine, which she gladly accepted.

He said, "I was planning on inviting a few of my former colleagues to join us, but they've scheduled a dinner for me at the Rotunda tomorrow night." He took a sip of wine. "You know what they say about too much of a good thing."

Kelsi said, "I read about that in the *UVA News*. The article said that Senators Warner and Webb are scheduled to attend."

"That's right. It's silly, really. Such a fuss. I'm still the same person I was before I got appointed to the Court, but now that I've got a different job everyone treats me like the second coming. Frankly, it makes me uncomfortable."

"You might as well get used to it. From what I've seen on C-SPAN, all of the justices are treated like royalty. I suspect that's why so many lawyers would like the job."

"C-SPAN? You don't get out much, do you? Seriously, I hope that's not the case. I hope my colleagues took the job because it's a chance to serve this great country of ours. That's why I did. I would've been more than content to live out my life teaching bright young students such as yourself, but when the president asked me if I would be willing to accept a nomination to the Court, I couldn't say no ... even after Jenny and Megan were killed. The president kindly gave me an out when he heard the news. I didn't take it, though. The Court is too important. And ..." McDonald's voice broke.

Kelsi finished his sentence: "and your wife would've wanted you to stick it out."

McDonald nodded. He stood up from his chair to check the chili, ... and to change the subject.

Kelsi followed him into the kitchen. "The chili smells great. I didn't know you could cook. I was expecting takeout from China Garden."

McDonald chuckled. "I can't cook. You're witnessing half my repertoire."

"What's the other half?"

"Pancakes. Megan used to love my pancakes. My chocolate chip smiles were a big hit with her."

Shoot, Kelsi said to herself. She had reopened the wound, and it had been closed for only a minute and a half. "Sorry," she said.

"Don't worry about it. You didn't know." McDonald dished the chili into two large bowls, handed the bowls to Kelsi to place on the table, and retrieved the cornbread from the counter next to the refrigerator. "I can make three things, actually. My cornbread ain't too shabby."

"I can't wait to try it."

"There's no time like the present." McDonald pulled out a chair for Kelsi. He made certain it wasn't Jenny's. He didn't think he would ever be able to allow anyone to sit in Jenny's chair. "More wine?"

"Yes, please."

McDonald refilled their glasses. "To better days to come."

Kelsi echoed McDonald's sentiment and touched her glass to his. "How are your clerks shaping up?"

McDonald reached for the cornbread. "Not bad. I was thinking of asking one of them to join us—a handsome young man from Yale. But I thought Agent Neal might object. How's that going?"

Kelsi blushed. "It's going good. He's sweet, and he doesn't play games. I'm tired of games. I swear, I think that's all law students know how to do."

McDonald smiled. "The law school always did strike me as an episode of *Beverly Hills, 90210*."

"What's that?"

"I guess I'm showing my age. It was a teen soap opera that was all the rage when I was in high school. The characters seemed to be playing musical chairs with their relationships in every episode. Dylan and Brenda. Dylan and Kelly. Kelly and Brandon. Brandon and—"

"—Brenda?"

"No. That would've been illegal. Brandon and Brenda were brother and sister."

McDonald and Kelsi laughed. They enjoyed more wine, chili, and each other's company. They were friends now. Nothing more.

McDonald had suspected when Kelsi was working as his research assistant that she had a crush on him. That happened occasionally. After all, he was smart, good-looking, and kind. But he had also known that Kelsi was too sensible of a young woman to act on her feelings. That said, he was delighted that she was dating Agent Neal. It took the pressure off.

Kelsi thanked McDonald for the wonderful evening, scrounged through her purse for her keys, and pulled out of the driveway.

She switched on her headlights and navigated the twists and turns of the dark country road. She smiled. It had taken a while—four months to be precise—but she was starting to feel normal again. She had Brian Neal's love to thank for that, in addition to small gestures of kindness such as being invited to dinner at Justice McDonald's house.

Kelsi was smart enough to know that she should have told McDonald about her most recent encounter with Clay Smith, but she just wanted to forget about it for a while. A desire to forget also explained why she had changed her mind about visiting McDonald in chambers during her recent trip to the Supreme Court. Besides, she said to herself as she popped a favorite CD into the car stereo, she never expected to see Clay again. The police had told her that he had left the state and was nowhere to be found.

CHAPTER 86

The police were wrong: Clay Smith was waiting for Kelsi Shelton when she arrived at her apartment. He had climbed through her bedroom window and was hiding in the closet. He knew the place well. He had been there before.

"Why are you doing this to me again?" Kelsi cried, while she struggled to free herself from Clay's powerful grasp.

Clay placed his hand over Kelsi's mouth and clung tightly to her waist with his other arm. He said, "I'm sorry. I have no choice."

Of course he had a choice. Everyone had choices ... even young men who belonged to the Ku Klux Klan. But human nature was such that most people tried to deny moral responsibility for the problematic choices they sometimes made. Clay Smith was one of those people.

He spotted a gym bag on the floor near Kelsi's desk. He snagged it by the strap and instructed Kelsi to fill it with clothes.

Kelsi said, "W ... why? W ... where are we going? I thought you felt bad about what you did before?"

"I did feel bad, and I still do. But like I said, I've got no choice. I'll let you know the 'where' part when we get there."

Actually, Clay didn't know the answer to Kelsi's question about where they were headed. He had a pocketful of possibilities—a stack of MapQuest printouts—but that was about it. He was playing it by ear. He had been taught at UVA that a good lawyer always knew where he was going with his case. He could only hope that another law school lesson—there was an exception to every rule—proved true instead.

Brian Neal tried to distract himself by watching ESPN's Sunday night baseball. He was addicted to ESPN—twenty-four-hour TV sports was a weekend warrior's wet dream—and he was nuts about baseball. But he cared more about Kelsi Shelton, and he knew how fond Kelsi was of Justice McDonald. The green-eyed monster frequently made appearances in new relationships, and it was rearing its ugly head at the moment in Neal's relationship with Kelsi.

Neal popped open a beer in the hopes of calming his nerves. Secret Service agents were schooled about the pitfalls of alcohol, and Neal rarely drank, but tonight he was making an exception. He knew that he didn't stand a chance in a head-to-head competition with McDonald—a glorified police officer versus a Supreme Court justice was like comparing a Division III swimmer to Michael Phelps—and he needed to try something to distract himself from that cold, hard fact.

He couldn't stop thinking about it, though. He couldn't stop his mind from racing ... from cataloging every weakness he possessed and every attribute of Justice McDonald. He muted the television and retrieved his cell phone from his pocket. Still no voice mail. Still no message from Kelsi. She had promised to call as soon as she arrived home, and it was well past midnight. He decided to call her instead. He hit her entry on his speed dial but was immediately directed to her voice mail. It said, "Hi. This is Kelsi. I'm out saving the world right now. Please leave a message."

Neal smiled at the "saving the world" remark. He always did. He often teased Kelsi about her unbridled ambition. He understood its origins, however. It had been like pulling teeth, but he had finally managed to pry the information out of her.

Kelsi Shelton was born in Appleton, Wisconsin, to a single mother who had to work two jobs to keep a roof over their heads and food on the table. Kelsi had never met her father. All Kelsi's mother would ever say when Kelsi asked about him was that he had left before Kelsi was born. She wouldn't even tell Kelsi his name or where he lived. Kelsi had discovered that information on her own. She had been in the process of trying to learn more about her dad when Clay Smith had abducted her.

CHAPTER 87

Clay pushed his baseball cap down on his forehead so that his eyes were barely visible. He was finding it difficult to see, but he didn't want to risk someone recognizing him. He had read in the local Charlottesville newspaper while he was waiting for Kelsi to come home that the police had given up almost all hope of finding him. Still, he needed to be careful. He glanced to his right. "How are you holding up?"

Kelsi said, "As if you care."

"Believe it or not, I do."

"You have a funny way of showing it."

"Like I said before, I'm sorry it has come to this. But I've got no choice."

"You said that last time."

"I meant it then, too."

"I don't believe you. You've said over and over that you care about me. If that were true, I wouldn't be sitting here."

Clay sat in silence, with no way to respond. What Kelsi said was true, and he knew it.

Clay turned onto State Road 250 and stepped on the accelerator. They were headed toward the Blue Ridge Mountains, about thirty miles outside of Charlottesville. They needed to find somewhere to spend the night, and Clay knew of a good camping site in the George Washington National Forest. He had spent several weekends there when he was in law school. He reached into his pocket and pulled out the stack of MapQuest directions. He flipped through them. He couldn't find the one for the camping site—it must have fallen out of his pocket somewhere—but he was pretty sure he remembered the way.

The George Washington National Forest extended from the entire length of the Blue Ridge Mountains to the North Carolina border. Seemingly every form of outdoor activity was available there: hiking, fishing, mountain biking, horseback riding, hawk watching, nature photography. Clay brought Kelsi to the Trout Pond Campground. Clay was a southern boy, and he loved to fish. But this particular campground was also a perfect hiding spot—remote, difficult to find, and rarely frequented.

Kelsi said, "It's a bit chilly for camping, don't you think?"

Clay said, "I've got plenty of blankets. We'll be fine." He unloaded the blankets from the backseat of his car. He pulled a tent from the trunk.

"One tent?" Kelsi asked.

"One tent," Clay answered. "I'll be on my best behavior. I promise."

"I don't believe a word you say. I never will again. But there's nothing I can do about it. You know it, and I know it."

Clay didn't reply. He set up the tent and unrolled the sleeping bags.

Kelsi stood and watched. She considered making a run for it, but she knew that Clay was a lot faster than she was. She also seemed resigned to her fate. Psychological studies revealed that was a common reaction for victims of kidnappings.

Clay removed a butane camping stove from his backpack. He opened a can of franks and beans with a Swiss army knife, poured the contents into a Sierra cup, and stirred the modest supper with the tiny spoon on his knife. He said, "Are you hungry?"

Kelsi said, "No." She was starving, but she didn't want to give Clay the satisfaction of thinking he was doing her a favor.

"Suit yourself." Clay ate a spoonful. "It's mighty tasty, though. Nothing beats franks and beans on a camping trip."

"That's what you're calling this, 'a camping trip'? I think the police will call it kidnapping."

"Like I said four times already, I've got no choice. I know you're upset, but I'm tired of your broken record." There was an edge to Clay's voice.

Kelsi picked up on it and wisely decided to stop twisting the proverbial knife. She knew from personal experience that Clay was willing to kill her.

Several minutes passed with nothing but the sounds of a back-country night: rustling trees, a symphony of crickets, the occasional howling coyote.

Clay broke the silence: "At least drink some water."

Kelsi did. In fact, she drank the entire bottle. She was parched. She wiped her mouth with her sleeve. "If I remember correctly, you're from Charleston, right?"

"Right. Why?"

"My dad lives there. Or at least he used to. I've never met him, but I found out recently that he's from there."

Clay smiled. "A southern belle, eh?"

"No. Charlottesville is as far south as I've ever been. I'm from Wisconsin. My mom's from Goose Creek, though. She met my dad during a high school football game. She was a cheerleader from the visiting team. He was the buddy of one of the players on the home team. There was a party afterwards. One thing led to another, and my mom got pregnant with me."

"How'd you end up in Wisconsin?"

"My grandparents sent my mom to live with her grandparents. You know, to avoid the embarrassment of a high school pregnancy."

"How old was she?"

"Fifteen."

"How old was he?"

"Seventeen."

"Is his name Shelton, like yours?"

"No. Shelton is my mom's name. My father's name was ... *is*—I don't know whether he's alive or dead—Collier ... Billy Joe Collier."

Clay almost dropped his Sierra cup. He knew whether Kelsi's father was dead or alive. He was the one who had killed him.

CHAPTER 88

Brian Neal jumped out of his car and hurdled up the stairs to Kelsi Shelton's apartment. He pounded on the door. It was three o'clock in the morning, but he was desperate. He needed to know. Had Kelsi made her choice? He knew it was *Kelsi's* choice. Beautiful women always got to choose. Beautiful women always had a parade of men chasing them... . Guys were almost never in control.

Neal continued to pound on the door. A light from the apartment next to Kelsi's flickered on. A disheveled young man—a UVA student, almost certainly—opened his door and said, "What the hell, man? It's ... it's, like, four o'clock in the morning."

Neal said, "It's three."

The sleep-deprived student said, "And that's supposed to make it OK to bang on my neighbor's door in the middle of the night?" He slammed his door in Neal's face.

Neal waited for the student to switch off the light. He reached into his pocket and pulled out a paperclip. He straightened one end, inserted it into the lock on Kelsi's door, and jimmied his way into her apartment. He had learned how to do it while he was being trained to become a Secret Service agent. The bodies that agents were assigned to protect were sometimes the targets of kidnapping plots, and locked doors sometimes had to be accessed. But Neal never imagined that he would use what he had learned to try to track down a girlfriend who was suddenly incommunicado.

"Kelsi," he said as he stepped over the threshold. "It's me ... Brian."

Nothing. The apartment was as quiet as a morgue. Neal flipped on the lights. Still nothing. Still no sign of where Kelsi might be. He walked to her bedroom and pushed open the door. Kelsi wasn't there, and her bed hadn't been slept in. Neal's mind raced through a series of possibilities: she was pulling an all-nighter at the law library ... she was sleeping with Justice McDonald ... she was spending the night at Sue Plant's apartment... .

Neal quickly dismissed the first possibility because Kelsi had told him as recently as the day before that exams were more than a month away and that she was caught up on the work she had missed when she was in the hospital. The thought of the second possibility—that Kelsi was having sex with Justice McDonald—made him sick to his stomach. He prayed it was the third. He jumped back into his car to find out.

Sue Plant was more polite than Kelsi's neighbor had been when Brian Neal appeared at her door in the wee hours of the morning. She was equally puzzled, though. "Is everything OK?"

Neal said, "Sorry to wake you, Sue. But is Kelsi here?"

Sue rubbed sleep from her eyes. "No. Why would she be?"

"I thought maybe you two were watching a movie or something. She said she'd call, but she never did... . She's not at her apartment."

Sue was Kelsi's best friend, and she obviously knew that Kelsi had been having dinner with Justice McDonald earlier that evening. She also knew what sometimes came after dinner, and it wasn't merely dessert. "I don't know what to say." She did, but she didn't want to say it. She also didn't *need* to say it. She patted Neal on the arm and watched him walk away.

Clay Smith waited until Kelsi Shelton was asleep and then quietly stepped away from the campsite. He didn't stray far. He needed to keep an eye on her.

He punched the power button on his cell phone and hoped he got a signal. He did, albeit only two bars worth. One reason he had selected the Trout Pond Campground was that it was remote, but not so remote as to be completely outside the range of a cell phone tower. The other campgrounds at which he had stayed in the past were dead zones.

He retrieved the scrap of paper from his wallet on which he had scribbled the telephone number he was about to call. He entered the digits: 1-434-555-7094. He placed the phone to his ear. It rang and rang and rang ... six times, seven times, eight times.

Finally: "H ... hello." The recipient clearly had been asleep.

Clay said, "Are you alone?"

"Wh ... who is this?"

"Are you alone?"

"Ye ... yes. But who is this? And wh ... what time is it?"

"It's three-thirty. It's Clay Smith."

"Clay! Where are you? What do you want? What are you doing?" So much for groggy ...

"None of that matters at the moment. The only thing that does is that I've got Kelsi. If you want her returned safely, you'll do what I say."

"Whatever you want."

"Good. I was hoping you would see it that way. I don't wanna hurt her. I don't. But I will if I have to. I think you know that."

Peter McDonald said, "I know it. I watch the news. Now what do I have to do?"

"Rewrite your opinion."

"What are you talking about? I haven't written any opinions. I just joined the Court."

"Don't play dumb with me, Professor." McDonald was still *Professor* to Clay. "We both know that's not true. We both know that I'm talking about your opinion in *Tucker v. University of South Carolina*."

"The Court hasn't released an opinion in that case, let alone an opinion written by me."

"I'm losing my patience. You're making me angry. And I don't wanna get angry. I might do something we'll both regret if I get angry. I read the draft. I need for you to rewrite the draft. The case needs to come out the other way."

"The draft? How did you get your hands on the draft? The courthouse is like Fort Knox."

"Don't worry about *how*. It's the *what* that matters now ... *what* you say in the opinion."

"It's not going to be as easy as you think, Clay."

"Why not?"

"You need five votes. The vote at conference was six to three. If I switch my vote, it'll still be five to four against Senator Burton's family."

An unanticipated obstacle had been placed in the way of Clay's plan. He was silent for a moment. He glanced over at Kelsi. She was still sleeping. He finally said, "I guess you better bone up on your skills in the fine art of persuasion. Justice Brennan was a master at persuading his colleagues to see it his way. The legacy of the Warren Court depended on it. Kelsi's *life* depends on it this time."

CHAPTER 89

Peter McDonald took a quick shower, threw on a suit, and headed for Washington. His Charlottesville home faded into the horizon of his rearview mirror. He wondered whether he would ever see it again. His life was very different now from when he and Jenny had purchased the house shortly after he had received tenure at UVA. Now, there was no Jenny. Now, there was no Megan. Now, there was no UVA. Why should there be a dream house? His life was mostly nightmares now.

McDonald maneuvered his car through the early morning traffic and onto the Theodore Roosevelt Memorial Bridge. He pondered the biographies of his eight Supreme Court colleagues. Of the five who had joined with him at the post-argument conference to vote against Senator Burton's family, four were partisan Democrats. Although the canons of judicial ethics forbade federal judges from participating in political events, the four were frequently spotted at Democratic fundraisers. He knew he would be wasting his breath if he tried to persuade them to switch their votes. You can't teach a yellow dog a new trick, he said to himself as he negotiated the well-planned streets of the nation's capital. Affirmative action was the sacred cow of the Left. But Donald Lowry was a different story. Donald Lowry was worth a shot.

At eighty-seven years of age, Donald Dickinson Lowry had served on the Supreme Court for nearly four decades. Nominated by a Republican president and confirmed by a Democratic Senate in the closest vote in modern American history, the Court's senior associate justice had become increasingly liberal over the years. He tended to side with the federal government when challenges were raised that the law at issue was beyond the government's power to enact; with regulators who wanted to reign in the free market preferences of the capital class; and with libertarians on free speech, the relationship between church and state, and the rights of those accused of crimes. But his most surprising vote by far was his decision to join a sharply divided Court in reaffirming, for the umpteenth time in a generation, the 1973 *Roe v. Wade* abortion case. Not only was Lowry a Republican, he was a Catholic. He was chastised by the Right for turning his back on the pro-life movement that had worked so vigorously to ensure his confirmation, and he was excommunicated by the pope himself for violating God's law that all life was sacred.

Justice Lowry had never publicly explained his vote. He had been pressed to do so many times over the years during the Q & A portion of the speeches he had delivered at a myriad of bar conventions and law school symposia, but his response was always the same: it was inappropriate for a judge to explain a decision issued by his court outside of the four corners of the written opinion itself. He insisted that this was especially true for a judge on a multimember court such as the U.S. Supreme Court.

Peter McDonald had long respected Justice Lowry for sticking to his guns, no matter how intense the pressure was on the elderly jurist to give the public what it wanted. Unfortunately, Lowry's willingness to fend off pressure would make McDonald's task of persuading him to switch his vote in *Tucker v. University of South Carolina* even more difficult than it otherwise would have been. But McDonald had to try. Clay Smith couldn't have been clearer: Kelsi Shelton's life depended on it.

Brian Neal had decided to double back to Kelsi's apartment the moment he arrived at his motel. A sudden tsunami of dread explained his decision. His insecurities aside, he knew that Kelsi wouldn't sleep with Justice McDonald. She had told him she wouldn't. She had *promised* him, and he believed her. Only one explanation remained: something terrible had happened to Kelsi; something horrific had been done to her again.

The same neighbor who had greeted Neal with grief when Neal first appeared at Kelsi's door tried to give it to him again. This time Neal didn't bother to try to win the neighbor's favor. This time he flashed his badge and told the kid to stay out of the way.

Neal felt guilty snooping around Kelsi's apartment, but he had no choice. The person who had tried to kill Kelsi remained at large, and there was no reason to believe that he wouldn't try again. In fact, the strong likelihood of a repeat performance explained why Neal's superiors at the Secret Service had permitted him to remain on the case. Of course, they would have decided otherwise had they known that Neal and Kelsi were sleeping together.

Much of what Neal discovered in Kelsi's apartment didn't strike him as unusual. The kitchen was stocked with fresh fruit, vegetables, nuts, yogurt—food that a busy but health-conscious student would enjoy. The living room was equipped with a big-screen TV and a DVD player. A dozen of Kelsi's favorite movies were stacked nearby. Neal had watched most of them with Kelsi and a bottle of wine. The bathroom was clean and decorated with scented candles and matching towels and washcloths. The bedroom was adorned with framed posters of major European cities—Neal knew that Kelsi liked to travel—and photographs of friends and family. Neal smiled when he noticed his picture prominently displayed on Kelsi's nightstand. The clothes in her closet were organized by season and style.

Neal returned to the living room and sat on a leather armchair that Kelsi had recently purchased from a local furniture store. He reached for his back as he remembered how heavy the chair had been to move from the roof of her car. He chuckled at how she had convinced him that he was strong enough to carry the chair himself. "You're strong, Brian," she had said. "You can lift it." She had added with a mischievous smile, "You'll also be saving me forty bucks in delivery charges."

Good memories, no doubt. Good times. But they did nothing to help Neal locate Kelsi *now*. He reached for the remote so he could check the news—so he could find out whether anyone had reported Kelsi missing—but just as he was about to press the POWER button he spotted a set of MapQuest driving directions to the Trout Pond Campground in the George Washington National Forest. The automatic stamp at the bottom of the paper indicated that the directions had been printed six hours earlier. Neal stuffed the directions into his pocket and raced to his car.

CHAPTER 90

Cat Wilson circled the Waffle House and refilled the coffee cups of a dozen grateful patrons. She had returned from D.C. and her manager was kind enough to assign her to the breakfast shift, which was the most lucrative time of day as far as tips were concerned. Cat was always strapped for cash, and her sojourn to the nation's capital had only exacerbated the problem.

Cat was never able to locate Earl Smith, and he still hadn't bothered to call. The same held true for Clay. Cat had waited for three hours at the Smithsonian for him—Clay had promised her a personal tour—but he never showed. Cat chastised herself when she realized that she didn't even know Clay's last name. Why the self-beratement? Because she and Clay had spent most of their two days together rolling around in the hay.

Getting stood up by men wasn't unusual for Cat, especially after they had slept with her a time or two and discovered that she had a young daughter. But she thought Clay was different. He reminded her of Earl in that regard... . Earl.

Peter McDonald arrived at the Court before all but one of his colleagues. The early bird? Donald Lowry.

"Good morning, Peter," the elderly jurist said. "To what do I owe the pleasure?"

It was half past seven in the morning and not even Lowry's staff had punched in yet. The justice had answered the buzzer himself. At his age, it took him a few minutes to make it to the door, but he eventually got there. He was sipping a cup of Earl Grey tea.

McDonald said, "I don't mean to disturb you at this early hour, Donald. I know how much you cherish it as your quiet time for writing. But I was hoping we could chat for a few minutes."

"Of course. Come in. Would you like a cup of tea?"

"I would love a cup. Thank you."

McDonald followed Lowry into Lowry's private chambers. Lowry motioned for McDonald to take a seat on the couch across from the coffee table next to the fireplace. McDonald watched Lowry pour him a cup of tea from an elegant china pot.

Lowry said, "This teapot was a gift from the chief justice of the Chinese supreme court. He presented it to me in Beijing at a dinner in my honor after the closing session of the first ever American-Chinese judicial conference. I cherish it."

McDonald observed Lowry shuffle toward him with a precarious grip on a teacup. The prudent course would have been for McDonald to meet Lowry at least halfway, but everyone who worked at the courthouse knew that Lowry always declined any concessions to his age. "Thanks, Donald," McDonald said when the cup finally reached its destination. He took a sip. "This is a rare treat. I'm a coffee drinker."

Lowry folded into the chair across from the couch on which McDonald was sitting. "I've been a tea drinker for nearly sixty years."

"What sparked your taste for it?"

"My year in England. It's true what they say: the Brits are obsessed with their tea. It's probably different now, what with us living in the age of Starbucks, but back in the dark ages, when I was across the pond, it was almost impossible to find a decent cup of coffee. It was Sanka or tea. I went with tea."

McDonald knew that Lowry's year in England was the year he spent at Oxford as a Rhodes Scholar, the most prestigious academic opportunity in higher education and an opportunity reserved for the best of the best. McDonald also knew that Lowry was too modest to mention his Rhodes Scholarship by name.

Lowry smiled at his junior colleague, and added, "I know you didn't drop by at this early hour to hear an old man's trip down memory lane. So, Mr. Justice McDonald, what do you need to talk to me about?"

McDonald reddened. "You're correct, as usual, Donald." He traced a finger around the lip of his teacup. He was stalling, and Lowry obviously knew it.

"Come on, Peter. Spit it out. I've been on this earth for almost ninety years, and I've been on this Court for the last forty of them. Nothing you say will surprise me."

"I need to change my vote in *Tucker v. University of South Carolina*, and I need for you to change your vote too."

Lowry almost dropped his teacup. "I stand corrected. You have surprised me. But if I may be so bold, *why* do we need to change our votes?"

McDonald fidgeted in his seat. His mind churned as he struggled to decide whether to tell Lowry the real reason for his request: to save Kelsi Shelton's life. He decided against it. He hated to mislead a colleague, but he feared he would be putting Kelsi's life in further jeopardy if he told Lowry the truth. Clay Smith had warned him to keep his mouth shut. McDonald couldn't afford to call Clay's bluff... . *Kelsi* couldn't afford it.

"Well," Lowry said, smiling. "I'm not getting any younger. What's the reason we need to switch?"

"Sorry, Donald. My mind was elsewhere for a moment. I'm not a morning person." McDonald took a sip of tea. He was still struggling with what to say. Finally he said, "The opinion just wouldn't write, so I reread the briefs. I now think Senator Burton's family has the better argument."

Lowry leaned forward in his seat. His eyes were locked on those of his younger colleague. Every Supreme Court justice took the job seriously—considered it a solemn responsibility—and Donald Lowry was no different. He said, "That might very well be, Peter. But my question remains: *why* do you think that?"

"Because I'm not comfortable with a decision that further entrenches the idea that precedent is sacrosanct.

As you know better than anyone, this Court overrules our own precedents, on average, about five times a year. I'm afraid my draft opinion is misleading in that regard."

"So you agree with Justice Witherspoon's dissent?"

Ralph Witherspoon was the most prolific member of the high Court. He had circulated a fifty-page draft dissent earlier in the week. It was a tour de force on the Court's approach to precedent from the early nineteenth century, when John Marshall was chief justice, to the present, and it provided McDonald with the cover he needed for the request he was making of Justice Lowry.

McDonald said, "Yes, I agree with Ralph's dissent."

"And you want me to help you turn Ralph's dissent into a majority opinion?"

"Yes."

"Have you spoken with Ralph?"

"No."

Lowry unfolded from his chair and shuffled to the credenza. He refilled his teacup. He didn't ask McDonald whether McDonald wanted a refill. The elderly justice appeared lost in thought. "This is highly unusual, Peter. Not only is this the most significant civil rights case the Court has decided in a generation, but it's your first opinion. The chief assigned it to you because he wanted you to hit the ground running. The media will savage you when they find out. And believe me, they'll find out."

"I know. But I don't care. I've never cared too much about what other people think."

At least that part was true. For example, many of McDonald's former colleagues at UVA law school used to pander to the students by abandoning the Socratic method and by awarding high grades. McDonald never did. He refused to spoon-feed lectures to his students, and he was a notoriously tough grader. He once wrote an op-ed for the *Wall Street Journal* about the latter, which he entitled with tongue firmly in cheek, *To B or Not to B.* He gave his students B's when they deserved them (and sometimes C's!). His colleagues, in contrast, handed out A's like Halloween candy. The dean would remind his grade-inflating charges that the law school needed to maintain standards, but chants of academic freedom always frustrated his calls for reform.

"What about what your colleagues think? Do you care about that?" Lowry asked next.

"Yes. But this case is too important to let that stand in the way."

Lowry studied his young colleague for a long moment.

McDonald raked his hands through his hair. His eyes wandered through the expanse of Lowry's elegant office. Forty years on the Court had generated many mementos: plaques from bar associations and law school officials, photographs with presidents and visiting dignitaries, and letters and expressions of appreciation from dozens of former law clerks.

Lowry finally said, "Let me think about it. Let me get back to you in a day or two. I need to reread Ralph's dissent. I need to reread the president's brief."

Peter McDonald stood up from his chair and extended his hand to Donald Lowry. "Thank you" was all McDonald could think of to say to his senior colleague. He knew that Lowry knew the merits of the case weren't what explained his request.

CHAPTER 91

Clay Smith gathered kindling for a fire so he could warm the oatmeal he had brought for breakfast. It reminded him of the camping trips he used to take with the Klan youth corps: a group of teenage boys and girls under the tutelage of a kleagle who would sleep under the stars and learn the ways of the sacred order. But there was a major difference between those days and this day: today, Clay was wanted by law enforcement around the nation for attempting to kill a UVA law student who once had worked as a research assistant for a law professor who was currently serving as an associate justice of the Supreme Court of the United States. To make matters worse, Clay had kidnapped that same law student to use as ransom to force the Supreme Court justice to change his opinion in the most important civil rights case the Court would be deciding in a generation. The plot had all the earmarks of a successful legal thriller—only this time the events were true.

Clay tried to clear his mind of the risks he was taking and the punishment that would be inflicted upon him if caught—life in prison, almost certainly; perhaps the death penalty—and focused his attention on starting the fire. He stacked the kindling to allow the flame to breathe, sprinkled dry leaves and grass over the pile, and struck a match. The fire promptly sparked, and Clay expertly crafted it into a manageable inferno. He grabbed the Sierra cup that contained the oatmeal and called for Kelsi Shelton. "Breakfast." Kelsi offered no response. "Breakfast," he said again. Still nothing.

He placed the spoon with which he was stirring the oatmeal on a cloth next to the fire and repeated his call from the front of Kelsi's tent. There was still no response from her. "I'm coming in." He pushed open the flap and discovered that she was gone. "Motherfucker!" he said. "I knew I shouldn't have trusted that bitch!"

Kelsi had promised Clay that she wouldn't stray if he allowed her to sleep in the tent by herself. She had lied, obviously. But who could blame her? Clay had tried to kill her once, and he was threatening to do so again. Frankly, she had been surprised when he acquiesced to her request for privacy.

Clay snuffed out the fire with the bottom of his boot and began a frantic search for Kelsi. Without Kelsi, he knew, he would have no leverage over Justice McDonald. Without leverage over McDonald, he had no way of forcing the desired outcome in *Tucker v. University of South Carolina*.

"Kelsi!" Clay called out while he stumbled through the brush. "Don't make this any more difficult on yourself than it needs to be." No response. He stopped walking. He strained to hear even the slightest sound that might identify where Kelsi was hiding. All he heard were the ebullient songs of the bluebirds nesting in the trees and the brook babbling at the bottom of the hill. He started walking again. "Shit!" he said, after a thorn bush scratched his cheek. He was wiping blood from his face with his handkerchief when his cell phone rang. He checked the number. Area code 202. Washington, D.C.

He said, "Hello."

"Clay?"

"Yeah."

"It's Professor McDonald."

"You mean Justice McDonald."

"Right. I still haven't gotten used to my new appellation."

"You better get used to it. That's the only reason Kelsi Shelton is still alive." Clay was an experienced poker player. He had no idea where Kelsi was, but Justice McDonald didn't know that.

McDonald said, "Calm down, Clay. That's why I'm calling. I managed to persuade Justice Lowry to change his vote. It wasn't easy, and he seemed skeptical, but he agreed to switch. And I'm switching my vote too, obviously. That makes it five to four for Senator Burton's family. That means the senator wins. It means you win. You can let Kelsi go now."

Of course, most of what McDonald was saying to Clay wasn't true—or at least it wasn't true *yet*. Justice Lowry had said that he would *consider* changing his vote; he hadn't *changed* it yet. But McDonald was afraid that Clay would overreact—that he would kill Kelsi—if he told Clay that Lowry hadn't made up his mind.

Clay's eyes searched the brush in front of him. There was still no sign of Kelsi. He knew that he had to continue his bluff too, although he had no way of knowing that Justice McDonald was bluffing. He said, "I'll let her go the moment the Court's decision is announced on the news. My cell phone has internet access, and I'll check CNN.com in the morning."

McDonald said, "No offense, Clay, but what guarantee do I have that you'll release Kelsi after the decision is announced? I'd be more comfortable if you let her go now."

"I don't care whether you're 'comfortable,' Justice McDonald. Either you do it my way, or I'll kill Kelsi. It's that simple."

Silence came from McDonald's end of the line. He finally said, "Can I talk to her to see if she's all right?"

Clay wanted to say, If I knew where she was you could. Instead, he said, "No. I'll call you tomorrow after I check CNN to let you know where you can pick her up. Now I've got to get off. My battery is low." He snapped his cell phone shut and continued his search for his UVA classmate. "Come on, Kelsi. I won't hurt you. I promise."

Kelsi Shelton would have been a fool to believe Clay Smith. That's why she fled. She heard him calling. She heard his pledge. She was tired, cold, hungry, and scared. But she was alive, and she intended on keeping it that way. However, everything changed the instant she tripped over a felled tree and twisted her ankle. Her situation went from bad to worse when Clay heard her scream in pain.

He stood over her. "I'm very disappointed in you. You gave me your word that you would stay put if I let you sleep in the tent by yourself."

Kelsi was clutching her ankle. She said, "Go fuck yourself. I don't care whether you're disappointed or not. You're a racist pig. And to think I shared my bed with you ..."

Clay smiled. "You're a big girl, Kelsi. You knew what you were doing when we slept together. You wanted it just as much as I did. More, in fact. You came on to me."

"Fuck you!" Kelsi said. She picked up a rock and threw it at Clay.

The rock hit Clay in the head. "Shit!" He rubbed his hand against his forehead. He was bleeding again. "Goddamn." He stared down at Kelsi with murder in his eyes.

Kelsi trembled. She finally saw Clay Smith, *klansman*. She finally saw the hate that lived in his heart.

"I should kill you right here and now, bitch." He studied the blood on his hand. He wiped it on his pants leg.

Kelsi knew Clay was serious. He had already tried to kill her once. "S ... sorry ..." She started to cry. It wasn't a howl. It was a weep.

Clay was immune to howls. The niggers he had lynched howled. He was a sucker for a woman weeping, though. Most men were. His mood softened. "Don't worry about it." He reached again for the cut. "I've had worse."

"N ... now what?" Kelsi said. She was hoping she didn't already know.

"Good news. I think I can let you go. Not today, but probably tomorrow."

"Why? Wh ... what changed?"

"Don't worry about that part of it. Just be glad that it looks like things'll turn out the way they should've turned out in the first place."

CHAPTER 92

Brian Neal took a swig from the plastic bottle that accompanied him everywhere he went. Many Americans were obsessed with bottled water, and Neal was among them. He sometimes regretted paying for something he could get for free, but at this particular moment he was glad he had something to drink. He wiped the sweat from his face. He glanced back at his car. He could barely see it. He could barely tell where he had parked it. That was good. He had made a conscious choice to hide it. He didn't want whoever might have kidnapped Kelsi to know he was looking for her.

Neal marched up a hill and through trees and brush. He swatted at gnats, flies, and other sundry insects. The MapQuest printout he had discovered on the floor of Kelsi's apartment directed him to the campground. It was a beautiful spot. He wasn't much of an outdoorsman, but his hike to the Trout Pond Campground persuaded him that he should give it a try. Perhaps he would invite Kelsi... . He would need to find her first.

He did. He did find her! He spotted her through the brush. She was several hundred yards away, but even from a distance he knew it was her—the blonde hair, the long legs, the porcelain skin. Kelsi Shelton was the most beautiful woman that Brian Neal had ever seen. He was about to call out to her when a rugged-looking young man appeared out of nowhere and handed her something to eat. Neal couldn't see the young man's face, which was obscured by a baseball cap pulled low on his forehead and a week's worth of stubble, but from a distance he resembled a young Colin Farrell, the Irish bad boy who no woman seemed able to resist.

Neal's heart sank. His insecurities resurfaced. He concluded that Kelsi had decided to date one of her classmates rather than him. He had been so jealous of Justice McDonald that he had forgotten that Kelsi was surrounded by scores of eligible young men every day in law school ... young men who had much more in common with her than he did.

Clay Smith said, "I'm glad you decided to eat."

Kelsi spooned the last of the oatmeal into her mouth. She stared into the horizon and watched a hawk circling above. "I suppose it's true what they say: prisoners on death row savor their final meal."

Clay shook his head. "Don't be so dramatic. You'll be OK. Justice McDonald will do what he needs to do."

Kelsi kept watching the hawk. "But will you, Clay? Will you?"

After a brief silence, Clay said, "You mentioned a while back that you recently learned who your father is ... that you found out his name and where he lives."

"Billy Joe Collier. So?"

"I'm from Charleston, too. Remember?"

"I remember. You mentioned that the day you tricked me into bed. But so what?"

Clay ignored yet another jab about conning Kelsi into sleeping with him. She had calmed down, and he didn't want to upset her again. He said, "I know him."

"You know my father?" Kelsi finally looked at Clay. Her eyes were wide and full of hope.

"I don't know him well, but I have met him a couple of times. He's a friend of my uncle's."

"What's he like? Is he nice? Is he married? Does he have kids?"

Kelsi Shelton was asking the sorts of questions children would ask about a parent they'd never met. Clay Smith—klansman, serial killer—didn't have the heart to tell her the truth.

"He's very nice. My uncle is always talking about how much fun they have hunting and fishing together." Clay noticed the hawk—a red-tail—that Kelsi had been watching. It had a dark brown band across its belly, formed by vertical streaks in its feather patterning. Its tail was brick red on top and yellow on the bottom. "He would love this place."

Brian Neal was halfway down the trail to his car when he heard Kelsi scream: "Fuck you! Get off me!" Apparently, Kelsi's new boyfriend had reverted to type. Neal had been in relationships before, and he knew that couples sometimes fought. But this didn't sound like a fight... . This sounded like rape.

Neal raced back up the hill as fast as his legs would carry him. He had never moved so quickly in his life. He had been involved in a few incidents as a Secret Service agent that required sudden bursts of speed, but trying to save Kelsi had shifted him into a gear he didn't know he had.

"Get off her, asshole!" Neal demanded as he crashed through the brush. "Get off her!"

Kelsi turned. She said, "Brian. Please help me. *Please.*"

Neal's fixation on the fear in Kelsi's voice—on the fear on Kelsi's face—caused him to commit a fatal error. It was a mistake that all Secret Service agents were constantly reminded to guard against... . He took his eyes off the bad guy.

When Neal did, Clay grabbed a log. When Neal reached Kelsi, Clay slammed the log against Neal's skull. *Pow!*

One hard smash was all it took. But Clay added a second for the sheer enjoyment of it.

Neal crumbled to the ground. Blood poured from the side of his head. It mixed with the dirt to form a muddy pool.

"Brian!" Kelsi cried out. "Please, God, not Brian!"

CHAPTER 93

Peter McDonald had an open-door policy at UVA law school. That meant that students were free to drop by and ask questions anytime they wished. Most of his colleagues saw students by appointment only; they met with them rarely, if ever.

The Supreme Court of the United States wasn't an academic institution, and security concerns dictated that visitors to the justices' chambers be few and far between. McDonald nevertheless almost never closed his door. Old habits were difficult to break. Today, he broke one. Today, he closed his door. Today, he was worrying about when he would hear from Justice Lowry.

There was a knock on McDonald's door. "Come in," he said. He was expecting a research memorandum from one of his law clerks concerning a statutory construction case the Court was scheduled to hear arguments about at the end of the week. The case involved ERISA—the Employment Retirement Income Security Act of 1974—the federal statute that regulated employee health and pension plans. McDonald had taught constitutional law at UVA and knew next to nothing about the ins and outs of one of the most important laws on the books. He had asked his law clerk to write a background memo for him.

But it wasn't his law clerk knocking at his door. It was one of the messengers who delivered communiqués from chamber to chamber. The outside world might've communicated via e-mail or telephone, but the members of the nation's highest court conversed the old-fashioned way

—by pen and paper. That was why it was so unusual for McDonald to have visited Justice Lowry in chambers.

The messenger said, “I’m sorry to disturb you, Mr. Justice McDonald. But Justice Lowry said this was urgent. Mrs. Jacobs told me to bring it right in.”

The messenger handed McDonald an envelope. The envelope was sealed, and it had Lowry’s signature written across the back to signal that it was meant for McDonald’s eyes only.

McDonald took the envelope from the messenger’s outstretched hand and said, “Thank you, Adrian.”

The messenger smiled at the thought that McDonald, a Supreme Court justice, knew his name.

McDonald watched the messenger close the door on his way out. The Court’s newest member opened the envelope. Justice Lowry’s note was only two sentences long, but they were the most important two sentences that McDonald had ever read:

> *I have decided to join Justice Witherspoon’s opinion. I have informed the chief justice that we have both agreed to do so.*

The note was signed, *D.D.L.* Donald Dickinson Lowry. McDonald folded it and placed it in his pocket. He thought about what Justice Oliver Wendell Holmes Jr. had famously written about making decisions, judicial or otherwise:

> *The character of every act depends upon the circumstances in which it is done.*

Then he thought about Kelsi Shelton.

CHAPTER 94

It took several minutes for the chief justice to gavel the courtroom to order. Ordinarily, one loud rap on the wooden block by the presiding judge was immediately met by cathedral-like silence. This was no ordinary day. Not only was the Supreme Court holding an unscheduled Thursday public session, but the chief had taken the unprecedented step of permitting live television coverage of the proceedings. Several of his colleagues had objected vigorously to the prospect of cameras in the courtroom. "We aren't *The People's Court*," one of the associate justices had insisted. The associate justice was referring to the long-running TV show. "I beg to differ," the chief justice had replied. "'We the people,' according to the preamble; in the United States, the people are sovereign." The chief justice was invoking the Constitution.

The calm lasted for only a moment. The storm returned when President Charles Jackson and Senator Alexandra Burton took their seats at their respective counsel's table. The two powerful political leaders acknowledged one another with a quick nod but otherwise directed their attention to the bench.

The chief justice again sounded his gavel. "Order!" he said. "The courtroom will please come to order!" He shot a hard glare at a CBS television reporter who was providing commentary from press row. The reporter didn't appear to notice. But he stopped in mid-sentence when one of the assistant U.S. marshals assigned to provide the day's security placed a large hand over his microphone.

Calm restored, the chief justice said, "The Court is ready to announce its decision in 11-426, Tucker and the University of South Carolina. Copies of the decision will be available from the Public Information Office immediately following this afternoon's session." The chief justice paused. Then he said, "The Court is well aware of the significance of today's decision. That's why we have taken the unprecedented step of permitting television coverage of the proceedings. Let me be clear, however: I have instructed the marshal's office to promptly remove anyone who creates a disturbance, no matter how small. Witness, for example, our friend from CBS News."

The spectators turned to their right and watched while a marshal escorted the reporter who had failed to heed the chief justice's decree from the courtroom.

The chief justice turned to his right—the spectators' left—and said, "Justice McDonald will announce the decision of the Court."

The chief justice had called an emergency private conference of the Court the moment he received word that Justices Lowry and McDonald had switched their votes. It was the chief's idea for Peter McDonald to be listed as the author of the Court's opinion in *Tucker v. University of South Carolina.* Justice Witherspoon didn't object. Ralph Witherspoon was a student of Supreme Court history and knew that William Brennan, the liberal lion whose seat he now occupied, wrote many a landmark opinion credited to others.

McDonald had gone along with the chief's suggestion because he wanted to reassure the nation that no member of the Supreme Court was beholden to the president who appointed him. Moreover, the opinion that an understandably nervous Justice McDonald was about to summarize from the bench went far beyond Justice Witherspoon's disquisition on precedent; the Court's newest member would be articulating a *substantive* basis for overruling *Grutter v. Bollinger.*

McDonald cleared his throat and said, "Thank you, Mr. Chief Justice. And thank you for the confidence you have shown in me by assigning me such an important opinion as my first for the Court. As my colleagues well know, I struggled mightily with it. I—we—know what's at stake."

McDonald's candor, a rare display of humility from a Supreme Court justice, caught the courtroom by surprise. The courtroom would have been stunned had McDonald also mentioned that he and Justice Lowry had changed their minds and decided to rule for Senator Burton's family. By custom, that information would be kept confidential until every member of the Court who had participated in the decision had left the Court and their private papers—draft opinions, internal memoranda, and the like—were deposited in the Library of Congress. McDonald had saved Lowry's note for precisely that reason.

McDonald reached for his legal pad and read aloud: "As those who were patient enough to sit through my confirmation hearings well know, I was a law professor prior to being honored with an appointment to the Supreme Court. As a law professor, I spent a lot of time thinking about how the Constitution should be interpreted. I have read scores of books written by colleagues at law schools across the country arguing that the Constitution should be interpreted in the manner they suggested in their books. I found the various books interesting but unsatisfying. Why unsatisfying? Because they didn't seem to be based on anything other than the specific law professor's idea about what he or she thought the law should be. Some made better arguments than others—Ronald Dworkin's insistence that the Constitution be read to advance the goal of human dignity was particularly difficult to resist—but that was only because some law professors have better argumentation skills than others. Professor Dworkin, for example, was a champion debater in college. Bluntly stated, I didn't think constitutional interpretation should turn on matters of rhetorical style."

McDonald lifted his gaze from the page and glanced out into the gallery. All eyes were focused directly on him. His mind flashed back to his first day in front of a classroom of students. He returned his attention to his legal pad. "You're probably wondering what any of this has to do with why we're all here today. Well, it has a lot to do with it. Frankly, it has everything to do with it. Although it's impossible to interpret the general provisions of the Constitution—'free speech,' 'due process,' 'equal protection,' and the like—without recourse to moral and political values, I wasn't comfortable with those values being those preferred by a particular Supreme Court justice simply because he or she was fortunate enough to serve on the Court. Consequently, I have tried to identify a set of moral and political principles that we have all agreed on. I—or more precisely, Douglas Scott in a fascinating book, *To Secure These Rights: The Declaration of Independence and Constitutional Interpretation*—have found the answer in the Declaration of Independence, the document that announces the *official* moral and political philosophy of the American regime."

McDonald flipped to page 3 of his legal pad. "In Thomas Jefferson's evocative words, 'We hold these truths to be self-evident, that all men are created equal, that they are endowed by their Creator with certain unalienable rights, that among these are life, liberty, and the pursuit of happiness.' When Mr. Jefferson penned those words during the summer of 1776, he was inspired by the prevailing individual rights political theory of the day ... most notably, the political theory of seventeenth-century British theorist John Locke. When Abraham Lincoln condemned slavery in the 1850s and 1860s, he was doing so on individual rights grounds. Slaves were people, Lincoln insisted, who were entitled to enjoy the rights of individuals—especially the right to be free. And when the Reverend Dr. Martin Luther King Jr. delivered his famous *I Have a Dream* speech in 1963, his 'dream' was that his children would one day live in a nation 'where they will not be judged by the color of their skin but by the content of their character.'"

McDonald paused and took a sip of water. "Most important of all for present purposes, the Constitution's commitment to the individual rights principles of the nation's founding document means that the affirmative action program at issue in this case, and similar plans in place at colleges and universities throughout the land, is unconstitutional. It—they—are inconsistent with the Declaration's mandate that an individual be treated as an individual, not as a member of a racial group. It was inappropriate for the University of South Carolina to treat Alexander Tucker as a member of the white race rather than as a young man with unique strengths and virtues. This Court's decision in *Grutter v. Bollinger* is overruled, the judgment of the U.S. District Court for the District of South Carolina is reversed, and the district court is hereby ordered to enter judgment for Patricia and Michael Tucker on behalf of their late son."

The courtroom quickly dissolved into chaos. Reporters rushed toward the exit so they could be the first to break the story, members of the Supreme Court bar dissected on the spot the merits of Justice McDonald's opinion, and tourists who managed to be in the right place at the right time mentioned to one another how they had just witnessed history.

Meanwhile, President Charles Jackson looked as if he had just seen a ghost, while Senator Alexandra Burton appeared like she had won the lottery.

Burton had won it. Thanks to Clay Smith, she had won.

CHAPTER 95

Kelsi Shelton stared into the horizon as Clay Smith drove away in a blue Toyota. She didn't bother to memorize the license plate. Clay had stolen the car when they were returning from the George Washington National Forest, and she was certain he would abandon it and steal a different one the moment he disappeared from sight. Besides, she was too tired to remember her name. There was no way she would be able to process a series of numbers on a speeding vehicle.

Clay hadn't said how Kelsi was supposed to get home from her present location: the parking lot of Crozet Pizza, about ten miles west of Charlottesville. She walked into the restaurant and asked if she could use the telephone. She dialed Sue Plant's number. But before her best friend could answer, Kelsi heard from over her shoulder, "Hey, kiddo." She turned to find Peter McDonald smiling and crying at the same time.

"Hey," Kelsi said. She started crying too.

They hugged.

"Are you OK?" McDonald asked.

Kelsi answered, "I'm cold and hungry, and ... and I miss Brian." Her tears flowed like waterfalls.

"Here." McDonald removed his jacket and draped it over Kelsi's slender shoulders. He noticed the manager behind the counter. "Can we get a large pepperoni, please? We'll be over there." McDonald pointed to a table near the radiator. He could warm Kelsi and he could feed her, but there was nothing he could do to comfort her about Agent Neal.

The pizzeria's manager was equally helpless. All he could say was, "It's on the house."

An old Bruce Hornsby song sounded in the background. Hornsby was a god in Virginia—a local boy made good. A Williamsburg native, he had recorded a series of hit albums in the late 1980s, he had won the Grammy for best new artist, and he had toured with the Grateful Dead after the Dead's longtime keyboard player died of a heroin overdose. McDonald himself enjoyed a personal connection to the gifted singer-pianist. Hornsby's brother John, who co-wrote a number of Hornsby's most popular songs, had graduated from UVA law school in the 1990s and had been one of McDonald's brightest students. More meaningful still, John had arranged for McDonald and Jenny to meet Hornsby backstage for soft drinks and snacks after one of Hornsby's sold-out concerts at UVA's basketball arena. Jenny was nuts for Hornsby's music—songs of lost love set to virtuoso piano grooves—and she used to tell her husband that, next to the day Megan was born, meeting Bruce Hornsby had been the greatest day of their married life.

Jenny ...

Megan ...

"Are you OK?" Kelsi said. The tables had turned; now Kelsi needed to console McDonald.

McDonald didn't respond.

"Peter?"

Finally, he said, "Sorry. I was thinking about Jenny and Megan. This was our favorite restaurant. Jenny loved the fresh ingredients they put on the pizza—everything but the olives are grown on site—and Megan liked to play with the toys they have for the kids." McDonald pointed to a large toy box in the corner by the door. "I wonder if Clay Smith knew any of that."

"I doubt it. How could he?"

"I don't know how Clay could know about it. But how could he know ... how could he *do* ... any of the things he has been doing?"

Kelsi glanced out the window. Clouds painted pictures above the mountains. She said, "I've asked myself that question many times during the last several days." She thought again about Brian Neal. She started to cry again. She whispered, "I guess it's true what my grandmother used to say: It's impossible to know what's inside someone's heart."

EPILOGUE

The State of the Union

CHAPTER 96

Peter McDonald hurried down the corridor. His Cole Hahn loafers snapped against the marble floor like a dancer's taps across the stage. McDonald was late for tea with Donald Lowry. Given what Justice Lowry had done for him, McDonald wanted to bring a gift, which explained his tardiness. He'd had a devil of a time locating the box that contained the author's copies of his new book, *The Ivory Tower*. It was a legal thriller set at a fictionalized University of Virginia. Court watchers were surprised when McDonald's publisher announced that the justice had penned a novel. Most observers had expected a treatise on constitutional interpretation from the former law professor. After all, several of McDonald's colleagues on the nation's highest court had published tomes about how they thought the Constitution should be read. McDonald knew about the justices' books—he had studied and benefited from them—but he had stated in a press release that he had always enjoyed John Grisham's novels and that he was eager to try writing one of his own. McDonald's closest friends knew the back-story, though: the Court's youngest jurist had written the book as escapist therapy ... for himself.

One of Lowry's law clerks welcomed McDonald to chambers: "Good morning, Mr. Justice. Justice Lowry is in his office. He's expecting you."

McDonald thanked the young man and knocked on Lowry's open door. "Sorry I'm late, Donald."

Lowry had his back to the door. He said, "Think nothing of it, Peter. Come on in and close the door. The tea is almost ready."

McDonald complied. He sat on the couch across from the coffee table next to the fireplace—the same spot from which he had asked Lowry to switch his vote two years earlier.

Lowry inched his way around a Persian rug with two teacups filled to the brim. McDonald was prepared to leap to the elderly justice's assistance at the first sign of unsteadiness. As before, there wasn't one.

"Thank you," McDonald said as he accepted the tea.

Lowry folded into the armchair closest to the fireplace. "You're welcome. I thought we would try some scented black tea this morning. It's a more aromatic version of Earl Grey's traditional blend. It's scented with even more bergamot than the original."

McDonald took a sip. "It's delicious. I have no idea what 'bergamot' is, but it smells good too."

Lowry chuckled. "I know I'm a bit obsessive about my tea, but everyone needs a hobby."

"Speaking of hobbies ..." McDonald pulled a copy of his novel out from underneath his trench coat and presented it to the senior associate justice. "I thought you might enjoy this. It's hot off the presses. I took the liberty of inscribing it for you."

Lowry smiled. "Thank you, Peter. In case you missed it, there's a glowing review in this morning's *Washington Post*. You're apparently the new Scott Turow—plenty of twists and turns but also plenty of insight about how the world really works."

McDonald blushed. "I'll have to read that review." He took another sip of tea. "Read the inscription."

Lowry willed his arthritic fingers to the title page. He read the inscription aloud: "To Donald Lowry, A hero to us all and a friend for life. Thank you for what you did for me." Lowry closed the book and said, "You're welcome."

The law clerk who had greeted McDonald knocked on Lowry's door and reminded the justice that he was scheduled to meet with a group of high school students in the cloakroom in five minutes.

Lowry's dedication to mentoring young people was legendary in legal circles. He said, "I'll be right there."

The law clerk left the two justices to conclude their conversation.

McDonald said, "Thanks again for the tea." He placed his teacup on the coffee table, shook Lowry's hand, and turned for the door.

Lowry said, "May I ask you something before you go?"

"Of course."

"Why did you need me to switch my vote? I know you needed my vote to get to five—the magical five—and I know what you said about not being comfortable with your original decision expanding our stare decisis jurisprudence. But four of our colleagues were comfortable with it, and scores of amici—including dozens of your former law professor colleagues—were comfortable with it. What was the real reason, Peter?"

McDonald glanced at the fire. Flames cast shadows across the room. "The 'real' reason?"

Lowry nodded. "Don't worry. I promise I won't tell."

Rain began to sound against the window behind Lowry's desk.

A tear came to McDonald's eye. He finally said, voice cracking, "I did it for Megan."

"Your little girl?"

"Y ... yes."

"What does your daughter—God rest her soul—have to do with the South Carolina case?"

Peter McDonald didn't have the strength to say any more. He didn't have the courage to describe how he had asked Donald Lowry to switch his vote to save Kelsi Shelton's life and how he needed to save Kelsi's life as a tribute to Megan.

Kelsi, McDonald always knew, was the kind of young woman that he hoped Megan would have grown up to be.

CHAPTER 97

Article II, section 3 of the U.S. Constitution specified that the president "shall from time to time give to Congress Information of the State of the Union."

Alexandra Burton was preparing to deliver her first address.

Burton had used her unexpected victory in *Tucker v. University of South Carolina*, and the sympathy that surrounded her grandson's death that led to the lawsuit in the first place, to catapult herself into the White House. The history books would record that the first woman president had defeated the first African American president by the paper-thin margin of three electoral votes. Those same history books would fail to note that President Burton was also the first member of the Ku Klux Klan to be elected to the most powerful office in the world. The oversight couldn't be attributed to any bias on the part of historians. Rather, historians didn't know about Burton's secret identity. Only one person outside of the sacred order knew.

That person?

Supreme Court Justice Peter McDonald, who had used his considerable research skills to confirm the rumor that Kelsi Shelton had shared with him when they were first reunited after Kelsi's kidnapping. Kelsi had told McDonald that Clay Smith was in the Klan and that Clay had let it slip during the unguarded moment when he was telling her about her father that Senator Burton—now *President* Burton—was also a member.

McDonald wasn't able to confirm that this explosive rumor was true by reading the U.S. Reports or the U.S. Code ... the answer wasn't contained in a Supreme Court opinion or a federal statute. Instead, McDonald had discovered the truth in a sacred scroll housed in the Masonic Temple of Capitol Hill. The scroll listed every man —and now woman—who had ever served as the imperial wizard of the Invisible Empire. Nathan Bedford Forrest's name was listed first. Alexandra Rutledge Burton was the most recent entry.

* * * * *

President Burton exchanged pleasantries with the congressional escort committee—senior leaders of the U.S. House and Senate—while she watched the House majority floor services chief announce the vice president and the members of the Senate, who then entered the House chamber and took the seats assigned to them. Members of the House were already seated. The House majority floor services chief next announced the president's cabinet, the dean of the diplomatic corps, and the chief justice and associate justices of the Supreme Court of the United States.

Two of the aforementioned dignitaries were absent from the speech. The first, a member of the president's cabinet, was quickly identified by the media horde covering the State of the Union as the secretary of agriculture. This particular official was the "designated survivor," the cabinet member who would provide continuity in the line of succession in the event that a catastrophe disabled the president, vice president, and other succeeding officers gathered in the House chamber for the president's annual address. The second missing dignitary—an absentee who went unnoticed by the press—was Peter McDonald.

President Burton arrived at the door of the House chamber. The House sergeant at arms loudly proclaimed, "Mr. Speaker, the president of the United States."

Cheers and applause filled the ornate room. President Burton walked slowly toward the Speaker's rostrum, followed closely by the members of the escort committee. She shook hands, offered hugs, and posed for photographs with a myriad of congressmen.

The president took her place at the House clerk's desk and then handed the vice president and the Speaker manila envelopes containing copies of her address. She was awash in good wishes. Her chest swelled with pride at the thought of all the good she could do for the country ... and for the Klan. Akia, she said to herself. A klanswoman I am.

The Speaker of the House introduced the president to the representatives and senators: "Members of the Congress, I have the high privilege and the distinct honor of presenting to you the president of the United States."

More cheers and applause ensued. The president held up her hands to try to quiet the crowd. One "thank you" was quickly followed by another.

Then, a *shot* rang out!

Then, a second *shot*!

The House chamber exploded into chaos.

A dozen Secret Service agents pushed aside everything and everyone in their path and rushed to the rostrum. But it was too late.

President Alexandra Burton was dead.

Peter McDonald—*Mr. Justice* McDonald—prayed for God's forgiveness as he retreated from the balcony and raced to his car.

Clay Smith would be next.

BIBLIOGRAPHY

Fiction should entertain. It also can inform. I consulted the following nonfiction sources when researching this novel:

Allen, James, Hilto Als, John Lewis, and Leon F. Litward. *Without Sanctuary: Lynching Photography in America*. Santa Fe, NM: Twin Palms, 2000.
This source provided the descriptions for most of the lynching scenes in this novel.

Booth v. Maryland, 482 U.S. 496 (1987).

Brown v. Board of Education, 347 U.S. 483 (1954).

Chalmers, David M. *Hooded Americanism: The History of the Ku Klux Klan*. 3d ed. Durham, NC: Duke University Press, 1987.
This source provided most of the history of the KKK described in this novel.

Dred Scott v. Sanford, 60 U.S. 393 (1857).

Gerber, Scott Douglas. "Justice Thomas and Mr. Jefferson." *Legal Times*, 5 May 2003, 60, cols. 1-3, 61, cols. 1-2.

Gerber, Scott Douglas. *To Secure These Rights: The Declaration of Independence and Constitutional Interpretation*. New York: New York University Press, 1995.

Grutter v. Bollinger, 539 U.S. 306 (2003).

Nomination of Robert H. Bork to be an Associate Justice of the Supreme Court of the United States: Hearings before the Committee on the Judiciary, United States Senate, 100th Cong. 1st sess., 1987.
This source was used in this novel for Peter McDonald's opening statement to the Senate Judiciary Committee.

Horowitz, David A., ed. *Inside the Klavern: The Secret History of a Ku Klux Klan of the 1920s*. Carbondale: Southern Illinois University Press, 1999.

McGinnis, John O. "Impeachable Defenses." *Policy Review* 95 (1999): 27.

Newton, Michael, and Judy Ann Newton. *The Ku Klux Klan: An Encyclopedia*. New York: Garland, 1991.

Parents Involved in Community Schools v. Seattle School District No. 1, 501 U.S. 701 (2007).
Payne v. Tennessee, 501 U.S. 808 (1991).
Planned Parenthood of Southeastern Pennsylvania v. Casey, 505 U.S. 833 (1992).
Plessy v. Ferguson, 163 U.S. 537 (1896).
Sims, Patsy. *The Klan.* New York: Stein and Day, 1978.
Tucker, Richard K. *The Dragon and the Cross: The Rise and Fall of the Ku Klux Klan in Middle America.* Hamden, Conn.: Archon Press, 1991.
This source provided most of the KKK terminology used in this novel.
Wikipedia, "Robert C. Byrd," last visited May 2, 2011, http://en.wikipedia.org/wiki/Robert_C._Byrd.
Wikipedia, "State of the Union address," last visited May 2, 2011, http://en.wikipedia.org/wiki/State_of_the_Union_address.

ACKNOWLEDGMENTS

I am grateful to various family members, friends, and colleagues who commented on drafts of *Mr. Justice* or otherwise provided encouragement. They include Jay Brennan, Dina Egge, Margot Gerber, Stanford Gerber, Kevin Hawley, Julie Hilden, Ken McDonald, Margaret McDonald, Sandra McDonald, Ron Mollick, Leslie O'Kane, and Dan Wewers. I am also grateful to Brown University's Political Theory Project for hosting me during my sabbatical while I finished both a nonfiction book, *A Distinct Judicial Power: The Origins of an Independent Judiciary, 1606-1787* (Oxford University Press, 2011), and this novel.

ABOUT THE AUTHOR

Scott Douglas Gerber is Professor of Law at Ohio Northern University, and Senior Research Scholar in Law and Politics at the Social Philosophy and Policy Center. He received both his Ph.D. and J.D. from the University of Virginia, and his B.A. from the College of William and Mary. He has had seven other books published, including *The Law Clerk: A Novel.* He finished *Mr. Justice* while on sabbatical at Brown University's Political Theory Project.

8404541R0

Made in the USA
Charleston, SC
06 June 2011